Readers love *Debt*
by K.C. WELLS

"*Debt* is a book that I recommend highly for lovers of LGBT romance and, for that matter, all romance."
—Happy Ever After, *USA Today*

"A wonderful, beautiful story with truly good, decent people. Something I don't get to see every day. Thank you, K.C."
—Rainbow Book Reviews

"This is not a story that you will EVER be bored reading. It's wonderful."
—Diverse Reader

"I really liked this book. I was hooked from the beginning...."
—Cat's Meow Reviews

By K.C. Wells

BFF
Bromantically Yours
First
Love Lessons Learned
Step by Step
Truth Will Out
Waiting For You

DREAMSPUN DESIRES
#17 – The Senator's Secret
#40 – Out of the Shadows
#76 – My Fair Brady

LEARNING TO LOVE
Michael & Sean
Evan & Daniel
Josh & Chris
Final Exam

LOVE, UNEXPECTED
Debt
Burden

SENSUAL BONDS
A Bond of Three
A Bond of Truth

With Parker Williams

COLLARS & CUFFS
An Unlocked Heart
Trusting Thomas
Someone to Keep Me
A Dance with Domination
Damian's Discipline
Make Me Soar
Dom of Ages
Endings and Beginnings

SECRETS
Before You Break
An Unlocked Mind
Threepeat

Published by DREAMSPINNER PRESS
www.dreamspinnerpress.com

BURDEN
K.C. Wells

Published by
DREAMSPINNER PRESS

5032 Capital Circle SW, Suite 2, PMB# 279, Tallahassee, FL 32305-7886 USA
www.dreamspinnerpress.com

This is a work of fiction. Names, characters, places, and incidents either are the product of author imagination or are used fictitiously, and any resemblance to actual persons, living or dead, business establishments, events, or locales is entirely coincidental.

Burden
© 2019 K.C. Wells.

Cover Photo
© 2019 Ethan James Photography,
ethanjamesphotography.com
Cover Design
© 2019 Paul Richmond.
http://www.paulrichmondstudio.com
Cover content is for illustrative purposes only and any person depicted on the cover is a model.

All rights reserved. This book is licensed to the original purchaser only. Duplication or distribution via any means is illegal and a violation of international copyright law, subject to criminal prosecution and upon conviction, fines, and/or imprisonment. Any eBook format cannot be legally loaned or given to others. No part of this book may be reproduced or transmitted in any form or by any means, electronic or mechanical, including photocopying, recording, or by any information storage and retrieval system, without the written permission of the Publisher, except where permitted by law. To request permission and all other inquiries, contact Dreamspinner Press, 5032 Capital Circle SW, Suite 2, PMB# 279, Tallahassee, FL 32305-7886, USA, or www.dreamspinnerpress.com.

Trade Paperback ISBN: 978-1-64405-232-7
Digital ISBN: 978-1-64405-231-0
Library of Congress Control Number: 2018963160
Trade Paperback published April 2019
v. 1.0

Printed in the United States of America
∞
This paper meets the requirements of
ANSI/NISO Z39.48-1992 (Permanence of Paper).

Acknowledgments

THANK YOU to my wonderful team of betas. As always, a stellar job!

And a special thank-you to Andrew Gordon, without whom the legal bits wouldn't have been... legal. You were there for *Debt*—it seems only right that you were there for this one.

Chapter One

May, 2016

NOW IS not the day for the judge to be running late!

Jesse Bryant pulled out his phone and glanced at it for what had to be the fourth or fifth time in the last ten minutes. Almost three months since the jury had found Mr. Richards, Seb, and the rest of their sleazy, low-life partners guilty of a long list of charges, and it all came down to this final day.

Sentencing. Mr. Richards's sentencing, to be precise.

Jesse had spent the whole morning trying to ignore the butterflies in his belly. At one point he'd sat on his hands to stop himself from fiddling with his phone, his bag—anything within reaching distance. All he wanted was to see that bastard go down, and for a long, long time. He knew he wasn't the only one. He'd spotted Baz, Jordan, and Steve coming into the courthouse that morning, all of them with tight expressions. They hadn't spoken, just given one another a brief nod.

Talking would be for when this was all *finally* over.

A gentle hand covered his, and Nikko Kurokawa leaned in to whisper, "Easy, Jesse. It'll be okay."

"Sure."

Nikko chuckled. "Look, we all *know* he's going down, right? The arguing is over, the prosecutor's asked for the maximum sentence…. And think about it. Gorton and Waters got fifty years each, and they were small fry. Seb got sixty." He snickered. "I don't think the prosecutor could've made it more obvious that he thinks Richards is scum, do you?" He pointed to the front of the courtroom, where Richards sat at one of two long tables, facing the judge's bench. Jesse stared at the back of his head as if he was trying to bore a hole into it.

Take your last free breath, because you're going down.

"What the judge says today isn't going to come as a surprise to anyone in this courtroom. Richards is going to be behind bars for decades to come." Nikko squeezed Jesse's hand. "So calm down, and enjoy watching it happen. Because they're going to make that piece of shit sorry for what he did for the remainder of his sleazy little life."

Jesse had to chuckle. "Wow. Where did my sweet, mild friend Nikko disappear to?"

For a moment Nikko's face hardened. "My brother has to start a whole new life because of him. Ichy almost *died* because of him. We had to wait for three months while the probation office conducted its investigations. We had to listen to their counsel try to make them sound like *choirboys*—"

"Yeah, like they were ever gonna get away with *that* one."

Nikki drew in a breath, calming visibly. "I'm just waiting for it all to finally be over, just like you are, just like Baz and the others are."

Jesse glanced down at their joined hands and saw Nikko's other hand was similarly engaged: Mitch had laced their fingers together.

They look so good together. A year since they'd met in the Black Lounge, and the couple were clearly still head over heels with each other. *I guess something good did come out of it after all.* Jesse loved the way Mitch gazed at Nikko, like he was the most precious thing on God's earth. *As he should.* Nikko was a beautiful man, inside and out, something Jesse had known from the moment they met.

"I see you brought your anchor with you," Jesse whispered back to him.

Nikko chuckled. "Oh, he's that, all right, and so much more besides. It's so good to know I'm not alone."

Jesse squeezed his hand. "I had noticed. You've brought your own support group, from the looks of it." Nikko had briefly introduced him to Mitch's parents and brother as they took their seats.

Nikko beamed. "Aren't they awesome? Valerie and Malcolm insisted on being here for the sentencing, and then Gareth announced he was coming too." He peered around Jesse, and his smile faltered. "I take it your parents haven't changed their minds?"

Jesse's stomach clenched. "Can we talk about something else?"

Nikko's expression was compassionate. "Aw, Jess. I'm so sorry. That isn't right." His gaze alighted on a point over Jesse's shoulder, and he smiled. "Look who *is* here, though."

Jesse twisted to look, and his heartbeat sped up. Detective Randy Michaels was standing at the rear of the courtroom, talking quietly with another cop. Jesse tried not to stare, but *fuck*, it was difficult. Of course Randy was there. Why wouldn't he be? It was his case, after all.

Randy hadn't changed a bit since the day the police had raided the Black Lounge. He still wore his long black hair tied in a ponytail, only now there was a pair of rimless glasses perched on his nose. Now and again Randy would push at them as they slipped, and the gesture took Jesse back to those weeks he spent in the Lounge. Randy had worn contacts then, and now at least the unconscious, habitual action made sense. Nearly a year had gone by, and he was still the same sexy fucker Jesse remembered. He'd lost a little weight, too, and it suited him.

Just then Randy glanced across at him, and Jesse did his best to remain calm when those beautiful blue eyes met his. Every single encounter he'd had with Randy throughout the trial, no matter how small, was burned into his memory. Randy gave him a nod and a smile before returning to his conversation.

One smile and my insides are dancing, while he has no fucking clue what he does to me. The irony of it all. *Surrounded by gay guys in that fucking club, and I had to fall for the straight undercover cop.* It was someone's idea of a joke. Out of all the guys Jesse fucked on a regular basis, not one of them stirred him like Randy. There were times when he told himself he was building this into more than it really was, only to recall Randy's smiles, the way they made him feel.

Like he mattered. Like someone was looking out for him, the way Mitch did for Nikko. The revelation came as something of a shock. Jesse was used to being self-reliant—since when did he need to lean on anyone?

Then it occurred to him. Since the raid, the only person he could rely on was himself.

He was on his own.

And he was still staring at Randy.

"Jesse." Nikko's urgent whisper jolted him back into the present.

Everyone was standing for the judge's entry.

Jesse lunged to his feet, his heart pounding. *Finally.*

When they were seated again, the judge cleared his throat and shuffled a sheaf of notes in front of him. "Having heard and read the arguments, letters, memorandums, and presentencing report, I am now ready to make my findings." He stared at Richards, his expression cool. "Daniel Richards, one might say your list of crimes appears impressive, but I prefer to think of it as vile. Running a network of brothels, where men were held against their will. Selling drugs on a vast scale, both here in the US and internationally. Moving drugs across state and international lines, in a manner that endangered human life. Human trafficking."

Even from a distance, Jesse felt the ice in the judge's stare.

"In this case, a lack of mitigating factors, combined with aggravating issues, requires me to impose as harsh a sentence as possible, as punishment for your heinous actions, and as a deterrent to those out there who might consider the same… how shall I put it… 'career path' that you have followed." His gaze flickered to the rows of chairs where Jesse, Nikko, and the others sat. "And finally, because your victims deserve justice."

Jesse swallowed hard, and Nikko's hand tightened around his.

"For this type of offense, there is, of course, a mandatory minimum term, but I have also taken into account that with good behavior, you may only serve 85 percent of your sentence. Therefore, I am sentencing you to 1140 months, so that you will serve at least 960 months."

Jesse did the math rapidly in his head. *Eighty years.* He let out a long sigh of relief. In front of him, Richards didn't flinch, his head held high.

The judge lowered his papers and addressed the courtroom. "I am delighted to say that the business of this court is done. My thanks to those individuals who gave testimony, many of whom I see here this morning. My hope is that you will not let these events blight your lives. Leave them behind, gentlemen. Leave them here. I wish you every success in whatever future you make for yourselves." And with that, he rose to his feet, pulled his robes around him, and left the courtroom.

Richards was led away by police officers, his icy calm no longer in evidence. Jesse thought he looked broken. *Good.*

When they were no longer in sight, Jesse sagged into his chair, bereft of energy.

Beside him, Nikko stared at the door where the judge had exited. "Have I said how much I like that judge?"

Mitch laughed, put his arm around Nikko, and kissed his cheek. "It's over, babe. It's really over."

Nikko shook his head. "Not yet, it isn't. When I get my brother back, *then* it will be over."

"Any idea on when that might be?" Jesse had been in court the day Ichy had given evidence. He could understand why Ichy had been taken into protective custody—Ichy knew where the metaphorical bodies were buried, and the verdict was due in no small way to all the information he'd revealed to the jury in his quiet voice.

Nikko leaned into Mitch, who gave Jesse a tired smile. "Now that the trial is over, Ichy gets a new identity. Once he's settled, he can start a new life." He kissed Nikko's head. "You'll see him again, babe."

"I know. I have to be patient. And at least I got to see him for a short while." Nikko peered at Jesse. "Randy arranged for us to spend some time together before they took him back into protective custody. Long enough to have a coffee and find out how he's doing."

"Randy's a good guy," Mitch affirmed. "He always was, even when he was undercover. He stuck his neck out for me, and that could've gotten him into serious trouble."

Jesse sighed. "I knew he wasn't like anyone else who worked there, that was for sure. Finding out he was a cop kinda made sense." And only added to his misery. What use was there in having the hots for a *cop*? In Vice, no less?

That, plus Jesse's present situation, added up to a Big Fat Zero.

"Are congratulations in order?" Mitch's mom looked like she was about to combust. "Because after that, they'd better be. Although, I have to say, I was expecting more of a flash-bang finale." She opened her arms wide, and Nikko rose to his feet, slipping free of Mitch's embrace and into hers. She held him tightly, standing on her toes to reach him, and Jesse's heart melted at the sight.

"And when she's done, it's my turn," Mitch's dad piped up from behind her, grinning.

Looks like Nikko found himself a family. Jesse was truly happy for him. Nikko had lost his parents when he was barely into his teens. But the love Mitch's family plainly felt for him only served to highlight Jesse's own family situation.

Yeah, thanks for that, Mom and Dad. Way to go. Ten months on, and the bitterness he felt toward them hadn't waned.

"How about we get out of here?" Mitch suggested. "Y'know, to someplace where there's room for all this hugging?"

His brother, Gareth, chuckled. "Just as long as you realize you get hugs too. You've been through this every step of the way as much as Nikko has."

His mom released Nikko. "Good idea. I've spent more hours than I care to remember in this courtroom. And now that it's finally over, I have no wish to see the inside of one ever again, even if it's as beautiful as this one."

Jesse knew where she was coming from. He'd barely paid any attention to the ornate room—his focus had been on other matters.

"Hey, Jesse." Baz waved to him. "What a result!"

Jesse laughed, momentary relief flooding through him. "I know, right? You okay?"

Baz shrugged. "Gettin' by. *You* know."

Jesse knew, all right. He'd caught sight of Baz on numerous occasions during the last ten months, enough times to know they were both "getting by" doing the same thing. Jordan and Steve were on a couple of the sites Jesse used, so they were in the same boat too.

Goodbye, Black Lounge—hello, streets of NYC. The venue might have changed, but they were still making a buck on their backs. Or on all fours. Or bent over a couch.

Whatever. The one thing that had changed was the atmosphere. There were times when Jesse yearned for the safety and security of the Black Lounge. Surviving outside its walls was a whole different ball game, as he'd already found out, to his detriment, on several occasions.

The Black Lounge's patrons observed the rules. On the streets, there were no rules.

"See you around, okay?" Jordan called as he followed Baz and Steve out of the courtroom.

Jesse nodded, conscious of Nikko beside him. He hoped to God Nikko wasn't about to ask any awkward questions, because Jesse had an inkling the answers might disappoint him.

He followed Mitch's family, Mitch, and Nikko as they exited the courtroom. The euphoria that had filled Jesse dissipated as quickly as it had arrived, leaving him sadly deflated. In the space of the ten months it had taken to arrive at this point, Jesse's life had completely changed.

Well, almost completely.

"Are you going home now?" Jesse asked Nikko. Home was Maine, and he had to admit, living there obviously agreed with Nikko. Jesse had hoped to spend a bit more time with him and Mitch.

"No, we're all staying at Gareth's place in Mount Kisco. It's only an hour by train from here, so it made sense." Nikko gave that shy smile Jesse recollected so vividly. "Gareth put Mitch and me in the guest cottage."

Mitch leaned in. "Which is my brother's subtle way of telling us we make too much noise," he said in a stage whisper. Nikko whacked him on the arm. "Hey! Are you gonna deny it?"

Nikko's cheeks were a charming shade of pink. "No, but you don't have to *tell* everyone."

Behind them, Gareth burst into an explosive snort.

"Jesse, we're going to have lunch, and we wanted it to be a sort of celebration. Won't you join us?" Mitch's mom took hold of Jesse's hand. "This is your day, too, after all. And we know you looked out for Nikko when you were both in… that place."

Jesse's throat tightened at the warmth in her voice. "Mrs. Jenkins, I—"

"And it's Valerie, dear. Don't refuse. We'd love to have you join us."

Whatever Jesse had planned to say escaped him as he caught sight of a handsome dark-haired man.

Randy was heading straight for them, smiling.

Chapter Two

"I THINK the detective might want to talk to you and Jesse," Valerie said quietly. "We'll wait over there. We're not in any hurry, and the table won't be ready for ages yet."

Jesse barely heard her. He was too busy trying to get his body under control. He breathed deeply, forcing himself to act calm as Randy drew nearer.

"Hey." Randy gave them both a huge smile. "Talk about a result." He reached for Nikko's hand, but to Jesse's surprise, Nikko ignored it and hugged Randy tightly. Randy flushed, his cheek pressed against Nikko's. "Yeah. I guess we *are* pretty much past the shaking-hands stage, right? After all we've been through together."

Nikko released him. "And I wouldn't have got through it without you." When Randy shook his head, Nikko held up one slim hand. "You were working undercover, and still you looked out for me. You went against Richards at least once that I know about, and that could've been disastrous for your case. But you did it anyway."

Randy shrugged. "You should never have been there in the first place. One look at ya and anyone could see that. I'm just glad it all worked out the way it did." His gaze flickered over to Jesse, and that smile didn't fade. "Hey. How are ya?"

What struck Jesse almost immediately was the lack of physical greeting. *What—I don't even rate a handshake?* That stung a little, but at least it quashed his nerves.

"I'm good. Glad it's over, like everyone else." Jesse kept his voice even, his tone cool.

Randy appeared faintly puzzled by Jesse's indifferent manner. "I see. So… how is life treating you both?"

Like Jesse wanted to answer *that* question. Thankfully, Nikko got in there first.

"I'm studying for my master's. When I'm finished, the plan is to teach music." Nikko snuck a glance over to where Mitch stood with his family, and his cheeks flushed. "Mitch keeps telling me I must be crazy."

"He still teaching up in Maine?"

Nikko nodded. "He loves it there. And we finally got a little place of our own, in Old Orchard Beach. It's about one block from the ocean."

Jesse liked the genuine warmth in Randy's blue eyes as he spoke. "That sounds great."

Nikko took Randy's hand and gave it a brief squeeze. "Thank you, by the way, for what you did. I didn't get the chance that day—by the time I looked around, you'd already left. But it really meant so much to me, to get a bit of time with Ichy."

Randy waved his hand. "Hey, it was no biggie. I figured you two needed to reconnect. It couldn't have been easy for ya, being apart like this." His gaze alighted on Jesse. "And how are *you* doing? Still studying?" He seemed to have recovered from his brief moment of bewilderment.

Fuck. There was no way out of this. Jesse couldn't tell him the truth, because how in the hell would *that* sound? *Hey, let's see. My parents have cut me off, both financially and in every other goddamn way, my studies are indefinitely on hold until I have enough money to continue with them, and I'm a full-time escort.*

Yeah, that would go down *really* well.

"Actually? My studies are on hold for a while. I wanted to take some time off to work, so I have part-time jobs as a server in a couple of places, although I *am* job hunting for something more permanent."

Randy nodded, as though all of that wasn't a total pile of bullshit. Then he reached into his jacket pocket and took out his wallet. He removed a card and handed it to Jesse. "Okay. If you ever need anything, here's my number. Don't hesitate to call me, all right?"

Jesse stared at the stiff card. "You still working out of Midtown South?"

"I'm working all over these days." Randy gestured for the card. "Lemme write my cell on that so you don't have to go through the precinct to get to me." He took the card, removed a small pen from his breast pocket, and scribbled a number. "There. Now you can reach me anytime." Randy handed it back to him.

"Detective Michaels?" It was Valerie. "We're all going for a celebration lunch. We'd love to have you join us. I already invited Jesse, but he hasn't given me an answer yet." Her eyes sparkled. "Though I don't think he'd want to disappoint an old lady."

Behind her, Mitch snorted. "Playing the old lady card again. Yeah, right. Pay her no mind, Jesse. The woman has a mind like a steel trap. Refuse at your peril."

Valerie merely raised her thinning eyebrows before smiling broadly at both Jesse and Randy. "Please, say you'll come."

Randy chuckled. "How could I refuse? Sure, I'd love to." He dug Jesse in the ribs with his elbow. "And if I'm going, so are you."

Jesse blinked, then shrugged. "Apparently, I'm coming too."

Valerie beamed. "Excellent. Malcolm will organize taxis for us all. We're going to the Palm Tribeca over on West Street. My eldest son, Gareth, has chosen it, so if you're not a fan of steak, blame him." And with that, she walked over to where her husband was standing with Gareth.

Randy shook his head. "Wow. I wouldn't want to cross her."

Nikko watched her with a gentle smile. "She's amazing." Then he grinned at Jesse. "Looks like I get a bit more time with you after all. We've got some catching up to do, because *someone* around here is terrible at answering texts and emails." His eyes twinkled.

Jesse couldn't come back with a witty reply, because Nikko had totally nailed it. The thought of him asking questions sent cold inching its way toward Jesse's heart. Then there was Randy, who seemed keen for Jesse to go too.

Lunch was suddenly a daunting prospect.

"So, YOU still working undercover?" Mitch asked Randy as the servers brought their appetizers. All around them was the chatter and bustle of a busy restaurant, full to capacity.

Looking at all the dishes being delivered to the table made Jesse's mouth water. He hadn't been tempted by the filet mignon, even though Gareth assured him it was delicious, and had gone for the salad instead, skipping the main course altogether. Jesse had a slim figure to maintain, but he was also acutely aware that some foods had unexpected benefits or drawbacks. Fruit was always a good idea. Spicy food? Hell. No.

"As a matter of fact, I'm not." Randy gestured to his face. "This is *way* too high profile now, after the media frenzy that followed the trial. So much so, it's haircut time."

Jesse gaped at him, appalled, and exclaimed, "But I *love* your hair."

Randy gave him a dazed glance, and Jesse kicked himself for the way he'd blurted it out like that. Thankfully, Valerie asked him some questions about Ichy, and Jesse was repreived. When his salad arrived, Jesse attacked it with gusto, trying not to attract Randy's attention again.

Beside him, Gareth stared at his appetizer—a glass bowl with three large shrimp hanging from its rim and a couple of dips beside it. "It always looks like a claw coming out of the bowl," he confided to Jesse in a low voice. "Reminds me of that movie, *you* know, when they're having dinner, and everything comes alive because these ghosts are trying to scare them away?"

Jesse chuckled. "*Beetlejuice*. Yeah, I know what you mean. Better eat it fast before it eats you."

Gareth laughed. "Thanks for that."

Jesse kept his gaze focused on his food, listening to Mitch tell funny stories about the kids in his class, Gareth sharing some of the architectural projects he was working on, and Malcolm trying to make sure everyone had plenty to eat. It was a pleasant lunch, but all the way through it, he was conscious of Randy sitting next to him, of the way he filled his pale blue cotton shirt. Not that he was overly muscular. Jesse liked his arms, the way his biceps curved gently, his large, capable-looking hands….

I even like the way he talks. Back in the Black Lounge, Jesse had only once seen Randy lose it, and that had been when he'd tried to maintain control during the police raid. The rest of the time, he'd spoken calmly and quietly, with the kind of voice that made you want to listen to him.

Then Jesse shook himself. *This is not good. Just quit thinking about him, why don'tcha?* Jesse lived in the real world, and much as he might fantasize about getting Randy between the sheets, he knew it was never gonna happen.

And that was a damn shame, because *Lord*, the man was gorgeous.

"You didn't eat much," Randy observed as the servers collected the coffee cups and Malcolm asked for the bill.

Jesse gave a shrug. "Guess I wasn't all that hungry." *And it's all your fault for making me so goddamn nervous.*

Randy glanced across the table at Malcolm. "What do you think the odds are on them letting me pay for my lunch?" he asked in a low voice.

Jesse snickered. "Pretty nonexistent. Besides, they made it clear why they invited us."

Randy gazed at Nikko. "They really do love him, don't they? Nikko had no idea when Mitch first walked into that room how his life was gonna change." He leaned closer. "D'ya think those two will get married some day?"

Jesse considered it. "Possibly. Mitch is pretty old-fashioned. And Nikko is already one of the family."

"Speaking of which, I didn't see anyone from your family in court today. I was gonna ask about that."

Jesse's heart sank, but before he could respond, Randy's phone buzzed.

He took it out and peered at the screen. "Dammit." He replaced it in his pocket and cleared his throat. "Sorry, everyone, but this is where I have to leave. It seems I'm wanted elsewhere."

Valerie nodded. "Thank you for coming, Detective Michaels."

Mitch snickered. "You know, the number of times I heard your name in court, and this is the first time it's occurred to me that it's the same as a friend of mine, who is also a New York cop."

Randy grinned. "That wouldn't be Donna, would it?" When Mitch's eyes widened, Randy laughed. "She's my cousin. And while we're on the subject, who do you think she called the night of the raid, to find out if Nikko was about to be released from custody?"

"That was you?" Mitch rose to his feet, walked around the table, and gave Randy a fierce hug. "Thank you."

A flush crept over Randy's cheeks. "You're welcome. And now I really gotta run." To Jesse's surprise, Randy pulled him to his feet and gave him a quick hug. "Take care of yourself, and be good."

Jesse gazed at him in mock indignation. "Me?"

Randy snorted. "You forget. I know you, remember?" He pressed folded bills into Jesse's hand. "Make sure Mr. Jenkins gets this, will ya? If I'm not here, he can't say no." And with that, he gave one more round of goodbyes before heading for the main door.

Jesse watched him go, stunned. *Talk about blowing hot and cold.* He could *not* make Randy out.

Nikko shifted into the seat Randy had vacated and leaned toward him with a conspiratorial air. "You still like him, I see."

Jesse gave him a bemused glance. "Course I like him."

Nikko fixed him with a hard stare. "Not what I mean and you know it."

Yeah, I do. Randy had been the topic of many conversations in the Black Lounge. Jesse sighed. "I'm not gonna torture myself, okay?"

Nikko regarded him closely. "What's really going on with your parents? Are they still mad at you because you got involved in the trial? Or is it more than that?"

It was time to tell the truth. "As soon as they learned about the Black Lounge, they cut me off. No more money for studying. No more money, period. And as far as they were concerned, I could forget about coming home too. They severed all ties. I was given one day where I could turn up to collect whatever stuff I could take away with me, and that was that."

Nikko's jaw dropped. "They... threw you out? Just like that?"

Jesse nodded. "Since then, I've been couch-surfing, moving from one friend's apartment to another." It sounded a lot more pleasant than it was in reality. Months of feeling like he was putting out his ex-college friends who lived in NYC, trying to keep a low profile, and above all, hiding what he was doing. They might have been his friends, but it was a sure bet they wouldn't want a hooker sleeping on their couch.

"But...." Nikko frowned. "How are you surviving?" Then his eyes widened. "You're—"

"We're not gonna discuss this," Jesse said softly. "Not here. Okay?" Much as he loved Nikko, he was not going to let him know how things really were. Nikko was happy, and Jesse wasn't about to burst his bubble.

Nikko swallowed. "Okay." He was obviously upset. "Listen, if you ever need a break, come see us, all right?"

Warmth spread through him. "You're a sweet guy, do you know that?"

Nikko set his jaw. "I mean it, Jess. If you have to get away from it all for a while, come and stay with us."

Mitch appeared between them, grinning. "No, don't do that, Jess. You'll never want to leave."

Jesse forced a laugh. "No fear of that. I'm a New York City boy. The change of pace would probably kill me."

Both Nikko and Mitch laughed at that.

Little by little, Jesse's heartbeat returned to normal. He gazed at Nikko and Mitch, both of them happy, settled…. *Look at me. Twenty-three years old, no fixed abode, living from day to day, and engaged in a risky business, to say the least.*

This wasn't good.

JESSE SAID goodbye to Mitch's family as they waited for a taxi to take the five of them to Grand Central Station. He figured the best way of making sure Randy's contribution made it to the right place was to give it to Mitch, after he'd explained who it was from. Mitch had winked and patted his back before giving Jesse a hug. He got an especially big hug from Nikko. Jesse knew what that was all about. Nikko was worried.

"I'm fine, okay?" Jesse assured him.

"But if you weren't, you'd tell me, right?" Nikko's anxious expression had Jesse kicking himself. *This is all my fault.*

"I would. I promise." Hell, Nikko was the closest thing Jesse had to a BFF. Then he gave Nikko a peck on the cheek. "Now go enjoy staying in Gareth's guest cottage."

"There's a pool," Nikko whispered, his eyes bright.

Jesse grinned. "You two could go skinny-dipping when no one's around."

Nikko gave an exaggerated shiver. "If I want to freeze my nuts off, I can go in the ocean every day at home. It's right on my doorstep." One last hug, and then the taxi arrived. Nikko gave him a fond glance before Mitch bundled him into the taxi.

Jesse stood and waved as the car pulled away from the curb, then headed for the Chambers Street subway station. He reached into his pocket for his phone. It had been on silent all morning, and he hoped to God he hadn't missed too many tricks, but there was no way he could have answered a call from a john. When he saw there'd been none, Jesse was both relieved and dismayed. *The day's nearly over and I have nothing to show for it. Why did I ever think I could make it in this game?*

Then he saw there was one missed call from Dale, the guy whose couch Jesse was currently occupying every night. This arrangement had gone on for the last month, and it had been working so well, Jesse had had visions of it becoming permanent. Then Dale found himself a new boyfriend, Tate, and the atmosphere in the apartment had changed. Nothing Jesse could put his finger on. He hadn't had all that many dealings with Tate, and even fewer conversations, but yeah, something felt off.

Jesse called Dale. "Hey. Sorry I missed ya."

"Oh, right, it was the last day in court, I forgot." Dale sounded more ditzy than usual.

"What's up?" When Dale sighed, Jesse came to a halt in the middle of the sidewalk. "Okay, what's wrong?" Because *something* sure was.

"I'm sorry to have to do this to ya, but…."

Jesse stifled a groan. He hated how these conversations always began the same fucking way. He'd heard plenty of them in the last ten months. Jesse said nothing, waiting for the hammer to fall.

"Look, it's not you, okay?"

Jesse snickered. "Sounds like we're breaking up. And if it's not me, then who *is* it?"

"Tate." A pause. "He's kinda given me an ultimatum."

Ah. Now the lack of conversation made sense. "Lemme guess. He doesn't want another guy in the apartment." He could see where Tate was coming from—no one wanted another body cramping their style, right?—but he'd only been Dale's BF for a matter of days.

"Got it in one. He said you don't have to move out right away."

Gee, how fucking magnanimous. "How long have I got?"

"A week, maybe?"

Great. Just fucking great.

Jesse sighed. "I'll get right on it." Not that he had any clue where to start looking. He'd just about exhausted his list of friends. Without waiting for Dale's reply, he disconnected the call.

Now what?

His imminent eviction took all the shine off the day. Richards in jail, Nikko blissfully happy, and Randy looking *awfully* fine….

Jesse pushed aside that last image. Right now he had to find a place to sleep, and pretty damn sharpish.

Chapter Three

RANDY EXITED the 191st Street subway and turned down Wadsworth Avenue, heading home, thankful to be leaving behind a long day of getting shit from his coworkers.

Jeez, all I did was get a freakin' haircut. To hear them all, you'd think I'd had a head transplant. He had to admit, it was a different look for him. After years of keeping his hair long, staring into the mirror and seeing black hair cut short and sleek was like looking at a stranger.

Isn't that the point? After months of having his face on TV, online, and in the newspapers, he felt he could finally do his job without someone asking him, "Hey! Ain't you that cop from the trial?" He'd enjoyed the long stint of undercover work, but it had been a trying time. Eighteen months working in the Black Lounge, slowly building the case against Richards and his mob, making sure his background story checked out, always being careful about every word that came out of his mouth….

Being back on the streets was something of a relief. And those contacts had been a bitch. Thank God he got to wear his glasses again.

As he walked along, his jacket wrapped tight around him—because hey, it might well have been May, but this was New York, babe—his thoughts turned to Jesse Bryant. Not that such thoughts had ever strayed all that far from him, ever since the lunch after the trial.

There's something not right there. Randy had always liked Jesse, with his happy-go-lucky attitude, that sexy smile, and abundant natural exuberance. How could anyone *not* like him? He'd been one of the most popular guys in the Black Lounge, and it was easy to see why. When Jesse greeted his clients, he was always relaxed, plainly looking forward to spending time with them.

Easy to like a hooker who obviously loved his job. Even easier to see why Randy had spent a lot of time thinking about Jesse, both when he was working and when he'd gone home for the night.

Randy shivered, and it had nothing to do with the sudden gust of wind that whipped around him. *Not gonna go there.* And then his mind went back to his original thought. Jesse hadn't been his usual self at all. Randy reasoned it might have something to do with his job situation. That would worry anyone.

He reached the ornate wrought iron gate that covered the entrance to his building on West 189th Street and climbed the steps. His mailbox was empty, so he went on up to the fourth floor. As he approached his apartment, his neighbor, Owen, from next door along the hallway, waved at him in greeting.

Owen beamed. "Hey. Just the man. I got a bottle of wine chilling in the refrigerator and my date just canceled. Wanna join me? You look like you could use a glass or three. Long day on the beat?"

Randy laughed. "It must be Friday. You're inviting me for a drink."

"Like I need an excuse." Sharing a bottle of wine was a regular occurrence.

Randy considered the idea for all of two seconds. "Sure. Give me time to grab a shower and change. And hey." He wagged a finger at Owen. "No putting any of your usual moves on me."

Owen grinned, his teeth gleaming. "Okay, I promise." As Randy opened his own front door, Owen muttered, "Besides. I got all new moves."

Randy shook his head, chuckling. "You are such a slut." He went into his apartment, suddenly in a much better mood. Owen had a habit of doing that, even if he was a terrible flirt. And God, did he flirt.

Half an hour later, refreshed and carrying two large bags of corn chips, Randy knocked on Owen's door. He'd already grabbed a bite to eat when he left work, but the chips would help to soak up the alcohol. *One bottle of wine, my ass.* Randy knew from experience that usually meant two, but it was Friday night, for God's sake, and the weekend beckoned.

Owen flung the door open, looking extremely casual in a pair of sweats and a white tank top that made his olive skin appear darker than usual. "Come on in." He stood aside to let Randy enter, then led the way into his living room. His black leather couch took up most of one wall, and in front of it sat a squat coffee table with a couple of glasses and a bottle of wine in an ice bucket.

Randy placed the chips beside the glasses, then flopped down onto the couch. "Thank God this week is over."

Owen snickered. "You say that every time. Liking the hair, by the way." He fanned himself. "Hot look." He went over to the kitchen cabinets on the other side of the room and extracted a bowl for the chips.

"According to you, I always look hot."

Owen emptied one bag into the bowl, then opened the wine. "Duh. That's because you always do." He got on with the business of filling the glasses.

"So who was your date with tonight, and why did they cancel?" Randy took a sip of the cold white wine. "Chardonnay?"

Owen's eyes lit up. "And they say cops are dumb. I've taught you well." He preened.

Randy snorted. "Sorry to burst your bubble, but I saw the label."

"Aw, why'd ya have to say that and spoil it? You could've left me feeling good, especially since I got stood up." Owen took a long drink from his glass. "And in answer to your question, my date was with Charles."

"Oh my. Sounds kinda snooty."

Owen nodded slowly. "You may be right. I asked him to join me here, and when he learned my apartment was in the vicinity of Washington Heights, he suddenly announced he had a *prior engagement* and called it off. You know what I say to that?" He raised his glass. "Fuck him."

"Amen to that."

Owen snorted. "I'm forty-three, for God's sake. That's too long in the tooth to be messed around by snobs." His eyes gleamed. "So when are *you* gonna make me a happy camper and go on a date with me?"

Randy laughed. "Don't you ever get tired of the constant rejection? It's never gonna work, and for two irrefutable reasons." He pointed at Owen. "You, gay. Me, straight as an arrow." That was his story, and he was sticking to it.

Owen laughed. "No one is completely straight, my friend. I've had enough so-called straight guys in my bed to know that."

"Maybe so." Randy took refuge in his glass. The chilled wine helped to counteract the heat that etched its way across his chest and up his neck, and he chugged it back.

"Oh, it's gonna be *that* kind of a night, is it?" Owen immediately filled his glass, and Randy arched his eyebrows. Owen smiled. "Relax, babe. I know better than to shit where I eat. Your precious bod is safe with me. Besides, we've gotten along so well all these years, I'm not about to spoil things now."

Randy chuckled. "Glad to hear it."

Owen nodded toward Randy's glass. "Now drink up. There's more where that came from." He gave Randy a speculative glance. "You're not usually this nervous. What's up?"

"Who says anything's up?" Randy gave him as innocent a stare as he could manage before grabbing a handful of chips.

"Mm-hmm. Of course, I could be imagining it, I suppose, but... I sort of got the impression you were a little uncomfortable just now. You know, when I gave my usual 'straight men aren't all that straight' spiel." Owen settled back against the couch, his gaze focused on Randy. "Then again, noticing people's reactions is part of my job, right?"

Randy groaned inwardly. Sometimes he forgot Owen was Dr. Owen Cardenas, psychologist. "You gonna go all Freud on me?" he joked.

Owen laughed. "Of course not. Now, just make yourself comfortable on my couch while I go get my notebook." He grinned. "Seriously, though, are you telling me you've never been attracted to a guy?"

Randy didn't respond right away but took another drink. "Know why they assigned me to the Black Lounge case? Because I felt comfortable around gay guys. And yeah, I might have mentioned that I have this gay neighbor who has the hots for me, just to prove my point."

Owen snickered. "Whereas we both know you're not my type, and I just love pulling your chain." He raised his glass again, and Randy clinked his against it.

"Ya know, some of my coworkers wouldn't touch that job with a ten-foot cattle prod." That still disgusted him. It was a job, for Christ's sake. *What the fuck did they think was going to happen in there?* Then he reconsidered. Some of the detectives he worked alongside would have run a mile if they'd seen what *he* witnessed on a daily basis.

Owen nodded. "Doesn't surprise me." He cocked his head to one side. "How long were you in there?"

"Eighteen months."

"Long time to be undercover." Owen peered at him. "Can I ask you something?"

"Sure."

"What did you see in there?"

Randy gave him a mild stare. "What you'd expect to see in what was basically a brothel."

"Nice deflection." Owen shifted a little until he was facing Randy. "Did you ever see guys fucking? And no, I'm not being salacious here."

Randy took another drink before replying. "Yes." His pulse quickened as he recalled walking through the main area, where there were couches and chairs. Where he'd watched a guy in a suit unzip his fly, slip on a condom, and sit back while one of the hookers sat on it and rode it until he came all over the red carpet.

Jesse. Holy fucking hell, Jesse, bent over that same couch, while two guys spit-roasted him. Christ, the noises he'd made. The way he'd looked.

"Lots of times?"

Owen's question yanked him back into the present. "Yes." So many times that he'd lost count. Another drink.

"And?"

"And what?"

Owen locked gazes with him. "How did you feel about that?"

Fuck. There was the million-dollar question. Randy took a deep breath. "It turned me on," he said quietly. And that right there was the fucking understatement of the year, pun most definitely intended.

"Did it make you curious?"

Randy frowned. "About what?"

Owen shrugged. "About what it might feel like. You know, in case you ever decided to do more than just… observe." He raised his eyebrows. "I don't have to spell it out, do I?"

"No, you certainly don't." Randy put down his glass. "And to answer your question… yeah."

"Thanks for being honest with me." Owen stared into his own glass. "So let me go back to my original question. *Have* you ever been attracted to a guy?"

There was no going back now.

"Yes," Randy whispered.

"More than once?"

Randy clasped his hands. "Jesus, I feel like I really *am* on your therapy couch."

Owen put down his glass. "I'm sorry. I went too far. But… one final question, if I may? One that's hopefully not too intrusive."

Randy snickered. "Hell, you've gotten this far—you might as well finish the job." His heart pounded.

"Have you ever wanted to see where that curiosity might lead you?"

Randy cleared his throat. "I like women."

Owen snickered again. "That wasn't what I asked. And so what if you like women? Nothing wrong with liking men *and* women, right?"

"If you say so."

Owen laughed. "I think I'd better quit at this point. If we carry on this conversation much further, you'll stop coming here for a drink on a Friday night, and I for one would hate that."

Thank God for that. Randy picked up his glass and raised it. "Here's to leaving the job where it belongs—at work."

Owen clinked his glass and sighed. "Okay, I got the message. I'll take off my psychologist's hat." He held out the bowl. "Have some more chips."

Randy took another handful, and the conversation slipped streams to end up being a discussion of weird people they'd seen lately on the subway. Sanity restored.

It wasn't until later, when Randy got into bed, switched out the light, and lay there, trying to ignore the sound of traffic, that he realized something. When Owen had asked if he'd ever been attracted to a guy, only one face flitted through his mind.

Jesse's.

And Randy wasn't sure how he felt about that.

Chapter Four

"SAME TIME next month?"

Jesse smiled. "Sure."

"Jonathon" wasn't exactly a demanding trick. If anything, Jesse felt more like a therapist than an escort. Their encounters always went the same way. Jesse would suck him off—which usually lasted less than five minutes—then they'd spend the rest of the hour cuddled up on the hotel bed while Jonathon talked about his lousy marriage, how his kids took advantage of him, how work was a ball-ache.... Jesse had learned not to offer advice, just to lie there, holding him and making soothing noises. Jonathon traveled to New York on business every month, and Jesse could count on getting a call the minute he checked into his hotel.

If only all my tricks were that easy. Jonathon was a walk in the park compared to some. And in a business where the customer was definitely king—at least, if he wanted them coming back on a regular basis—sometimes that meant putting up with whatever they threw at him.

"Whatever" covered a lot of ground.

Jonathon saw him to the door, and Jesse patted him on the shoulder. No kisses on the cheek for this guy. The first time Jesse had gone to give him a peck, Jonathon had visibly recoiled, and Jesse got the message real fast.

He walked along the hallway to the elevator, checking his phone. His next "appointment" wasn't for a couple of hours. Jesse sighed. *What has a guy got to do around this city to drum up more business?* He already had his details on three online sites, and always asked the few regulars he had to spread the word, but that wasn't working out all that well for him. Word-of-mouth was infinitely preferable to the johns who saw his ad. At least with the former, he had an idea what to expect. With the latter, he had no clue, and he couldn't exactly afford to be fussy.

You take what you can get, right?

Jesse shook his head. *Pretty Woman* might have been a great movie, but it bore little resemblance to reality. He couldn't picture Richard Gere manhandling Julia Roberts, for one thing, or wanting to fuck her straight for a solid hour. Jesse had caught on damn quick to the tools he could employ to make sure that didn't happen too often. Offering a john a full-body massage meant minutes ticking away when he wasn't getting fucked, and that was just fine.

Jonathon's hotel was located in the East Village, which meant only one thing—the chance to meet up with a few friends at Nowhere on East Fourteenth Street. He could afford the time, right? It wasn't as if he was inundated with calls. *And besides, when was the last time I went for a drink?* It was nine o'clock, his day wouldn't end until after midnight, and he fucking deserved a beer.

His phone pinged, and Jesse smiled. Steve was already at Nowhere. *Great minds think alike*, he texted back. *Be there in five*. He called the elevator, still smiling. He hadn't had the time or the opportunity to talk with Steve at Richards's sentencing, and he hadn't seen him during the intervening three weeks. *Time to catch up on the latest gossip.*

By the time he walked into Nowhere's heavily red interior, Steve was already at the pool table with two beers on the shelf behind him. Jesse grinned as he approached. "Who's winning? And is one of those mine?"

Steve nodded without taking his eyes off the ball at the end of his cue. "The one on the left. And shh, gotta concentrate." His partner snickered, and Steve glared at him. "Hush, you. I'm just warmin' up."

Jesse walked behind him and grabbed the glass. He leaned against the wall, taking in the guys who were packing the place. Having a social beer was a rarity. Normally he bought a Coke and made it last all night while he kept his eyes peeled for possible hookups. Not that it was an easy task—Nowhere was a dark joint. Jesse loved it. The drinks were cheap, and the place had this whole dive-y vibe going for it. Better yet, the DJ played a great selection of music at a volume that didn't deafen you. Nowhere was a gay bar, but not obviously so. It was the kind of bar you went to if you wanted a cheap drink before going out to somewhere else a helluva lot more expensive.

"Aw, shit."

Jesse bit back his smile. Apparently something had broken Steve's concentration. Jesse grabbed an empty table in the corner, amazed to find one, and waited for Steve to join him.

Steve took the chair facing him and chugged back a third of his beer. "How's tricks?"

Jesse snickered. "We talking specifically or generally?"

To his surprise Steve didn't smile. "You heard what's been happening?"

Okay, that killed his good mood. Jesse put down his glass. "Apparently not. Enlighten me."

Steve frowned. "Something's up. Another site has just closed down."

"What do you mean, another?" Jesse was genuinely perplexed.

Steve cocked his head to one side. "How many escort sites are you listed on?"

"Three."

He nodded. "And you haven't heard any whispers? How maybe they're gonna close down?"

Jesse blinked. "All right, what have I missed?"

Steve shrugged. "Maybe you've just been lucky so far, but I know of at least three sites that have closed in the last month."

"They weren't doing enough business?" Jesse couldn't see *that* being the case. One couldn't go anywhere in Manhattan without tripping over an escort. Business was brisk.

Well, for *some* escorts it was. He'd give anything to be one of those guys, the ones who were charging three hundred a time and got it, the ones who did cam work too. *Maybe that's something I need to consider doing.* Because at this rate, he'd never have enough to finish his MBA. In fact, the way things were going, he'd be looking at finishing in his thirties.

That was a sobering thought.

Steve shook his head. "More like the owners are getting nervous. Something's in the wind."

"Like what?"

"The word on the street is that the current administration is cracking down on sex trafficking—"

"Which has nothing to do with us," Jesse interjected.

Steve held up his hand. "Maybe so, but as a result, sex workers are being affected. Sites are being watched. I tell ya, being online is getting riskier by the minute."

Fuck. That was *not* good. Those three escorting sites might not bring Jesse a lot of business, but at least they brought *something*.

Steve stared gloomily into his glass. "If the site I'm on goes tits-up, that means it'll be back to doing things the old-fashioned way. Word of mouth, on the streets, in the old spots. But what makes that *really* bad is the cops are getting more vigilant. I swear, everywhere I go nowadays, there's a cop watching."

That didn't surprise Jesse. "If they're cracking down on sex trafficking, it stands to reason they've got prostitution in their sights too." God, it had been so much easier in the Black Lounge. Guys coming to them, facilities….

Except he couldn't think like that. Because easy as it had been, behind the Black Lounge was all that shit that cost people their lives.

Steve cackled. "What you *really* need these days is a friendly cop in your corner. Y'know, one who'll turn a blind eye, take backhanders to keep his mouth shut—hell, even take payment in kind. There *are* cops out there who'll do that, right? You hear some guys talking about them all the time."

Jesse's mind went straight to Randy. "I do know a cop, but… I don't think he'd do that." Like Jesse was ever gonna let Randy get *one whiff* of what he was doing. He smirked. "You know him too."

Steve's eyes widened. "That undercover guy? Fuck no. He works *Vice*, for chrissakes. Stay away from that guy. No, I'm tellin' ya, the way this is going? Your best bet is to have guys watching your back. Safety in numbers, an' all that." He peered at Jesse. "Where are you staying? Last I heard, you were at a friend's place."

Jesse gave a bitter laugh. "Which friend was that? I moved out of one place just after the trial finished, but where I am now? Not gonna work out. I have to find somewhere else." Again.

His heart sank at the thought.

Steve gave him a thoughtful stare. "I got a place. Not huge, but it's in a good location." He grinned. "An abso-fucking-lutely *perfect* location."

"Where?" Jesse's heartbeat quickened. *Please, tell me he's offering….*

"You know the XL Lounge on West 42nd Street? There's an apartment block next door, and lots of guys stay there." Steve's eyes gleamed. "And I *do* mean lots. Hookers, rent boys, escorts, sex workers… whatever you wanna call 'em, they live there. And we look out for each other."

"Any apartments available?"

"No idea, but I can find out." Steve's face lit up. "But I got a better idea. Move in with me. Okay, so it's not that big, but there's a couch. You do outcalls only, right?"

Jesse nodded.

"Then that works out just fine. It makes sense. We share the rent, instead of you forking out for your own place."

Jesse had to admit, he really liked the idea. "You sure I wouldn't… cramp your style?"

Steve guffawed. "Hell no. And it would be good to have someone I can trust around the place. I mean, it's not like we don't know each other, right?"

He had a point. Jesse nodded. "Then, yeah, I'd love to."

"When could you move in?"

"Well, not until the weekend. I'm gonna be busy until then." He smirked.

Steve raised his glass. "Amen to *that* kind of busy."

Jesse clinked his against it, then pulled out his phone. "And speaking of business, I gotta run. Got a guy waiting for me on the Upper East Side." He drained his glass, then reached into his pocket for three dollars.

Steve shook his head. "Keep your money. You can buy the next one. Now that I know where you're gonna be living." He waggled his eyebrows.

Jesse laughed. "Thanks, Steve, you're a lifesaver." He leaned across and gave him a peck on the cheek before getting up from the table. "I'll text you about moving in, all right?"

Steve nodded. "Now get your cute ass to the Upper East Side an' work it, baby."

Jesse gave a little wiggle as he walked toward the door, hearing Steve's laughter behind him.

Despite Steve's revelations about possible changes on the horizon, Jesse was feeling more positive. Things were looking up, finally.

RANDY WALKED into the Stitch Bar and scanned the tables. He smiled when he caught sight of Donna waving at him and made his way over to her table. She stood as he approached, beaming, her arms wide for a hug.

"Hey, how's my famous cousin? And where did all your hair go?"

Randy laughed as she released him. "Why? You don't like it? And not so famous these days, thankfully. What are you drinking?"

Donna rolled her eyes. "A cocktail, what else? It's goddamn happy hour."

"Ah, is that why we're here?" Randy couldn't have cared less where they met up. He hadn't seen Donna in a long while.

"That, and the fact that they serve amazing pizza. I've got one ordered." Her eyes glittered. "If you're good, you can share. Now, what are you having? And don't go all boring on me. Choose a cocktail. Live adventurously. You must be missing all that, now that you're back to everyday policing."

Randy huffed. "It's certainly not boring."

A waitress appeared at their table, but before he could utter a word, Donna ordered him a cosmopolitan. As the waitress walked away from them, Randy stared at Donna.

"That's it? I get no choice?"

"Suck it up. I'm buying this round. You can buy the next."

Randy laughed. "Oh Lord. Last time we went to a bar, you drank me under the table."

Donna buffed her nails on her blouse. "That's 'cause a beat cop can outdrink a detective any day of the week." She leaned back in her chair. "God, it's good to see ya. I meant to call weeks ago when the trial finished, but life kinda got in the way."

"Is that why you called? Because it has been a while? Not that I'm complaining, you understand. I love seeing you." He grinned. "It's that suspicious nature of mine. Can't turn it off." Donna bit her lip, and Randy gaped. "My God, are you blushing? You don't blush, ever."

She gave him a mock glare. "Hey. Course I blush. And I asked you here because… I have news." She held up her left hand, and something glinted on her ring finger.

Randy's jaw dropped. "No. Seriously? When did this happen? And who's the lucky guy?" Before she could reply, he got up from his chair, came around to hers, and hoisted her to her feet in a fierce hug. "That's wonderful," he said quietly, his cheek pressed to hers. He released her and took a step back. "Yeah, happy is a good look on you."

They sat down, and Donna took a long drink from her glass. "Okay, now to answer your questions. This happened last week, and you might know him. His name is Andy Varrio."

Randy blinked. "He's a cop, isn't he? Works Vice?"

She nodded. "He just transferred to Brooklyn. And this is all Mitch Jenkins's fault."

"Mitch?" Randy laughed. "How is this his fault?"

"I took him to talk to Andy—you know, about Nikko? And he asked me how long I'd had the hots for him. Well, it got me thinking. Hell, if Mitch could see it, maybe everyone else could too. Including Andy. So I… asked him out for a drink. That was nearly a year ago. Anyhow, last week he popped the question."

Randy had to admit, she looked ridiculously happy. "How did Aunt Carol take the news?"

Donna snickered. "Oh my God. I swear, I've *only* just gotten Mom to stop saying, 'Well, it's about time.' To hear her, you'd think I was an old maid. I'm only thirty." She grinned. "Not as old as some folks I know, right, cousin? You're, what, thirty-six? Isn't it time you found yourself a good woman and settled down?" She rolled her eyes and shuddered. "Christ, I'm turning into my mom."

Randy snickered, but all the muscles in his stomach tensed. "Any date set for the wedding?"

Donna shook her head. "This is gonna take some organizing. Andy has this *huge* family, and they're spread out all over Brooklyn, Queens, Long Island…. Thank God *our* side isn't that ginormous." She fell silent as the waitress approached with Randy's cosmo and a large wooden slab with a delicious-looking pizza on it. When they were alone again, Donna gave him an inquiring glance. "I didn't put my foot in it, did I? I mean, I have no idea if you're seeing anyone…."

Randy smiled. "Still single, and happy to stay that way." He helped himself to a slice of pizza, moaning when the flavors burst on his tongue. "My *God*, this is good."

"Didn't I tell ya?" Donna took a bite, nodding. "Mmm." She swallowed and peered at him again. "And how is my old friend Mitch?" She sighed. "I miss him. I comfort myself with the knowledge that he's happy up in Maine. He *is* still happy, right?"

"Blissfully." Randy envied him. He and Nikko were obviously such a good fit.

"Hey, what did you mean about work certainly not being boring?"

He sighed. "Long story."

"Then give me the sound bite."

Randy took a sip of his cocktail. "It's like someone lit a fire under the police commissioner's ass. Get this—I now have 'targets' to meet." He air-quoted.

"What kind of targets?"

He paused. "We're being pushed really hard to get the sex workers off the streets, like they've suddenly become an eyesore or something."

Donna's sigh echoed his. "Yeah, that's what Andy was saying too. I guess it's happening all over the state." She gazed at him thoughtfully. "Can I ask you something? How do you feel about that? Seeing as you worked undercover in a brothel. Does it make you see things differently?"

Randy let out a sigh of relief. "Yeah. I can't help it. I got to know those guys. More importantly, I got to know why they were there. And yeah, it does color how I see things."

Donna inclined her head toward the pizza. "Less talk, more pizza. And just to lighten the mood, I'll tell you some of Frank's latest exploits."

Randy groaned. His cousin Frank was gay, and not exactly a good judge of character when it came to the men he dated. "What's he done now?"

Donna bit her lip. "I'm just gonna say a few choice words. Emergency Room. Candles. Doorknob. Inappropriate use thereof."

Randy winced. "Ouch. And by the way, we're eating here."

Like that ever stopped Donna.

RANDY KISSED Donna goodbye and headed for the subway. As he neared the station, he glimpsed a familiar figure: a tousled-haired blond, slim man leaning against the wall next to the entrance, his hands in his jacket pockets. Randy's heartbeat sped up, and he hurried over.

"Hey, Jesse!"

The young man turned, frowning when he saw Randy. "Were you talkin' to me?"

It wasn't Jesse.

Randy held up his hands in apology. "Sorry. I… thought you were someone else."

The guy nodded amiably, and then his face lit up as another man walked over to him, his arms open wide. "Hey, you got here."

Randy tried not to stare as they kissed, clearly lost in each other and not giving a shit for those who observed them.

When they parted, the blond guy looked in Randy's direction, and he tensed. "Can I do somethin' for ya?" His partner jerked his head up and stared at Randy, too, just as tense.

Fuck. Randy gave him as relaxed a smile as he could manage. "It's fine, honest. Just good to see people in love."

Just like that, the blond guy's features softened, and he smiled warmly. "Hey, no problem." He took the other man's hand, and they walked away, not letting go.

Randy waited until they were out of sight, then expelled a long breath.

Talk about Jesse on my mind.

It was getting to be a common occurrence.

Chapter Five

JUNE WAS turning out to be very pleasant—warm enough that Jesse was wearing his jeans and a pale pink shirt with only the middle buttons fastened. The perfect day to be taking a walk in Isham Park.

Not that Jesse was there to take a walk. He was scouting for business. The entrance to the park on 212th Street and Broadway had proved profitable a couple of times in the past, but this was obviously not one of those days. It was usually easy to spot those who were interested—there was no way to hide it when a guy walked past you but kept looking back. *Busted.*

The tricky part was when a guy wanted to take him into the park and fuck him up against a tree. *That* got the adrenaline pumping.

In the end it hadn't mattered that it was a perfect summer's day. It was past four o'clock and Jesse had spent a couple of hours there, with nothing to show for it. If the day wasn't going to turn out to be a complete bust, he needed to move on to a more profitable location. At least, that was the idea—until he caught sight of a familiar figure, heading right for him. Jesse peered a little closer and stiffened. His hair was a damn sight shorter, but it was definitely Randy. He wore jeans and a white shirt, as if he was trying to blend into the background.

Because he looked nothing like a cop.

What's he doing way up here? Then Jesse gave himself a swift mental kick. *What are you, a fucking* moron? *He's hardly out for a walk in the park, is he? He's a fucking* Vice cop. *And it's a solid bet he's looking for guys like me.*

Jesse thought fast. Because it was a sure bet Randy would want to know what *he* was doing there too. He breathed in deeply, then smiled, standing still as Randy drew nearer. "Hey." His pulse raced with the effort he was putting into looking relaxed.

Randy's face lit up. "Hey. What brings you to this neighborhood?"

Jesse gestured to a spot behind him. "Oh, I had a job interview at a pizza place around the corner, but they took on someone else." He tried to look suitably upset about the outcome, aware that he couldn't lie for shit. His mom had told him that often enough.

"Aw, that's a shame. Have you got time for a coffee?"

The unexpected question took Jesse aback for a second, but he recovered quickly. "Sure. Where'd you have in mind?"

Randy pointed across the street to where a cafe stood, its white-framed windows open, with seating outside behind a red barrier, and a red-and-white striped awning above. "How about there? It's a great day for sitting outside."

Jesse peered at the sign above the cafe. "My, how French. Sure. Cafe De Broadway it is."

Randy chuckled. "The name might be, but inside it's pure all-American." He walked over to the crosswalk, and they waited until the traffic came to a halt.

Jesse chuckled. "Yeah, good idea. You wouldn't wanna get caught jaywalking, right?"

Randy snorted. "I've missed that sassy mouth of yours."

They crossed the street and went inside the cafe. The server led them out to a table, and they sat.

Randy looked him up and down. "A word of advice? If you're serious about finding a job, maybe a less casual look next time might be the way to go?" He smirked. "I mean, I know it was only a pizza place, but still, first impressions, right?"

Jesse forced a laugh. "That might've had something to do with the outcome, don'tcha think? Thanks for the advice." He perused the menu, his mouth watering when he saw one item. "When was the last time I had flan?" he murmured.

"Flan?" Randy frowned. "You mean, like a tart?"

Jesse shook his head. "It's like a creme caramel, only with more substance. Great if you have a sweet tooth."

Randy sighed. "Damn. Your X-ray vision saw my weakness right away."

"Oh really?" Jesse snickered, and when the server returned, he ordered two portions of flan, plus a couple of lattes. Once the server had left them, he relaxed into his chair and gazed at their surroundings. "This is really nice." How in the hell he managed to sound so calm, he would never know. *What is it about Randy that gets me all tongue-tied and wound up tighter than a clock spring?*

Like he didn't know the answer to that one.

"I'm glad I got the chance to get you on your own," Randy said after a moment's silence. "That lunch after the trial wasn't the best time to talk."

A rolling sensation unfurled in Jesse's belly. "Oh? What about?"

Randy rested his chin on his steepled fingers and gazed at him. "I asked about your family, but you didn't answer."

"Not quite. You got a call, remember?" Jesse knew he wasn't going to get away with it a second time.

Randy smiled. "Nothing wrong with your memory, is there, Jesse? But now you can answer. Because I got the feeling all wasn't right with you and that your family might be one of the reasons for that. Of course, I could have everything backward, but I doubt it. Nothing wrong with *my* memory either." He regarded Jesse closely. "You were always such a happy, laid-back soul. Used to make me smile to hear the way you went on."

Jesse couldn't resist. "Except you never used to smile at me, only Nikko. I'd joke with him about it. Thing is, when you stopped smiling, I knew that was bad."

Randy stared at him. "And there *I* was, thinking I was doing such a good job of remaining objective in there."

Jesse sighed. "You were easily the most human person in that place." When Randy didn't break eye contact but held his stare, Jesse shrugged. "We held on to that."

"I see." Randy cleared his throat, the faintest flush creeping up his neck.

The coffees arrived, and soon after, the flans, each one sitting in the center of a plate, caramel sauce drizzled over it, along with raspberry sauce, and a cherry on top of it, with a couple of mint leaves as the finishing touch.

Randy beamed. "This looks amazing." He patted his stomach. "And definitely wicked." He took a forkful, and closed his eyes as he tasted it, his tongue darting out to lick the sauce from his lips.

Jesse tried not to stare. *This was a bad idea.* He attempted to concentrate on his flan, but Randy had other ideas.

"So are you gonna tell me now? About your family?"

Sighing, Jesse put down his fork and slowly recited the whole sorry mess, dismayed as Randy's expression morphed from shock into anger. When he'd finished, Randy was staring at the tabletop, his jaw set.

"I am so sorry," he said at last. "I had no idea it ended up that way. And I can't help feeling that I'm partly to blame."

Jesse stilled, gazing at him incredulously. "How can any of this be *your* fault? I was the one who chose to work there, remember? You were just doing your job. And because you did your job, Richards and the rest of them are behind bars tonight."

That jaw hadn't so much as quivered. "Yeah, but I got you to testify. You didn't have to do that."

Jesse huffed. "Of course I did. You said it yourself. For the case to succeed, you needed as many of us as possible to say what went on there."

Randy stared at him for a moment, then went back to his flan. "So where are you living now? Obviously you're still in New York."

Jesse smiled. "Like I could live anywhere else." Except that wasn't quite true, not anymore. The Big Apple had lost a lot of its luster during the past ten months.

"And yet you still haven't said where exactly it *is* that you're living." Randy's lips twitched.

"Oh, I'm sharing with a friend. It made sense to have a roommate," Jesse said vaguely.

That careful scrutiny was once more in evidence. "Do you need anything? And I'm being serious here, so don't just wave me off. I mean it. If you need something, ask."

Randy's quiet, earnest voice found its way under Jesse's skin, and he swallowed hard, genuinely touched. "I'm fine, honest, but thank you." Too much emotion, way too close to the surface. He gestured to Randy's hair. "I thought I'd hate the new look, but you know what? It suits you." His blue-black hair was glossy, cut close to his head, and had Jesse itching to run his fingers over it. The combination of dark hair, creamy skin with a hint of facial scruff, and those startlingly blue eyes behind wire frames was stunning. Randy's eyes had always had the capacity to make Jesse weak at the knees, but now?

Why did you have to make him straight, God? I mean, really?

Randy beamed. "Thank you. I still keep catching sight of my reflection and going, 'Who *is* that?'" Jesse laughed, and Randy gazed at him critically. "Seems I'm not the only one who's gone for a new look. You've changed your hair."

Automatically, Jesse reached up to touch his head. "Yeah. It was getting a little too long. Besides, summer's coming. Short hair is always better when the weather gets hotter." Who was he kidding? It had nothing to do with the heat, and everything to do with creating the right look.

"Well, to quote you… it suits you."

Jesse didn't know how to respond. He cleared his throat. "So… you still in Vice?" Like he didn't already know the answer to *that* one. It was way too big a coincidence finding him in that spot.

"Yeah." Something in Randy's less than enthusiastic tone got through to him.

"I thought you liked your job."

"I did—I mean, I do—but…." He forked off another piece of flan but didn't eat it. The sigh that rolled out of him was so heavy that Jesse gazed at him in concern. Randy put down his fork. "I ran into Baz last week."

"Our Baz?"

That brought a faint smile. "Yeah, our Baz. Anyhow, it was pretty obvious he's soliciting."

That wasn't news to Jesse, but hearing Randy's words sent a quake through him. "Wow. What did you do?" Jesse could feign surprise. That was child's play compared to some of the emotions he faked during sex.

"I *should* have arrested him. That's what I *should* have done." Randy's words were tinged with anger, and Jesse couldn't tell if they were directed at himself or at some other unknown entity.

"But you didn't," Jesse said finally. What puzzled him was that he'd seen Baz a couple of days before, and Baz hadn't said a word about it.

Randy shook his head. "His husband is incapacitated. He had an accident that left him unable to work. What Baz earns on the streets is the only thing keeping their heads above water." When Jesse gaped at him, Randy smiled. "You didn't know he was married, did ya?"

"No." The subject had never come up those occasions when they'd worked together.

Randy nodded sagely. "Most of the guys who worked in the Black Lounge were there because they really needed the money to survive. Well, apart from you." He laughed. "You were the exception."

"Huh?"

Randy's smile didn't falter. "You needed the money, sure, to supplement what you got from your family for your studying, but you also did it because you loved the sex." He picked up his fork and continued eating.

"I was that obvious?" Jesse had to laugh too. "What can I say? You nailed me." He snickered. "Well, not literally."

Randy coughed, and he reached for a napkin. "Christ, warn a guy before you say stuff like that." He wiped his mouth, then chuckled. "I've missed you."

Jesse's breathing hitched, but he covered it with a cough. "Really?"

Randy nodded, his eyes bright and his mood visibly lighter. "Life was never dull when you were around." He put down his napkin. "I'm really glad I ran into you today. I'm sorry the job interview didn't work out, but I'm sure something will turn up. And now that I know what your situation is, I'll be keeping my fingers crossed that you find something soon."

"Thank you," Jesse said sincerely. "And I've enjoyed this too." It felt like they'd connected in a way that hadn't been possible in the Black Lounge, which was hardly surprising.

"But now I have to go." Randy got out his wallet and extracted a few bills.

"You're running out on me again?" Jesse joked. "And can I pay for my half?"

Randy shook his head. "When you've got a job and things are looking better, then yes, we'll do this again. Right now, I'm taking care of you." He grinned. "We all need a treat now and then, right? And yes, I'm running out on you again. I got bad guys to put away, remember?" Except his smile faded a little as he said the words.

"Where are you going now?" Jesse didn't want to let go just then.

"Right this minute? The Metro on 215th Street."

"Me too. I'll walk with you."

Randy's smile blossomed. "Great." He put the bills under his coffee cup, along with a tip, and they left the cafe, heading up Broadway. While they walked, Randy talked about all the open-air concerts taking place at various locations around Manhattan that summer. It turned out they both liked live music, and by the time they reached the Metro, Randy was already suggesting meeting up one evening to go to a concert.

It felt... unreal. Not only that, it felt like a dream. Until Jesse reminded himself savagely that *dream* was the perfect word for the situation, and that he needed to *wake the fuck up. Vice cop, remember? What would happen if a john saw you with Randy? Ever think about that?* Randy had changed his appearance, sure, but there might still be guys who'd recognize him, especially after having his face all over the media.

No, it was time to face reality. Nothing was ever gonna come of it, no matter how much he wanted it.

Sometimes Jesse hated being a realist.

STEVE WAS out when Jesse got back to the apartment, and that was fine because he had a phone call to make. He settled on the couch that doubled as his bed and clicked on Nikko's number.

"Hey." The genuine happy note in Nikko's voice warmed him. "I was just thinking about you."

Jesse chuckled. "Whaddaya know, I'm psychic."

"I was going to call you this weekend. Something you said at lunch that day has had me worrying, and I can't shake it off."

Aw fuck. Jesse knew it was time for honesty. "Okay, before you ask, yes, I'm escorting, all right? But I'm being careful, and at least I have a place to stay where I'm not waiting for someone to throw me out on my ear. It's a safe place too." He knew he was sanitizing the whole situation, but Nikko didn't need to hear the bad parts. *Give him the* Pretty Woman *version.* Nikko was gullible enough to believe it.

"You couldn't find a job?"

Jesse snorted. "You have no clue what it's like here, do ya? And let's be honest, I'm good at what I do. So it's a case of sticking with what you know works." Silence. "Nikko?"

A sigh filled his ears. "I guess you know what you're doing. Just keep on being careful, okay?"

"Always." Time to change the subject. "Hey, guess who I ran into today?"

"No idea."

"Randy. We had coffee and dessert." In spite of his initial panic, the memory still gave him a good feeling.

"Wow. I bet you enjoyed that."

"Yeah. It was a toss-up which was better—the dessert or the company."

Nikko chuckled. "I think it's a no-brainer which one came out on top." He paused. "You know what? You need a man."

Jesse laughed. "Sweetheart, I have lots of men. Well, most of the time they have *me*, but I'm not complaining." Who was he kidding? He knew full well that to most of the guys who paid him, Jesse was nothing more than a convenient hole. Scrap that—a pair of holes. And holes were easy to find in New York. There was plenty of competition out there.

"You know what I mean. You *need* someone."

Jesse was silent for a moment. "Yeah, but the one I want, I can't have."

"Why not?" Nikko asked softly.

"Let's see. One, he's straight. Two, he's out of bounds. I'm sure there are more reasons, but those two are more than enough." Yeah, because *three* was the real doozy. *He's a Vice cop.*

"That doesn't sound like the Jesse I know. If you want this guy, go after him."

Jesse couldn't hold back his sigh. "Let's not talk about this, okay?" Besides, it was time to get busy. He had money to earn.

"Fair enough. Call me soon?"

"I will, I promise." Jesse disconnected the call. He stared at the screen, wishing life was as simple as Nikko plainly thought it was. *Go after him. Yeah right. And what if that route only leads to torture?*

Jesse didn't need that kind of pain.

Chapter Six

RANDY SWITCHED off the TV, not that he'd really been watching it, and threw the remote onto the seat cushion beside him. His mind had been all over the place that evening, and he knew a lot of that was because of his meeting with Jesse.

It was just a coffee, for God's sake. Then why had it felt like so much more?

Thinking about Jesse seemed to be a common thread running through his days and nights, but Randy told himself he was just worried about him. That was all. It wasn't as if he was attracted to him, right? It wasn't like he was picturing Jesse with that new sexy haircut, and those pale blue eyes that seemed to see right into him, right? Because Randy was straight, no matter what Owen said.

His thoughts went back to that conversation with Owen, and his words were right there. *No one is completely straight, my friend.* Randy huffed. "Oh yeah?" he muttered. "We'll see about that." He reached for his laptop on the coffee table and fired it up. A quick online search found him exactly what he was looking for—a quiz.

Can we guess if you're gay? the headline screamed at him. There were only ten questions. Randy got comfortable and clicked on the icon to start.

The first question made him blink. *What the hell?* It wanted to know if his index finger was shorter than his ring finger. *Okay, not what I expected, but hey, let's play.* He clicked on the answer, then went on to the next question.

That was even weirder. Music artists appeared, and he was asked to choose his favorite. Beyoncé was there, so that was easy, but he could easily have chosen Katy Perry or Rihanna.

The third question had him laughing out loud. *Can you do this?* There was a video of a guy with his legs in the air, juggling five balls between his hands and feet. *Hell no.* Randy was still laughing as he went on to the next question. A pattern emerged, as he had to choose his favorite movie from a list, between *Batman* or *Superman*, his favorite chocolate…. The only time the questions got vaguely serious was when it asked how old he was when he had his first kiss.

Randy chuckled. He didn't think Tilly Kendrick stealing a kiss at a family wedding when he was seven was likely to affect the outcome much.

At last he was through them all and clicked for the results. When a rainbow flag popped up, filling the screen, with a single word—*Gay*—beneath it, Randy stared at it in disbelief.

Uh-uh. No way.

He got up from the couch, poured himself a glass of whiskey, and sat back down to redo the test, only this time, he varied his answers, because obviously some of his previous choices had screamed *gay*. The second time, he got a different response.

It said *Bi-curious*.

This stupid test is defective. Randy did another search and found one that appeared less inane and more scientific, with multiple choice answers. *That's better.* He took a drink from his glass and clicked on the screen. The opening words were a comfort.

This quiz will also cover bi-curiosity, so you can find out if you are straight, but with exceptions. Don't be worried about your result—you are lovable just the way you are.

He smiled to himself. *I'm lovable*. Then he went to the first question.

Do you have any same-sex crushes?

Shit. Okay, that was a dilemma. Did he answer truthfully, or what? Randy decided to be honest and see where it took him. But after that, the questions grew increasingly more… intimate.

Have you considered marrying the same sex? That one was easy. *No.*

Have you considered kissing the same sex? Oh dear God, he didn't want to get into *that* one.

Have you imagined having intercourse with the same sex? Randy swallowed. *Holy fuck.* He knew that any of the answers except *No* was going to steer his result down a certain course, but he couldn't in all honesty hit *No.* Because that would have been a lie.

The next two questions dealt with hypothetical situations in which Randy might find himself and his reactions to them. That wasn't so bad. But the seventh question froze him, because there it was, the heart of the matter.

Do you think you are homosexual?

He moved his finger across the mouse pad, deliberating. The answers ranged from *Not at all* to *Yes*, with varying degrees between. *I don't know how to answer!* In the end he went for *Not at all*, because he wasn't, and that was that.

Do you support homosexual marriage? The responses weren't as simple as yes or no, however. *Yes, but anonymously* felt like a lie, as did *I do not think much of it*. Randy thought it was one of the most important decisions the Supreme Court had ever made. But the three remaining choices were all about the possibility that it would happen for him one day, and he was stumped. In the end, he had to pick something, so he went with the anonymous one.

Have you taken a sexuality quiz before? What was the result?

Randy laughed. "Which time?" He lied and clicked on *This is my first sexuality quiz*. That left him with the final question, and he braced himself for whatever was about to appear on the next screen.

In your ENTIRE LIFE, have you been sexually attracted to the same sex?

His heartbeat quickened. His throat dried up. He ached to click on *No*, but that was a lie. *Multiple times* was equally a lie, and that left him just one answer that got near to the truth. Randy took a deep breath and chose his response. *Only once.*

His breathing still rapid, he clicked on Test Results and waited.

40%. Bi-curious.

Okay, it wasn't as bad as the first test, but that didn't mean he was happy with it. And that meant only one thing—do the test again, altering his responses to the ones he felt a straight person would give.

By one in the morning, he'd done two more tests on other sites and no longer knew which way was up. His results ranged from *Gay* to *Bi-curious*, all the way down to *Straight*. That last result should have made him happy, but it didn't.

It was false, and he knew it.

Beyond tired and confused as hell, he stumbled into bed and was asleep within seconds.

RANDY LEANED against the washing machine, its white noise strangely relaxing, and closed his eyes. The basement was empty, and his was the only machine in operation. He rubbed his hands over his face and caught the smell of the fabric softener, a mixture of lavender and chamomile. He inhaled, letting it soothe him.

"Someone looks like he's had a rough day."

Randy opened his eyes. Owen stood in the doorway, a white plastic basket in his arms. "Hey."

Owen nodded toward the dryer in the corner. "Came to collect my stuff." He walked past Randy and proceeded to empty his clothing from its innards. "So am I right? Rough day?"

"Lately, every day's a rough day." Randy was kind of getting used to it, but that didn't mean he liked it.

"What's up?"

Randy placed his hands on top of the washing machine, letting its rumblings shudder through him. "This job is getting tougher. That's what's up."

"In what way?" Owen asked as he folded a cream shirt carefully before placing it in the basket.

Randy huffed. "Seems like there are more and more guys working the streets. I should explain. I deal mainly with male hookers. My job is to arrest the *bad guys*," he said, air-quoting. "Only, that's the problem. I don't see them as bad guys." That had turned up during his debriefing sessions, once he'd finished his undercover stint.

"Apart from a sudden influx of hookers and rent boys—and I can't see how that could be, unless they've suddenly started bussing in from all over—what else has changed?"

"You know how this administration likes to be seen doing the right thing?"

Owen rolled his eyes. "Lord yes. 'Let's crack down on the homeless.' 'Let's get the beggars off the streets.' 'Let's crack down on the motorcycles.' Seen it all before." He peered at Randy. "I take it you're under the microscope this month?"

Randy snorted. "More like this year. 'Let's crack down on prostitution.' 'Let's stop sex trafficking.' Now when it comes to the latter, I got no problem. You can recognize who the real bad guys are—the ones behind the scenes, selling people. Guys like Richards and his brother Seb, y'know, real scumbags. Earlier this year, NYPD added another twenty-five detectives to their Vice squad, just to investigate sex trafficking. Plus they set up a twenty-four-hour hotline, staffed by Special

Victims Division investigators, so people can call to anonymously report trafficking."

Owen frowned. "But... that's good, isn't it?"

Randy nodded fervently. "Oh, sure it is! Human trafficking is one of the fastest growing enterprises in the world. Why'd you think the judge threw the book at Richards? New York is the fourth-highest state for sex trafficking. And I think it's great that they talked about 'altering the mindset,' switching the emphasis away from the prostitutes and focusing more on the pimps who sell them and the johns who pay for their services."

Owen folded his arms across his chest. "Then what's changed? What's taken the status from *great* to *not so great*?"

Randy stared at the tiled floor. "You wanna know what I was doing all day? Posting fake ads and sending text messages. Posting phony listings to prostitution sites."

"That doesn't sound like policing."

He shrugged. "All part of the latest initiative. We post the ad, go to a hotel, wait until the john shows up, then arrest him."

Owen frowned. "That sounds like it could be dangerous. Just thinking how *I'd* react if I turned up at a hotel, expecting to find a hooker, and instead I'm confronted by a cop. Some guys might decide to beat the shit out of you. Tell me you cops work in pairs for this."

Randy laughed softly. "You bet your ass. Most of the time, they don't react too violently." There had been some, however, and a couple of incidents had resulted in additional charges of assaulting a police officer. "Except I think the word is out. Some of them aren't showing up, so then we send text messages."

"Saying what?" Owen asked with a smirk. "Sorry I missed you, please call again?"

Randy cleared his throat. "The NYPD sent you this message because you responded to an online ad for prostitution. Offering to pay or paying someone for sexual conduct is a crime and punishable by incarceration up to seven years." He shook his head. "I've sent so many of 'em, I could type it with my eyes closed." He shook his head. "I'm seeing a helluva lot of hotel rooms on a weekly basis, 'cause there's a sting at least once a week, including ones run by female officers. But to be fair, the ads are aimed at people trying it for the first time, hoping to scare 'em off, or legit guys with jobs or families who don't want to get arrested."

"Then I still don't get what the problem is, because this all sounds like good sense to me."

Randy nodded slowly. "So we crack down on the guys buying sex. Good deal. But when you move away from that and start to look at the people who are selling on the street? That's when the lines start to blur." He shook his head. "The world isn't black and white anymore, just... shades of gray. Suddenly you got people whose livelihood is being altered by what we do."

Owen blinked. "You're feeling sorry... for the hookers?"

"You forget, I got to know a lot of those *hookers*. I know what forced them to sell themselves in the first place. Don't be thinking Richards strong-armed them into working in that place. They *wanted* to be there because it put food on the table, clothes on their backs.... And they didn't put Richards away for eighty years just for running a brothel. They put him away for pushing drugs and moving people across the States, and a whole lot more besides. But yeah, it's the ones making money on their backs I feel sorry for. Because their lives just got a damn sight harder."

Owen finished folding, came over to him, and laid a gentle hand on Randy's shoulder. "Are you okay? I've never heard you sound this low before."

Randy sighed. "When I first became a cop, I felt like I was doing some good, ya know? Making a difference. But now? The job has changed, and I'm not so sure I like what it's become." He expelled a long breath. "Ignore me. I went to bed way too late last night, and I'm feeling really tired."

Owen nodded, squeezing Randy's shoulder. "Tell you what. Why don't you come over to my place when you're done down here, and we'll have a drink and watch some TV. Just for some company and to take your mind off things." He held up his hands. "One drink, I swear. I wouldn't let you have more than that, not if you're so tired. You won't sleep tonight either. But I don't like the thought of you being alone this evening. Seems to me like you could use a friend."

Randy smiled. "That is exactly what I need. Sure. Let me put the clothes in the dryer, and I'll be up there."

"Great. I'll see if there's anything worth watching. I'm thinking a comedy or something else equally light on the brain." Owen picked up his basket. "Just knock when you're done."

"Thanks, Owen." Randy waited until he'd gone before taking his phone from his jeans pocket. He went into Contacts and pulled up Jesse's number, staring at it for a few minutes. He wasn't sure why Jesse had come to mind. Randy supposed it was because he was still worried about him. Something about finding him at that spot near Isham Park the other day had bothered him. Randy knew why *he'd* been there—it was a favorite haunt for hookers picking up trade—but seeing Jesse there had given him a moment's unease.

Please, tell me you're not doing what I think you're doing.

Randy didn't want to be scoping Jesse out.

In the end he put his phone away. *What reason would I give for calling him? "Hey, Jesse. Just thought I'd give you a call and check you weren't soliciting. How's tricks?"*

Yeah, that would go down *really* well.

The best thing he could do would be to keep an eye out for Jesse. And hope to God he wasn't hiding something.

Randy didn't listen to that small voice in his head, telling him he already knew exactly what Jesse was up to.

Chapter Seven

JESSE COULDN'T believe he was considering asking Randy to go with him to a concert, of all things. When he'd first seen the details, Randy had leaped to mind immediately. It was only after Jesse'd thought about it for a while that he saw the downside to this plan.

Spending time with Randy was... risky.

Randy wasn't stupid. He was more than capable of putting two and two together and coming up with Jesse hooking, especially if he had a suspicious nature.

Excuse me? Cop, remember? Isn't that a prerequisite?

And the more Jesse considered the idea, the more convinced he became that Randy would never go for it. Never mind that they'd discussed this—asking Randy to come along felt too much like inviting him on a date, and why would he say yes to that?

For fuck's sake, just ask him. He can only say yes or no, right?

Jesse summoned up his courage, pulled out his phone, then paused when he saw the time. It was late. Like, *really* late to be calling. He found Randy's card and composed a quick text instead. *Hey. You around?*

Jesse laughed when Randy's reply flashed up. *Around what?*

Okay 2 call U?

Seconds later a text pinged in. *Sure.*

His heart hammering, Jesse dialed.

"Shouldn't you be in bed?" Randy said in a stern tone. "And yeah, that was a joke. Just in case my delivery was crap."

Jesse snickered. "Don't give up the day job."

"So you called me just to sass me? I'm hanging up now."

"Wanna go to a concert?" Jesse blurted out. When the line went quiet, he pressed ahead. "Remember we talked about the open-air concerts this summer? Well, there's one next week in Central Park. I don't know if you've ever heard of Lucy Wainwright Roche, but—"

"Are you kidding? I *love* her stuff. One of my favorite New Yorkers. I loved her cover version of James Taylor's 'America the Beautiful.'"

"Seriously? Me too." And just like that, Jesse's nerves took a back seat. "Does that mean you wanna go?"

"What night are we talking?"

"Saturday, six till nine. It's not just her playing the whole time, of course. There's also the Indigo Girls." He had no idea if Randy was into folk rock, but learning they were playing, too, had been the icing on the cake for Jesse.

Silence, and then Randy spoke softly. "I love their songs. 'Power of Two' is one of my all-time favorites. It's got one of the best lines ever. 'I'm stronger than the monster beneath your bed.'"

Wow. Randy was just full of surprises. Jesse loved their music, but apart from that, he followed them because they were LGBT activists, both of them lesbians, both in committed relationships. He doubted that was why Randy liked them, however.

"Then it's a yes?"

Randy chuckled. "No—it's a *hell yes*. Are we talking Rumsey Playfield?"

"Uh-huh."

"Then we'd better get there early, because that place will be packed. How about I meet you by the Bethesda Fountain at five o'clock? Maybe even a little earlier, if you want to get close to the stage."

"That sounds great." Jesse's head was still spinning. *He said yes.*

Randy yawned. "Oops, sorry. Been a long day. But you know what? I'm really looking forward to this."

"Yeah, me too. See you then." Jesse disconnected the call and let out an undignified squeal that thankfully no one else got to hear. Thank God Steve was out.

Then it hit him.

Hey. I should be out. Somewhere in Midtown was a john expecting him for a late-night booty call. *So get Randy out of your head and get your ass in gear.*

Literally. Because the last thing he wanted was a pissed trick.

Pissed equaled unpredictable. Not good.

BY THE time Jesse got back to the apartment, it was almost 1:00 a.m., and Steve wasn't around. Jesse grabbed a quick shower, then wrapped a towel around himself, poured a glass of juice, and sat on the couch, checking his phone for messages. When he opened his emails, Jesse noticed one from one of the sites he used.

It wasn't good.

"What the fuck?" Jesse read it through again, his stomach churning. He was still reading when Steve walked through the door. Jesse gazed at him, shaking his head. "Looks like you were right."

"About what?"

Jesse held up his phone. "One of the sites I'm on is closing down. Seems some of their ads were placed by cops, and people got arrested when they showed up. The site owners don't want to continue, not if they have no idea which ads are real and which are put there by the cops."

Steve scowled. "I don't blame 'em. And it's getting worse. The next thing you know, we'll be getting calls from guys, only when we show up, it'll be a cop. I tell ya, we're never gonna know who's a john and who's a cop. It's enough to make you stick with the guys you've serviced before."

"Yeah, but if I do that, I'm not gonna survive." Jesse felt sick. "I rely on those sites to bring me new guys. Sure, I've got my regulars, but they're not enough." He growled at the back of his throat. "Fucking NYPD. Don't the cops have anything better to do—y'know, like solve murders and shit like that? What harm are *we* doing? The johns wanna fuck, and *we* want them to fuck us. I call that win-win."

There was a time when he'd loved this, but that was when he'd worked at the Black Lounge a couple of nights a week, more during vacation time, to have a bit more money in his pocket. It was an enjoyable way to make a buck.

But times had changed. This was different. This was tougher.

This was survival.

"Maybe it's time to think about a change of career," he joked halfheartedly. Except he knew deep down it wasn't a joke. At this rate he'd be going under in a matter of months.

Steve snorted. "What—and work in a restaurant for minimum wage? You can earn more on your back in one day than you can earn in a week waiting tables. You just gotta be careful. That's all." He yawned. "I'm gonna hit the sack. Gotta look my best for my public, right?" Steve grinned. "Not all of us have your looks."

Jesse snickered. "Was that a compliment? Gee, thanks."

Once Steve had gone into his bedroom, Jesse pulled out the couch, his sheets still in place, and got ready for bed. Outside, the traffic continued with its dull drone, despite the hour. Jesse lay there, his mind going over their conversation.

A change of career. Yeah right. Jesse didn't want to think it had come to that. Not yet, at any rate. The way he looked at it, guys were paying him to do something he loved. Because Randy had nailed it for sure. Jesse loved sex, loved everything about the act. Most of the time he bottomed, but that was fine by him. It made those rare occasions when a john wanted to get fucked all the sweeter.

Except....

In the stillness of the apartment, Jesse took a long, hard look at himself. Everything was different. Sure, he'd enjoyed the sex in the Black Lounge. What was there not to like about it? He got to have fun, plus added income, with a steady stream of guys wanting him. Now? Sex had become his lifeline. And yes, there *were* days when he didn't feel like getting on his knees, or all fours, or his back. These days it was getting riskier by the minute.

And what about my goals? Back then he'd had a clear picture of what he wanted, where he was going. He'd left Michigan to study for his bachelor's in New York. When he'd completed that and spent what seemed like forever trying to get a job, he'd told his parents he wanted to do an MBA, and they'd been totally behind him. *Pity they forgot all that when they learned how I'd been supplementing what they gave me to live on.* He sighed. *Maybe I should've stuck with waiting tables after all. They'd have been okay with that.* Because right then he was achieving nothing. Real life had been put on hold, and the chances of earning enough to both keep himself going *and* save up to fund his education were looking remote.

Maybe waiting tables *as well as* hooking was the way to go. Another string to his bow.

Jesse recalled one of his first conversations with Nikko, who'd expressed surprise that Jesse was a student. *I told him selling myself wasn't what I wanted to do in life, and yet here I am.* Then he smiled to himself. That had been the day Jesse had noticed how often Randy smiled at Nikko. Jesse had been a little pissed at that. Oh, he really liked Nikko, who was obviously a sweet guy, but dammit, he'd wanted Randy to smile at *him*.

Jesse closed his eyes, picturing Randy's face, that sexy smile, those blue eyes that could be so warm sometimes. He pictured Randy as he'd been in the restaurant that day, those strong arms, those large hands.... Jesse shivered, imagining Randy's hand on his belly, his chest... and lower. *Oh fuck.* Jesse threw back the sheet and palmed his cock, his mind veering off into some blissful fantasy where Randy was touching him, caressing him... kissing him. Wrapping that big hand around Jesse's dick. Holding it around the root while he moved in to—

Jesse came with a shudder, all over his belly.

He lay there, his breathing returning to normal, his come cooling on his skin as the pleasure slowly ebbed away. *Talk about hot.* He wiped himself with the towel he'd left beside the bed, then closed his eyes once more.

Even if I can't have him, I can dream about him at least.

It was a poor consolation.

And jerking off to thoughts of Randy amounted to avoidance of the real problem.

RANDY MADE his way toward the fountain, asking himself for the umpteenth time why he'd agreed to this. Sure, he loved live music, and this particular artist was worth seeing any day, not to mention the Indigo Girls, so why was he regretting his decision?

There was only one answer. The prospect of spending an evening with Jesse.

Randy had really enjoyed their coffee the other week. He liked Jesse's company. But being around him was... tricky. Ever since Randy had taken those damn stupid tests, he'd become more aware of how often he thought about Jesse—and the *way* he thought about him. Because all that did was highlight the conflict within him.

I like women. I don't like guys.

Except Jesse was a guy, right?

There were times when he wondered why he was fighting this. What would be so wrong about liking guys too? What bothered him was how it was so out of the fucking blue. *You don't just wake up one morning and say, "Hey, I think I might be bisexual." That's not how it works.*

Except Randy had no clue how it worked.

Then he faced the facts. This was *not* out of the blue. This was only a continuation of what had started back in the Black Lounge—that slow dawning of interest, the realization that Randy's sexuality was not a done deal.

He had a fair idea what lay at the heart of his battle. His father.

Don Michaels was a "man's man." Macho. Tough. The kind of man who would never understand how guys could be attracted to guys, because "hey, you got everything you need right there between a woman's legs." The kind of man who joked with his work buddies in the meatpacking district, mouthing off about "the fags," and "the fuckin' queers takin' over the place." The kind of man who'd brought up his only son to believe that men were strong, unemotional, macho….

And yet there was Owen. Strong, intelligent, masculine, in touch with his emotions—and gay. And the guys in the Black Lounge. Some would have fitted right in there with his dad's description, but not all. Jordan, for instance. Baz was another. Randy had spent the last few years questioning the stereotypical images he'd accepted as a youth, because he'd finally come to realize there wasn't a mold out there somewhere for a gay man.

Or a straight man, for that matter.

And where do I fit in? Bi-curious? Bisexual?

He knew one thing for sure. "Randy" was a work in progress.

As Randy neared the fountain, he caught sight of Jesse, with shades covering his eyes, wearing white sneakers, a pair of denim cutoffs that revealed long, slim, tanned legs, and a white top emblazoned with the word *Love* in rainbow lettering, complete with glitter. Randy smiled to himself. *Nothing subtle about you, baby*. Then his heart skipped a beat as Jesse stretched, his top riding up. Randy couldn't take his eyes off Jesse's lean torso, barely an inch of fat on him. Something sparkled at his navel, and Randy realized it was a piercing. *That's new*. Some part of his mind went off in another direction, wondering if anything else was pierced too. Randy's pulse quickened at the thought.

Jesse's gaze swiveled in his direction, and he broke into a smile that made Randy's pulse quicken even more. *Lord, he could light up a room with that smile*. Jesse strolled toward him, his pace languid, moving easily, his arms at his sides. By the time he was close enough that Randy could see the outline of his phone in his front pocket, Randy had gotten himself under control.

"Have you been here long?"

Jesse shook his head. "Only about ten minutes. I was walking through the park, enjoying the sun." He tilted his head up, the light glinting off his sunglasses. "Isn't it a beautiful evening?"

It is now. Randy coughed. "We should get going if we're gonna get a good spot."

"Sure."

They walked side by side, following the gradually swelling noise of voices that led them to the concert area. They climbed the shallow steps that led to the main gate, and then they were out into the open air, a green artificial surface with a stage set up at one end and a large circular canopy above it. People had already started to gather close to the stage, sitting on the ground, where they talked and enjoyed the evening sunshine.

Randy led Jesse to the front, where they sat down. One of the concertgoers had brought along his guitar and was playing softly. He turned out to be really good, and before long, people were calling out requests. It proved to be a pleasant hour, sitting there in the evening light, listening to beautiful music.

When the concert began for real, Randy forgot about his job concerns and his self-doubts and lost himself in the music. Now and again he glanced at Jesse, finding him equally absorbed in the atmosphere, that smile never far from his face. It was a joy to sit there and listen to such wonderful voices, such thoughtful lyrics.

Then there were those moments when his gaze met Jesse's, and the contentment Randy saw in his eyes gave him reason enough to be glad he'd accepted the invitation. When the concert came to a close, he was genuinely sorry. He didn't want the night to end.

The concertgoers filed out of the playfield, Randy and Jesse heading for the nearest exit on East Seventy-Second Street.

When they reached the street, Jesse gave him a dreamy smile. "Wasn't that awesome?"

Randy had to agree. "Thanks for suggesting it. I had a great evening." He paused. "Do you want a coffee or a drink or something?" He wanted to hold on to the moment a little longer.

Jesse bit his lip. "Would you be offended if I said no? It's just that… I have another interview in the morning, and I want to be ready for it. And for me, that means getting a good night's sleep."

Randy smiled. "No problem. Thanks again for tonight." He tilted his head. "Which way is home? I go thataway." He pointed north.

Jesse chuckled. "And I go south. Thanks for coming with me." He paused, and Randy wondered what was coming. To his surprise, Jesse jerked his head forward and gave him a peck on the cheek before heading down Fifth Avenue.

Randy watched him walking away, still reeling from the unexpected display. He waited until Jesse was no longer in sight, then headed up Fifth Avenue, feeling light.

JESSE SAT on the train, his mind replaying the concert. It had been a fantastic evening, but having Randy there with him made it all the more memorable. Randy's presence was kind of a two-edged sword, however. Jesse had been constantly aware of him, and it had been difficult to concentrate fully on the music. Now and again, he'd caught Randy looking at him, and his heartbeat had sped up. Trying to appear unruffled had taken all his effort.

That last-minute invitation….

He'd wanted to say yes, to grab more time with Randy, but it was too much of a temptation. And besides, he really didn't need to torture himself like that. Jesse felt bad about lying, though.

Why did I have to go and kiss him?

That was easy. It had seemed like a good idea at the time.

"Did you have a good time tonight?"

Jesse blinked and looked around. The train car was half-empty, and a guy was seated next to him, smiling. "Excuse me?"

"The concert. In Central Park? I saw you there."

Jesse frowned. "Yeah, sure." *Okay, this is weird.* He glanced at the guy again, taking in his brown, straggly hair, brown eyes, and thin lips. Then he realized with a shock that he'd seen him before. The guy was a trick, from maybe a couple of months before. He'd given Jesse a bad feeling. Jesse hadn't felt safe and had been relieved to get the hell out of there.

"Yeah, I was gonna say something, you know, let on to ya, but then it occurred to me the guy you were with might not know about your… occupation." He smirked.

Holy fuck. That had been a close one. Panic slid through him in a cold rush, and Jesse fought to suppress a shiver. He couldn't reply, his throat was so tight.

The train drew to a halt, and to his utter relief, the guy got up. "This is me. Nice seeing you again. I might give you a call soon. You were… good." He leered, and Jesse wanted to throw up.

The doors opened, and he got out. Jesse waited until the train was moving again before putting his head in his hands, breathing deeply. He tried desperately to recall the trick's name so that if, God forbid, he did call again, Jesse would know to turn him down. Better than that, he'd pass the guy's name around. He was bad news—Jesse felt that in his bones.

Then reality slammed into him like a sledgehammer.

You can't afford to turn down jobs. Beggars can't be choosers, remember?

Another line of business was looking more and more like a really good idea.

Chapter Eight

JESSE CAME out of the hotel room and immediately reached into his work bag for some gum. Anything to take away the taste of the trick's cock. Jesse had wanted to use the shower, but had been refused. It happened, now and again, hence the reason for a supply of baby wipes in his bag. He huffed. Some guys were real dicks. Still, he couldn't complain, not with two hundred dollars in his wallet. The john wasn't complaining either, judging by the noise he'd made when he came all over Jesse's back. A job well done.

He smiled as he went down to the lobby in the elevator. *Not a bad day's work.* There were some days where he felt like he was continually reinventing himself. Where he made sure the trick felt like some kind of sex god at the end. Not that Jesse was paying all that much attention during the act. He imagined himself on a movie set, playing before an unseen camera, where he slipped into porn mode, making all the right noises in all the right places. There was skill involved, but it wasn't so much about positions or flexibility. It was the ability to make a guy feel like he was in complete control, when in truth, Jesse didn't let go of that control once.

Not quite truth. There were some times when Jesse just held on until the end, waiting for it to be over.

It was the end of a long day, and his last trick of the evening. That meant only one thing: back to the apartment for a long shower. Baby wipes were okay for a quick cleanup, but no substitute for a shower nozzle that could find its way into all his nooks and crannies. Not to mention the hot water that pummeled away any aches.

When his phone vibrated in his bag, Jesse stifled a groan. He'd had enough for one day. Then he sighed. Since when could he turn down work? Each dick represented cash to pay his share of the heat, the electric, the food.... And maybe have enough left over for that cute pair of sneakers at Macy's.

Except he knew better. Cute sneakers were a luxury he could ill afford.

Only one more day until the weekend. Not that Jesse's weekends were any different from his weekdays. Guys wanted to fuck, regardless of what day it was, and business was actually better on the weekend.

Sometimes. At other times, it was like walking through a fucking desert with no watering hole for miles.

He pulled out his phone and peered at the screen as he walked through the lobby, not bothering to pretend like he was staying there. The guy at the desk knew different anyhow—the hotel was used by a lot of escorts. Jesse smiled when he saw the text from Randy.

I'm done for the day. Want a coffee? Near Union Square if that works for ya.

Jesse was about to type *Sure* when he stopped. That business with the guy on the train gave him pause. What if another john spotted him when he was with Randy?

He pushed aside the thought. *Christ, if I think like that, I'll never go anywhere with him again.* And that was a situation he didn't want to contemplate. Besides, it was just coffee, right?

Jesse smiled as he typed. *Yup. Name the place.* The shower could wait. He was clean enough for coffee.

A second later he got the reply. *The Coffee Shop, 30 mins.*

Perfect. *I'll be there.* Jesse headed for the train.

By the time he walked into the cool interior, Randy was already sitting at the bar, his back to the door. Jesse crept up behind him, then said loudly, "We gotta stop meeting like this."

Randy gave a start and swiveled to glare at him. Then Jesse saw the spilled coffee all over the countertop. *Shit.* He reached quickly for the napkins, mopping up the liquid. "I'm sorry. I had no idea you already had your coffee. I'll get you another."

Randy chuckled. "Just sit down so you don't get into more trouble."

Jesse widened his eyes. "Me? Trouble?"

Randy gave a loud snort. "Christ, you can't do innocent to save your life." He signaled to the server and ordered two lattes. After the server walked away, he regarded Jesse closely. "You look tired. Are you okay?" Concern laced his voice.

Jesse gave a half smile as he climbed onto the stool next to Randy's. "I'm not sleeping well, that's all." He guessed it really had been a long day after all, because right then, he was bone-tired. But not too tired to have a glance around the coffee shop, looking for familiar faces.

God, look at me. Talk about paranoid.

"You know what you need to do?" Randy said suddenly, his eyes bright. "You need to go home, shove a pizza in the oven, put your feet up, and fall asleep on the couch watching a movie."

God, you're sweet. Jesse sighed. "In theory, that sounds awesome. In practice? Not gonna happen."

"Why not?"

"My roommate's apartment has the bare essentials. In this case, a combined microwave and toaster oven. So it's French bread pizza or nothing. The more serious flaw to your plan is no TV, no iPad, and no laptop. And I am *not* watching movies on my phone." He smiled. "Not that it wasn't a great idea. I can't remember the last time I watched a movie." Their lattes arrived, and Jesse took his, inhaling its aroma. "I've only had one cup of coffee today. God knows how I've survived." He sipped at the frothy beverage.

"I don't know what I'd do without coffee." Randy snickered. "Maybe twenty-five to life."

It took all Jesse's efforts not to blow froth everywhere. When he caught sight of Randy's grin, Jesse knew that had been his goal. He shook his head, chuckling. "You bastard."

Randy gasped. "You can't say that to me. I'm a police officer." His eyes sparkled with humor, and something rolled over deep in Jesse's belly.

Why can't you like guys, Randy?

He pushed down hard on the pleasurable shiver that threatened to ripple through him. "So, you're done for the day?"

Randy nodded. "I'm going to follow my own advice. Drink a cold beer, order in a pizza, and watch a movie." He stilled. "Say, here's an idea. Why don't you join me?"

Jesse frowned, the words not computing. "Join you?"

Randy grinned. "Movie. Pizza. My place."

Oh my God. "Seriously?"

"Sure, why not? I've got a great selection of DVDs, but if there's nothing you like, you can choose something from Netflix. And you get to choose the pizza."

Say yes. Say yes. Say yes, you dumbass.

Say no. You could be earning a few bucks. Sitting on your ass watching a DVD earns you nothing.

"You know what? You're on." Jesse's heartbeat nudged up a gear. "Just one thing? Can I go home and change first?" Because *no way* on this planet was he going to Randy's place without a shower.

Randy laughed. "Of course you can. Look, it's six o'clock now. Why don't we say seven thirty at my place?"

Jesse coughed. "That would be awesome—if I actually knew where you lived."

"Oops." Randy snickered again. "I'll send you the address, along with a map." He gestured to Jesse's tall glass. "Now drink your coffee. I need to get home ASAP."

"Why?" Jesse couldn't resist. "What is it you need to do before I see your place?"

Randy gave him a hard stare. "If I went to your place right now, with no warning, would you be happy?"

Jesse thought about the bag of toys he'd cleaned the night before that was sitting on the couch, next to his latest supply of condoms and lube. He cleared his throat. "Probably not."

"Exactly. So drink up."

Jesse drank his latte. Despite his fatigue, the prospect of spending an evening in Randy's home had him buzzing.

Until that voice in his head piped up.

Calm down. It's just a movie and pizza. Don't go making it out to be anything more.

There were times when Jesse hated being a realist.

THE MINUTE Randy got through his front door, he performed a quick assessment of what urgently needed done. Thankfully there wasn't a lot of clutter—he could have been a poster boy for the minimalist look—but that didn't mean he hadn't left clothes, magazines, and other items lying around.

I can't believe I asked him back here. Whatever possessed me?

It had been a spur-of-the-moment suggestion, but as soon as he'd uttered it, Randy had been seized by a panic that surprised him. *It's just a movie and pizza, right? Then why does it feel like so much more?* This irrational reaction didn't make sense. It was just two guys sharing a pizza, for God's sake.

Then why does it feel like... a date?

He pushed aside such thoughts and got down to the real-life business of making his apartment presentable. Clothes went in the hamper, books back on the shelf, mugs were washed, dried, and put away. A quick check on the beer situation—because he *had* mentioned beer, right?—to find all was well in that department. As he tidied, he kept up a running conversation with himself in his head.

Why am I doing this?

Because I want to make Jesse feel good. He looked like he needed a pizza night. That's why.

So it's just for Jesse, then.

Yeah, right. Randy wanted to spend time with him, and he knew it.

When the door buzzer sounded, it made him jump. He pressed the intercom button. "Hello?"

"Lemme in. I'm starving!"

Randy laughed. "Fourth floor, apartment 4A." He pressed the release button and opened his front door.

Jesse soon appeared, wearing jeans, sneakers, and a loose-fitting blue shirt that matched his eyes. In his hand he carried a plastic bag. He grinned when he saw Randy. "No elevator, huh? Now I know why you're in such good shape."

It took a second for his words to fully register. "Thanks for the compliment." Randy peered inside the bag Jesse thrust at him, and smiled. "Aw. You brought beer. How thoughtful."

Jesse snickered. "Hey, it goes well with pizza, right? What am I saying? Everything goes well with pizza." He sniffed the air. "Which I can't smell, so I'm assuming you haven't ordered yet."

Randy rolled his eyes. "I was waiting for you." He pulled out his phone and brought up the page for Charlie's Pizza. "Pick one. And don't worry if I'll like it or not. I've been through every pizza on their menu."

Jesse laughed. "Now I know why you live on the fourth floor. It's to work off the pizza." He peered at the screen. "Ooh, they've got meatball. Nice. *And* ground beef. Now I'm spoiled for choice."

"Then we order two. What's the best thing about pizza, after all?" Randy laughed when they said in unison, "Leftovers for breakfast." He made the call, while Jesse wandered around the living room, pausing at the shelves where Randy kept his DVD collection. By the time the pizza was ordered, Jesse was pulling out cases and reading the backs, looking relaxed.

What hit Randy was how natural it felt to have Jesse there. His earlier panic had fled, replaced by quiet anticipation.

This is going to be okay.

Chapter Nine

"OH MAN. These garlic knots are *amazing*!" Jesse moaned as he took another mouthful.

Randy chuckled. "Yeah, I couldn't tell you liked 'em." Thankfully he'd gotten two orders.

Jesse flushed and swallowed. "Oops. My bad. You can have another slice of pizza to make up for it."

"Gee, how generous." Not that he really minded. Jesse's obvious enjoyment was adorable. "Did you decide on a movie?" Jesse had insisted they eat first, and Randy had been fine with that. He'd been hungry too.

Jesse bit his lip. "Well, kind of. You have an old movie on your shelf that I just love, but I don't know…. You really have to be in the mood for that kind of thing."

"What kind of thing?" Randy was intrigued, mentally going through his DVDs.

Jesse smiled. "*Notting Hill*."

Randy blinked. "Okay." That was… unexpected.

"Yeah, I know, it's a real chick flick, but… it makes me smile every time I see it. And that killer line—'I'm just a girl, standing in front of a boy, asking him to love her'—makes me tear up when I hear that."

Randy couldn't help smiling. "I'll make sure I have tissues handy." He shook his head.

"What?"

"I guess I expected you to choose something more modern, with more action…."

"And less romance?" Jesse suggested with a grin. "Gotta tell ya, I'm a sucker for a good romance."

"Then let me clear all this crap out of the way, and we can put it on. Unless you want another slice of pizza?"

Jesse groaned. "Are you kidding? I'm gonna have to work out extra hard tomorrow. I haven't eaten so much in ages."

Randy picked up the pizza boxes and the bag containing what was left of the garlic knots. "Want a beer?" he asked as he dumped them on the countertop.

"Ooh, yeah. And I really like your place. All this exposed brick is great."

"Thanks." Randy reached into the refrigerator and pulled out two cans. "You want a glass?"

Jesse smirked. "Hell no."

"A guy after my own heart." Randy handed him a can, then went over to find the DVD. "I guess this says something about me too," he said as he loaded the disc into the DVD player.

"I did notice there were quite a few similar movies on your shelf."

"Damn. My secret is out."

Jesse chuckled. "Yeah, who'd have thought it? Randy Michaels, the big bad cop… who likes mushy romance."

Randy sat beside him on the couch and smacked him on the leg. "Less of the mushy, you." He aimed the remote, and the TV screen burst into life.

Jesse settled back against the cushions, a contented smile on his face. "You were right, y'know. This is exactly what I needed."

"Then I'm glad I suggested it." Randy got comfortable, his gaze fixed on the screen.

His mind was focused on other things, however. On not sitting too close to Jesse, although he badly wanted to. On the smell of him, because *damn*, he smelled good, a pleasant mix of soap and something else—not cologne, but hey, he didn't need it. Jesse's scent stirred Randy's senses, and he breathed him in, wanting more. Jesse shifted a little closer, and Randy had to fight the urge to put his arm around Jesse's shoulders.

Jesse made comments throughout the movie, laughing at Hugh Grant's roommate as he flexed in his underwear for the press, and sighing when Julia Roberts impulsively kissed Hugh. His eyes started to close before the end, however, not that Randy was all that surprised. Jesse really had seemed tired when he'd turned up at the coffee shop. When Jesse leaned into him, his breathing more regular, Randy knew he'd fallen asleep.

Randy sat there, not wanting to move, Jesse's golden head against his shoulder, his breathing slow and even. Randy craned his neck to look at him, trying not to disturb him. *God, he looks so peaceful.* Jesse had changed a little since the Black Lounge days. He was leaner in the face, for one thing, but it suited him. He'd always been a slim thing back then, but there seemed to be more definition in his arms these days. That haircut made his face appear softer, accentuating his beauty.

There. Randy could admit that much to himself. He found another man beautiful.

He switched off the TV and closed his eyes, drinking in the moment. A warm feeling of peace washed over him, and Randy exulted in the unfamiliar sensation. It felt… good.

Better than that, it felt… right.

The call of nature was not going to be ignored, however, and Randy had to move. He got up very slowly, conscious of Jesse's weight against him. Jesse stirred a little, then sighed as Randy eased him down onto the couch. By the time Randy got back from the bathroom, Jesse was fast asleep.

Randy didn't have the heart to wake him, not when he clearly needed the sleep. He went into his bedroom, removed a sheet and pillow from the closet, and brought them back to the couch. He covered Jesse with the sheet, but as he tried to gently lift Jesse's head to slip the pillow under it, Jesse awoke, blinking.

"Oh wow. I was totally gone there," he said groggily. He struggled into a sitting position. "I should leave."

Randy gently but firmly pushed him back down onto the couch. "You can sleep here. It's a comfy couch. I should know—I've fallen asleep on it enough times. Stay. Have breakfast with me in the morning before I go to work." Jesse opened his mouth to protest, but Randy gave him a firm stare. "You got anything else you need to be doing right now? Anywhere you need to be?"

After a moment, Jesse shook his head. "No."

"Fine. Then you stay." Randy nodded toward the kitchen area. "There are glasses in the cabinet above the sink if you want water. There's a new toothbrush in the bathroom cabinet. I'll put out a towel for ya. If you need anything, my room is the far door on the left of where you came in, all right?"

Jesse nodded, smiling faintly. "Thanks."

"No problem. Now go back to sleep."

Jesse snickered. "God save me from bossy cops." He kicked off his sneakers. "I should brush my teeth," he said, midyawn. "I hate waking up with garlic breath." Another yawn, this one longer.

"Sure. Whatever." Randy watched, amused, as Jesse lay down and rolled over to face the back of the couch, stuffing the pillow under his head. Randy stared at him, the long line of his body beneath the sheet, the slow movement as he breathed evenly. He clicked off the lamp in the corner and crept toward his room.

Once inside, he softly closed the door. He undressed quickly and got into bed.

What a great evening. Randy had loved every minute of it. He could have woken Jesse and let him go home, sure, but he hadn't wanted Jesse to leave. They'd had more than a few laughs during the movie, and they hadn't put away all that much beer. What had surprised Randy most was how relaxed he felt in Jesse's company.

Well, we're not exactly strangers, are we? Granted, Jesse hadn't been working in the Black Lounge the whole time Randy had been there undercover, but Jesse had been an easy person to get along with. Plus, there had been all the times they'd met up during the trial. *Maybe that's why it feels so natural to be around him. We've moved on from being cop and witness to being friends.*

Except *friend* wasn't the right word for Jesse. It was a hell of a lot more complicated than that.

Randy closed his eyes, trying not to think of Jesse in the next room.

I'd love to do this again.

He didn't want this to be a one-off.

JESSE STRETCHED and yawned. He had no clue of the time, but he'd slept like a log. He patted his jeans pockets for his phone before realizing it was on the floor beside the couch where he'd left it the night before. Jesse picked it up and peered at the screen. Six fifteen.

He had no idea what time Randy usually left for work, but he figured it would be early.

In that case, I'll put the coffee on. Then he reconsidered. First priority was cleaning his teeth, because… yuck.

Jesse got up off the couch, folded the sheet neatly, and deposited it on top of the pillow. Randy had been right about the couch—it had been supremely comfortable. Jesse padded through the apartment to the bathroom and located the toothbrush Randy had mentioned. *What the hell was I thinking last night? Garlic?* Gum was definitely going to be on the agenda for the rest of the day, not to mention a damn good shower when he got home. Garlic was usually a no-no, but Jesse had been so hungry, and those knots had smelled so damn good, he hadn't been able to resist.

His ablutions finished, he went into the kitchen area and did a quick hunt for the coffee. The red plastic container of Folgers wasn't hard to find, and Jesse set up the coffee machine. Next, he found a large white ceramic container with the word BREAD on it, sitting next to a toaster. *Perfect.*

By the time the coffee had dripped its way into the pot, the toast was done. Jesse went to Randy's door and knocked gently. No response. He knocked a little harder. "Randy? There's coffee and toast when you're ready."

"Huh?" A pause. "Really?"

Jesse chuckled. "Yes, really. Come and get it." He went back to the living room, where he'd placed two mugs and two plates of toast on the coffee table.

Randy emerged from his room, looking bleary-eyed and pretty damn cute.

"Good morning."

"Mornin'." Randy sniffed the air. "That's nice to wake up to. You'll have to stay over again." He flopped down onto the couch and reached for the coffee, then smiled after the first mouthful. "*And* you make good coffee."

Jesse snickered. "What's difficult about making coffee?"

"You'd be surprised. My dad can't make coffee for shit." Randy took another drink from his mug. "Oh yeah. You can definitely stay here again."

Jesse laughed. "You just love me for my coffee." It was a joke, of course, but one that gave him a pang. *What I'd give for you to love me for real.* Jesse gave himself a swift mental kick in the ass. *Enough with the torture.* He glanced over at Randy, who appeared not to have reacted to his words. Good.

They finished the toast and coffee in silence. Randy took the mugs and plates over to the sink. "I'm gonna grab a quick shower before work.

If you want, you can go now, or you can leave with me. We'll be heading in the same direction, after all."

Jesse liked that. Anything to spend more time in Randy's company. "I'll leave when you do."

"Great. Then I'd better get my ass in gear. I won't be long." He disappeared toward the bathroom.

Jesse proceeded to wash the dishes, listening to the sound of running water on the other side of the wall. He had to smile when Randy started singing. *Whitney Houston? Really?* Jesse chuckled, then started singing along to "I Wanna Dance With Somebody." He caught Randy's laugh, and then both of them were singing, Randy slapping the bathroom wall in time to the music.

Now there's a new experience.

By the time Randy was ready to leave, Jesse had put away the dishes and made sure the living room was tidy. Randy gave him an appreciative glance. "You just wanna be sure of an invite back, don'tcha?"

Jesse sighed dramatically. "Damn. You saw straight through me." As Randy unlocked the front door, Jesse stopped him with a hand to his arm. "About last night. Thanks. I had such a good time. And thanks for letting me sleep on the couch."

Randy peered at him. "Looks like it did you some good. And you're welcome. Seriously. I had a great time too." He paused. "By the way, joking aside… I'd really like it if we could do this again sometime."

And that right there made Jesse's day. "I'd love to."

Randy's smile lit up his face, reaching his eyes. "Great." He opened the door, and Jesse stepped out into the hallway to wait while Randy locked up. Randy's words gave him a warm feeling that he knew would stay with him.

What a perfect way to start a day.

Too bad it was back to reality.

Chapter Ten

Randy stared at the tickets in his hand. "You sure about this?" He still couldn't believe his luck.

Detective Mona Lawrence laughed. "Course I'm sure. I'm not gonna be able to use 'em, now, am I? Not with the in-laws suddenly decidin' they're gonna visit for the whole damn weekend. I'm glad you want 'em. Thing is, are *you* sure you can find someone to go with ya at such short notice?"

"Oh yeah." That was a no-brainer.

She grinned. "You got someone in mind, don'tcha? Who's the lucky girl?"

"Just a friend." Randy smiled to himself. *Jesse is gonna flip when he hears this.* "Thanks again, Mona." He smirked. "By the way. Nice outfit."

She rolled her eyes. "Yeah. What you *really* mean is, nice tits." She adjusted her cleavage in her tight-fitting cerise top. "I swear, some of the guys' eyes were out on stalks when I walked through here this morning. The sooner I'm off these stings, the better. I'm gettin' real tired of playin' the hooker."

Randy patted her arm. "I feel for ya, really. I'm on next week." Time to once again wait in a seedy hotel room for johns to show up so he could arrest them.

She nodded. "Oh well. I'm outta here. See ya." She walked away from him, and he couldn't resist.

"Really rockin' those killer heels, Mona. You should wear those more often."

Without even turning her head, she flipped him the bird.

Randy laughed. He'd worked with Mona ever since the squad had been put together. She was a damn fine detective and had worked her ass off on the sting operations. *And probably her feet, too, in those heels.* Thank God Randy could wear pretty much what he damn well pleased.

He went over to his desk and got out his phone to compose a text. *Hey, got a minute?*

Jesse's reply was swift. *Sure. What's up?*

Okay to call?

Seconds later, his phone rang. "Hey."

"Do you have anything planned for the Fourth?"

A moment of silence. "Not at the moment. I'll be busy over the weekend, though. Got a shift in a restaurant, but that's just Saturday and Sunday morning. Why?"

"How'd you like to go to Coney Island?"

Jesse snickered. "Really?"

"Wait, hear me out. There's a new venue opening up, the Amphitheater, and they've got a concert Monday night to celebrate. And I've just been given a pair of tickets to it."

"Oh, cool. Who's playing?"

"Well, it might not be your kind of music, but—"

"Quit stalling and tell me," Jesse said with a laugh.

"The Beach Boys."

Another pause. "Seriously? Hell yeah. You know me, I love music concerts. The Beach Boys? Talk about iconic. Wow."

Randy loved the excitement in Jesse's voice. "Hey, I just had an idea. I'm not working the Fourth, so why don't we make a day of it? You know, Luna Park, ride the Cyclone, the Ferris Wheel…. There's the hot-dog-eating contest at Nathan's too. Have you ever been to Coney Island?"

"A couple of times, when I first came to New York. The whole day?"

"Sure! We can catch the train from midtown, maybe midmorning. The hot-dog contest, then a stroll along the boardwalk. Fried clams and a beer at Ruby's, then spend the rest of the day in the park. The concert starts at seven, and then there's the fireworks. Just be prepared for it being real busy there. It's *the* place in NYC to celebrate the Fourth."

"Are the seats good?"

Randy laughed. "Would it matter if they were all the way at the back? Gimme a sec." He pulled the tickets from his wallet and peered at them. "Wow. I'm really gonna owe Mona. These are damn good seats." They were in the front half of the amphitheater.

"You sure you wanna go with me? I mean, isn't there anyone else you could take along? Not that I don't love the idea, you understand. I just don't want to take someone else's place."

Randy closed his eyes. *There is no one I would rather spend the Fourth with than you.* He cleared his throat. "Yes, I'm sure. I wouldn't have asked you otherwise."

"Then okay. Let me know nearer the time where you want to meet. And... thanks, Randy. This is so cool."

"You're welcome. Have a good weekend, and I'm glad you've got some work lined up. I'll see you Monday." Randy disconnected the call, then put away his phone. Jesse hadn't hesitated to tell him about the work he'd be doing, and it sounded plausible, but Randy couldn't help wondering if it was a lie. Because there was some part at the back of his mind that was certain Jesse was soliciting.

Right then, Randy wanted to believe he had it all wrong. Except he didn't have time to think about such things.

He had work to do.

RANDY HAD just gotten out of the shower when there was a knock at his door. He grinned. *Like I don't know who that is.* He opened it to find Owen standing there, looking smart-casual in a pair of black jeans and a white shirt, with a slim gold chain around his neck.

"It must be Friday," Randy quipped.

Owen looked him up and down. "That towel doesn't suit you. Take it off." He leered.

Randy rolled his eyes. "Get in here." He stood aside to let Owen enter. "Go sit while I put some clothes on." He didn't wait for a response but went into his bedroom, leaving the door ajar. "I keep telling ya, you really need to try out these lines on a boyfriend, you know, not your straight neighbor," he called out.

He caught Owen's chuckle. "Sorry. Not buying the straight part, not anymore."

Randy opened his closet and removed a clean pair of jeans. "Was there something you wanted, or did you just come over here to cast doubts on my sexuality?" He had more than enough of those himself. He squirmed into his jeans.

"How would you feel about going for a drink tonight?"

"What, and miss our Friday night in with a bottle or two of wine?"

There was a pause, and then Owen spoke from the other side of the door. "Are you decent?"

Randy laughed. "Like you haven't already peeked. Yes." He pulled the door open. "Okay, what's this about a drink?"

Owen stared at him and sighed. "I always guessed there was a hairy chest lurking beneath your clothes. You just made me a happy man."

Randy flung the damp towel at him. "When you've finished lusting after what you can't have…. You said a drink?"

Owen placed the towel at the foot of Randy's bed, then stepped back. "Ever been to a gay bar?"

Randy snorted. "Lots of times."

"You mean for work, right?" When Randy nodded, Owen smiled triumphantly. "As I thought. Well, I'd like to take you for a drink in a gay bar I know."

It sounded innocent enough, but Randy's heartbeat quickened and something fluttered in his stomach. "Why a gay bar in particular?" Except he already knew the answer to that one.

Owen leaned against the doorframe. "The last time we spoke, I sensed a great deal of curiosity in you. I just wondered if you'd like to satisfy that curiosity. Nothing heavy, mind, just a drink in a bar, surrounded by gay men. Actually, not just gay men. Probably all shades of the LGBTQI spectrum." He gave Randy an easy smile. "What harm would it do to go for a couple of drinks in a public bar?"

No harm that Randy could think of, apart from the fact that his heart was pounding at the mere thought.

He could refuse.

He could make an excuse.

Except Randy knew Owen had nailed it. He *was* curious.

"Fine. A couple of drinks, no more."

Owen's eyes lit up. "Excellent. In that case, choose what else you're wearing, and we can go."

Randy burst out laughing. "Excuse me? There's this little thing you might have heard of, it's called *food*. Really useful. Keeps you from fainting after a long day at work."

Owen waved a hand. "We can eat near there. Tons of places to eat. And if I wait until you've eaten, you'll change your mind, so uh-uh." He pointed to the closet. "Shirt. Choose one. Casual."

Randy gave up and pulled a black shirt from its hanger.

"Ooh, the man in black. Very sexy."

Randy glared at him. "Down, boy. Or I *will* change my mind."

Owen mimed zipping his lips and left the room.

Randy slipped his arms into the short-sleeved shirt, his heartbeat still not back to its normal level. "What am I getting myself into?" He knew this was irrational. He had nothing to fear from a drink in a gay bar. He'd been in gay bars before.

Then why am I nervous?

RANDY PERCHED on the high white barstool and gazed at his surroundings. Rise was in Hell's Kitchen and, at first glance, appeared to be very popular—and *not* what he'd expected. The music was a great mix of modern and throwback, with two large screens showing videos at one end of the bar. The place was packed, and what surprised him was the clientele. He'd anticipated a very young crowd, but what he saw was a mix of all ages, including older guys maybe in their fifties who seemed perfectly at ease with the fun, upbeat, happy vibe that filled the bar. The bartenders.... *Oh my.*

"They *are* gorgeous, aren't they?" Owen said quietly into his ear.

Randy jerked his head to glare at him. "How do you do that?"

Owen laughed. "What's my job again? Hmm? I'm an observer of human nature."

Randy sighed. "Okay, so they're gorgeous. I have no problem admitting that. I can appreciate a good-looking man." He sipped the cocktail Owen had ordered for him, a heady mix of rum and juice, which was delicious. It was also his second, and he was feeling more relaxed.

Owen leaned against the bar. "And speaking of men… who is this guy you were attracted to?"

Randy blinked. "You've lost me."

Owen smiled. "You have to be good at listening in my line of work. And even better at remembering. I asked you if you'd ever been attracted to a guy before, and you said yes. So… who was he? Though maybe I should be asking, who *is* he?"

Randy took a long pull on his straw. "It's complicated."

"I can deal with complicated. That's my job. Try me."

Randy shook his head. He wasn't ready to talk about Jesse, not yet. "If your goal was to get me here, get me drunk, and get me to talk, it's not gonna work."

Owen's eyes glittered. "Who says that was my goal?"

Randy did an eye-roll. "Oh please. When is your goal *not* to get me to talk?"

"Have you at least enjoyed the experience so far?"

He smiled. "Yeah. It's nice to get to see things from a different angle. I only get to see the seedier side." Rise was nothing like the gay bars he usually found himself in. "This was relaxing." He enjoyed sitting there, soaking up the atmosphere, watching the people around him having fun, with none of the airs of pretentiousness or snobbery that he'd witnessed in a lot of New York bars. Everyone was just there to enjoy themselves.

Owen nodded. "Which is precisely why I brought you here to *this* bar. Believe me, there are others where you wouldn't feel so comfortable."

Randy laughed. "At this point there's not much that can shock me. Been there—hell, I *worked* there."

Owen picked up his cocktail glass. "Now *that* sounds like a challenge."

Randy stilled. "And that was the last thing I intended doing, knowing you."

Owen was gazing at him in a thoughtful way that set off those flutters in Randy's belly all over again.

"Owen." He forced a warning note into his voice. "We are *not* going to any more gay bars."

To his surprise Owen smiled. "Oh, I have no intention of doing that. I have something else in mind."

When nothing else was forthcoming, Randy sighed. "You're not going to tell me, are you?"

Owen's only response was a grin, and Randy's mouth suddenly grew dry.

Oh dear God, what now?

"We can go when you're ready," Owen told him before handing bills to one of the bartenders. Then he turned to Randy. "Do you trust me?"

His throat tight, Randy nodded.

"I learned a lot about you, that time we talked. And I got the feeling that you're going through something, maybe a kind of… evolution. Making discoveries about yourself. Well, I want to help. But for me to do that, you *do* have to trust me."

Fuck. Randy's heartbeat raced, and he was suddenly grateful he was sitting down. "Okay," he managed to get out.

Owen nodded, then patted Randy's arm. "Good man. Now let's go home." He got off his stool.

Randy did the same, amazed that his legs held him upright. The idea that Owen was planning something both terrified and excited him, but he liked the way Owen put it.

Am I... evolving? He wasn't sure. When it came to the crux, Randy thought it was less a matter of changing from one state into another, and more a case of acknowledging what he'd known for a while.

All he had to do now was accept it.

Chapter Eleven

JESSE WAS having maybe the best Fourth of July of his life, and it wasn't even noon yet. Most of his enjoyment boiled down to the man walking at his side. Randy wore a pair of shorts and a white sleeveless T-shirt, perfect for the warm day. He appeared at ease, possibly the most relaxed Jesse had ever seen him. His eyes were hidden behind his shades, and that was Jesse's only regret, but the sight of Randy's firm calves, covered with a light down of hair, made up for it. The low scooped neck of his T-shirt revealed another surprise: Randy was hairier than Jesse had suspected.

Dammit. He loved hairy guys.

After Randy bought them cards for the rides, they'd strolled along the boardwalk, stopping at a bar when Jesse had seen the sign for margaritas. Randy had rolled his eyes but hadn't argued. What appeared was the largest strawberry margarita Jesse had ever drunk, so large they had to share it, and the alcohol gave him a pleasant buzz.

That meant he'd needed food, so a huge pretzel with mustard was the obvious choice. They'd walked along some more, Jesse pulling off pieces and handing them to Randy. They'd missed the hot-dog-eating contest, but the smell drifting out of Nathan's was heavenly. And of course that meant Jesse had to have one.

By midday he was stuffed.

Randy laughed. "Where do you put it all? Have you got the kind of metabolism that burns everything up?"

"I wish." Jesse patted his belly. "This requires a lot of work." He grinned. "But it was worth it. I don't eat this shit at home. So, what next?" To hell with watching what he ate. It was a *holiday*, for Christ's sake.

Randy pointed up and to the right. "How about that?"

Jesse followed his finger and swallowed. "Are you kidding? I am *not* riding the Cyclone after eating a humongous pretzel *and* a hot dog, and drinking the world's largest margarita. Not unless you really *want* me to throw up all over ya?"

"Then how about a nice, gentle ride on the Wonder Wheel?"

Jesse glared at him, not taken in for a second by Randy's innocent expression. "You forget, I've been here before. And I wouldn't put it past you to choose one of the swinging cars. You know, the ones that go on rails and scare the shit out of you?"

Randy smirked. "It was worth a try."

"We are gonna have a pleasant stroll along the boardwalk, maybe check out the amphitheater for later, and by the time we've done that, I *may* be ready to tackle some rides without fear of heaving."

"So I guess that means the Steeplechase is out. And the Luna 360. And the Soarin' Eagle." Randy's lips twitched.

Jesse gaped at him. "Oh my God. You are evil incarnate, aren't ya? You look like butter wouldn't melt, but behind those gorgeous blue eyes lurks the brain of a fiend." Then he realized what he'd said, and he snapped his mouth shut. Randy regarded him with slightly widened eyes, and Jesse leaped in before he could get a word out. "I tell you what. Why don't *I* choose a ride?"

Randy narrowed his gaze. "Okay, I'll bite. Which ride did you have in mind?"

Jesse beckoned him with a crooked finger, and they picked their way through the crowds, heading toward the Wonder Wheel. Facing it was something that was much more Jesse's level. "There," he said, flinging his arm out.

Randy bit his lip. "Spook-a-Rama? You want me to go on a… ghost train?"

Jesse snickered. "Don't tell me the big bad cop is scared."

Randy narrowed his gaze. "Did you see anything *remotely* scary on my shelves? Hmm?"

"Oh, for Pete's sake. It doesn't even look scary." Above the frontage was a carved hideous monster, and the track was lined with panels depicting various horrific images that managed to not be horrific at all. Jesse pointed to a hand-painted sign on the right. "This was built in 1955. How scary can it be?" He was enjoying himself.

Randy let out an exaggerated sigh. "Oh, come on, then." They went through the turnstile and got into a brightly painted car. As it moved off, Randy pointed to the lurid panels. "Yeah, you're right. I mean, look at this." When they passed the sign screaming *Danger* at them in giant red letters, he chuckled. "Yeah, right."

They burst through the doors at the end, on which were painted huge eyeballs, and then they were plunged into complete black.

"Okay, this is spooky," Randy said quietly.

Jesse snickered again. "Scared of the dark too? I'd never have— Jesus *Christ*!" A skeleton lunged at them through a curtain, lit up by red lights, and Jesse reached for Randy's arm.

Randy laughed. "This might be more fun than I thought."

"Hey, it surprised me," Jesse protested, recovering quickly. As ghost trains went, this was pretty tame, the usual combination of strobe lighting, glowing eyes, hideous creatures, and of course, skeletons all over the place, with flickering lights playing over them to make it look like they were moving. Being in the dark, however, was seriously spooky.

An air jet blasted over them, and they grabbed each other, both of them laughing. When a zombie half fell out of a closet, lit up eerily, it was Randy's turn to clutch Jesse's arm, his fingers digging into the muscle.

"Hey, it's just a zombie who wants to eat your brains," Jesse said soothingly, amid chuckles.

"Ha! You're nearest, so you're first on the menu." Randy sighed when they passed a couple of corny ghosts lit up by a glimmer of daylight. "Aw, it's over."

"See? You liked it." Jesse had loved the sheer campiness of it all, but mostly he'd loved being alone in the dark, holding on to Randy's arm. As they burst through the doors into bright sunlight, he reluctantly let go. "So, where next?"

Randy laughed. "Anywhere you like."

Jesse was loving the day more and more—right up to the moment where they walked out of the ride and into the path of a very familiar guy….

Jesse felt like the marrow froze in his bones. What the fuck was Jonathon doing in New York? He lived in *Wyoming*, for God's sake, with his wife and kids—

The same wife and kids who were strolling along with him, the boy giving the Cyclone long glances, the girl yelling that she wanted to go on the Wonder Wheel. His wife looked bored out of her skull.

Jonathon caught Jesse's eyes, and all the color slid from his face.

Don't stop. Don't say a word. Please. Jesse's heart hammered, and sweat popped out on his brow. Then he found he could breathe again as Jonathon looked away, pointing to the Spook-a-Rama.

Jesse walked on, picking up the pace a little, praying silently that Randy hadn't noticed a thing.

"Are we in a hurry or something?" Randy sounded amused.

Jesse forced a light laugh. "Hey, we've only got one day. That's a lot of rides to fit in before the concert." He didn't look back, his heartbeat calming down a little.

By the time they'd reached the Wild River, he was thinking logically. Of course Jonathon wouldn't have said anything. Why would he? He had a damn sight more to lose than Jesse did. Still, the moment had given Jesse quite a jolt.

Randy can't find out. And Jesse would do everything to make sure Randy stayed in the dark.

RANDY WAS having an awesome day. He couldn't remember the last time he'd let loose and really enjoyed himself, but this Fourth so far was ranking at the top. They rode the Wild River, both of them laughing as they hit the water at the bottom, the spray wetting them thoroughly. The Tickler had Jesse screaming every time the car went backward, and Randy loved every minute of it. Both of them screamed on the Steeplechase, which was way too short.

As they walked to the Cyclone, it occurred to Randy that the rides he'd enjoyed most were the ones where Jesse was sitting beside him.

"Ready for this?" he said as they lined up to get on the ride.

Jesse was staring up at the roller coaster. "It's so high." As they waited for the next car, his eyes widened. "Oh my God. I think we're gonna be at the front."

Randy couldn't have planned it better if he'd tried.

They climbed into the car, and it began to chug its way up the steep incline. As they neared the top, Jesse pointed to the sign above their heads. "Remain seated? Like who'd be dumb enough to stand up in this thing?"

They reached the top, and Randy grabbed hold of Jesse's hand, raising it aloft.

"*No!*" Jesse screamed.

"Yes!" Randy whooped as they plunged down, the wind hitting their faces, the sudden rush of adrenaline spiking through his body. Every dip he did the same thing, and every time Jesse screamed with delight.

By the time they reached the tunnel, Jesse was laughing his ass off. The car came to a stop and they got out, Jesse still beaming.

"That was great!" They stumbled toward the exit, Jesse's arm around Randy's waist. Randy didn't know if that was instinctual on Jesse's part. He only knew it felt really good. When Jesse released him, lowering his arm, Randy sighed internally.

As days went, this one was freaking perfect, and he didn't want it to end.

"It looks like some giant white bug," Jesse said as they waited to enter the amphitheater.

"I guess it does." Above, white canvas stretched between curved steel girders, so the venue was covered but left open to the elements on three sides. Their seats were in one of the front three blocks behind the orchestra pit.

When they finally sat down, Jesse gazed at their surroundings. "This is amazing."

Jesse's hand lay on his thigh, and Randy longed to cover it with his own, but that was a step he dared not take. It wasn't the action of a friend—more of a lover. Those times throughout the day when they'd grabbed each other, laughing and screaming, had already been burned into his memory.

Randy clasped his hands in his lap. "Have you had a good day?"

Jesse shook his head, his expression almost solemn. "No," he said simply, before breaking into a gentle smile. "I've had an awesome day, and it isn't even over." Then the lights went down and he focused his attention on the stage. "Here we go," he whispered.

Randy took in very little of the concert. The music washed over him, adding to the atmosphere, but all he was aware of was Jesse beside him, his warmth, his scent. Spending the day in his company had been incredible but had only added to Randy's confusion. What scared him most was the thought that he didn't want to be Jesse's friend.

He wanted to be more but was too terrified to do anything about it.

Randy could take as many tests as he liked, could fake as many results as he wanted, but it didn't alter what he knew to be the truth.

He wasn't straight.

He was attracted to Jesse.

He wanted to spend more time with Jesse.

And that scared him to death.

RANDY STOOD with Jesse on the boardwalk, watching the night sky fill with starbursts and showers of light as the firework display brought the day to a close, accompanied by car horns as their alarms were triggered by the vibrations.

"Fireworks always make me feel like a little kid," Jesse said quietly.

Randy knew what he meant. "I still *ooh* and *aah* when I watch them. Maybe they make everyone feel that way." Jesse was standing close enough that Randy could smell the lingering scent of coconut sun cream. It was the smell of summer.

After ten minutes or so, the display came to an end, and he sighed. "They never go on long enough."

Jesse chuckled. "I know what you mean." Around them, people had already started walking off.

Damn. Randy knew the day had to end, but he wasn't ready for it. That meant back to reality, and he didn't want to go there.

"I guess we'd better make tracks." Jesse gazed at him, the lights from the park catching in his eyes. "This was a great idea. Please thank whoever gave you those tickets."

"I will." Mona was going to get the biggest bunch of flowers Randy could lay his hands on. "Thanks for coming with me."

Jesse's face lit up. "I haven't had this much fun in a long time."

"Me too." Randy didn't move, unwilling to break the fragile bubble of time they'd enjoyed together. Except he couldn't put it off any longer. "Come on. Let's head for the train."

Together they walked slowly, neither of them speaking, and that was just fine by Randy.

Words were superfluous.

Chapter Twelve

RANDY GLANCED at his phone—11:25—and sighed. *He's not gonna show.* Another one.

"Shall we call it?" Detective Rich Glover said from the bed, where he lay staring at his phone.

Randy nodded. "I'll do it." He called up Detective Harris, who was leading the sting operation that day. "Hey. Another no show here."

Harris's sigh equaled his. "Great. I'll get them to send the message. You two have no more booked for this morning, do you?"

"Nope. I'll go visit the usual haunts, see who's around."

"Tell him I'm coming back to the precinct," Rich called out.

"Did you hear that?" Randy asked Harris.

"Yep. Good luck this afternoon. Well, more luck than you had this morning."

"Yeah, sure. I'll see you back there later." Randy disconnected the call, then got up out of the armchair where he'd been sitting for the last forty minutes, taking one more look around the hotel room, and headed for the door. *This is such a waste of time.* There'd been more success on the previous sting, and he wondered if it might not be time to switch to another hotel. There was always the possibility that someone working there had tumbled to what was happening and was warning the johns. *Anything is possible, right?*

"I'll leave first." Rich patted his back. "See ya later." He left the room, and Randy waited for a minute or two before opening the door again. He stepped into the hallway—and his instincts kicked in, forcing him to step back into the room and peer around the doorframe.

Jesse had just gone into a room down the hall.

Randy's heart pounded. He was sure Jesse hadn't seen him. As for what he was doing there, Randy didn't need to be a genius to work that out. He crept quietly past the door and along to the elevator. No sound emerged from the room. When the elevator arrived, Randy got in and went down to the lobby, out of the hotel, and across the street to the

Starbucks. He grabbed a coffee and sat at a table in the window, giving himself a clear view of the hotel. Randy noted the time, then sipped his coffee and waited, feeling sick to his stomach.

An hour later, Jesse emerged from the hotel and turned left.

Dammit. Randy hated being right.

He waited a moment, then left Starbucks and followed him, making sure to keep to a safe distance. The last thing he wanted was for Jesse to spot him. Trailing him like that felt… wrong, but Randy had to know for sure.

Jesse walked about ten blocks, then turned onto West Forty-Second Street, and not long after, disappeared into an apartment building.

Randy's heart sank. *Fuck.* He knew the place. It had once been a hotel, but had since been turned into an apartment building, one that was frequented by a lot of hookers. Not the kinda of place worth busting—plenty of guys lived there, but didn't bring their johns home. Randy could understand that. Too risky if a trick went tits-up and they were suddenly dealing with a crazy. No one wanted *that* turning up on your doorstep.

He crossed the street and waited under the scaffolding that covered the front of the building, his gaze locked on the entrance Jesse had used. A short while later, Jesse emerged in different clothing and started walking along the street. Randy watched from a distance, until he saw him go into a coffee shop. He hurried along the street and stopped at the edge of the coffee shop, peering inside. Jesse was sitting at a table, staring at his phone. Five minutes later, a guy turned up who made straight for Jesse. From the way they greeted each other, it was obvious they weren't strangers.

Randy breathed a little easier. *He's just meeting a friend.* Then the friend got up and headed for the restroom at the rear. Less than a minute later, Jesse followed him.

Five minutes passed.

Ten minutes.

Randy kept checking his watch, his heart plummeting with every passing minute. When the friend came out first, Jesse following after a minute, Randy's mind got to working. How many arrests had he made in restrooms in the past? Sure, sometimes it was just a couple of horny guys, but there *had* been occasions when money changed hands.

Maybe this was all aboveboard. Maybe they'd just been talking. *But in the restroom?*

Randy ducked out of sight as Jesse left the coffee shop, thankfully crossing the street and heading toward Ninth Avenue. Randy didn't follow. He needed to think.

I could have this all wrong. Except the hotel incident was leading him down another path. Suspecting was one thing—knowing for sure was something else. *And where does that leave me?* Randy knew what he *should* do. That was a no-brainer.

I need to talk to him. I need to ask him straight. Except he didn't want to do that, for fear he wouldn't like the answer. Especially if that answer meant he should arrest his friend for soliciting.

Whether he *was* going to arrest Jesse was another matter.

Randy was a mess. His body felt heavy as fuck, and his chest was tight. He couldn't focus. *I don't know what to do.* Only, that was a lie. He *did* know what to do—he just didn't want to do it.

Three days previously, he'd felt on top of the world. Spending the Fourth with Jesse had been the best day ever.

Now?

He was conflicted as hell.

RANDY SLOWLY climbed the stairs, with no enthusiasm for the coming evening. All through the day, his mind had defaulted to Jesse, and yet he was still no nearer to working out what to do about the situation. Several times that afternoon, he'd been at the point of messaging Jesse to ask him to meet up for a coffee at the end of the day, but each time he'd chickened out.

He didn't want it to be true.

As he reached his floor, footsteps sounded behind him. "Wait up!"

Randy paused, his hand on the rail, and lingered for Owen to catch up.

Owen was grinning like a lunatic. "Good evening!"

"I'm glad someone's happy," Randy murmured, continuing toward his front door.

Owen stopped him with a hand to Randy's arm. He frowned. "Well, *you're* obviously not. Which is a pity, because I was *about* to invite you in for a drink to help me celebrate."

"Celebrate what?"

Owen beamed. "You know the clinic where I'm working? How it's been a temporary post for the last six months, as I was covering for a long-term absence? Well, I found out this morning the psychologist concerned has decided to call it quits, and they've offered me a permanent position."

Randy couldn't remain down in the face of such elation. "That's great news," he said sincerely.

"So will you? Come in for a celebratory drink? I'm sure I've got at least one bottle of something fizzy in my refrigerator." Owen batted his eyelashes. "Pretty please?"

Randy laughed. "You're a goof."

Owen's eyes lit up. "And that's a yes, if ever I heard one." He opened his front door and waited.

Randy shook his head, chuckling. "Fine. One drink." He reasoned Owen was just the distraction he needed right then. He stepped into Owen's apartment and went into the living room.

Owen marched over to the refrigerator and yanked open the door. "Now, *please* let there be a bottle of champagne or prosecco or *something* in here." He let out a little triumphant cry and pulled out a bottle of prosecco. "Perfect!" He thrust the bottle into Randy's hands. "You open that. I'll get the glasses."

Randy laughed. "You know, you're even bossier when you're in a good mood." He tore off the foil and began twisting the bottle carefully.

Owen reached into the cabinet and removed two long glasses. "And speaking of good moods, what's happened to yours? When I saw you on Tuesday, you looked like you'd won the lottery. What happened?"

Randy gave the bottle one last twist, and the cork popped out. Owen held both glasses while he poured, and then they both sat on the couch. "First things first. Congratulations. That's wonderful news."

Owen smiled broadly. "Yes, it is. I hated the fact that my job was up in the air, so to speak. I feel a lot more secure now. At my age that really matters." He peered at Randy. "And now tell me what's wrong."

Randy took a sip of the sparkling liquid. "My job just got a lot more complicated, that's all."

Owen snickered. "With you, everything is *always* complicated."

Randy took another drink, then told him about Jesse, how they'd met, and what he'd suspected, before moving on to the morning's incident.

He left out the two concerts. That would only add fuel to Owen's already fertile imagination.

Owen frowned. "Maybe I'm being a little dense, but I don't see the problem here. Either he's soliciting, in which case you arrest him, or you've got it wrong and it's all totally innocent."

Yeah, like it was that easy.

"Okay, why are you hesitating?" Owen cocked his head to one side. "What is it with this Jesse?"

Randy couldn't answer. Randy didn't *dare* answer.

Except he'd forgotten about Owen's powers of observation—again.

Owen's eyes widened. "Oh my God. *Oh*. It's like that, is it?"

There seemed little point in hiding the truth any longer. "Okay, so… yeah, I'm interested in him."

"Aha. The mystery guy."

Randy shook his head. "And before you get carried away, nothing is gonna happen between me and Jesse. Nothing ever could." It was all such a fucking *mess*.

Owen remained silent for a moment, sipping his prosecco. Finally he met Randy's gaze. "If I may make a suggestion? What you need right now is a distraction."

"And you provided it." Randy raised his glass. "For which I'm grateful."

Owen smiled, his eyes sparkling. "Not exactly the distraction I had in mind."

Oh God. "Why do I get the feeling this is not going to end well?"

Owen ran a finger around the rim of his glass. "A couple of friends of mine have invited me to a party Friday night. I thought you might want to come with me."

Randy blinked. "A party?" Then he grew aware of the knot in his belly. "What kind of party?"

Owen gave a casual shrug. "Just a gathering of men. Who all happen to be gay or bi. And… it's the kind of party where 'things' might occur." He air-quoted.

Randy's breathing quickened. "What kind of things?"

"Nothing you wouldn't have seen in the Black Lounge, I assure you."

He snorted. "That's not saying much. I saw a lot."

Owen smiled. "I'm sure, but with one important difference. Everything you might see at the party would be consensual."

That wasn't exactly a comfort. Some of the things that took place in the Black Lounge were also consensual. Randy's heartbeat matched his breathing. "We're not talking anything… illegal here, are we?"

Owen arched his eyebrows. "Define *illegal*."

"Drugs." Randy couldn't believe he was asking questions, as though he were actually interested in going. *But I* am *interested.* Well, maybe curious was a better word.

Owen held his hands up. "Okay, there might be poppers, but that would probably be it." He focused his gaze on Randy. "None of your bad guys there. Just ordinary men, having a good time. From what I've gleaned, it sounds like a group of friends getting together, that's all."

Then why didn't it sound like an ordinary evening? Randy considered that it might be just a consequence of his present assignment.

Owen put down his glass and sighed. "If you see anything that makes you uncomfortable, you leave. Just like that." His eyes were kind. "What I'm trying to give you is an opportunity to be among gay men in an environment where it's okay to 'let loose.' No one to judge you. A place where you're safe. A place where if you feel you want to take things a step further, you can."

Fuck. Randy's curiosity went into overdrive. "About taking things further…." His throat dried up, and he quickly took a drink from his glass.

"Totally up to you. If you want to leave, fine. If you just want to make out with a guy, that's fine too."

Make out with…. *Oh God.*

He was conscious of Owen's careful gaze, aware of just how much Owen saw, because he'd seen it all before, right? What Randy knew to his bones was that Owen wasn't judging him, and that knowledge eased a little of the tension in him.

Only a little.

"Like I said, you don't have to *do* anything. Watching might be your thing." Owen paused before continuing. "What I'm trying to say is, *you* control it."

There was no use denying it. Owen's words painted a picture that both intrigued and excited him, fueling his curiosity to almost fever pitch and overriding his instincts.

Randy took a deep breath. "Okay," he said slowly. "Friday night, you said?" That was only the next night. The *next freaking night*.

It was Owen's turn to blink. "Yes." Then he smiled. "Good man. It takes courage to push at your boundaries, to step outside your comfort zone. But you won't be alone."

Randy knew Owen was right. He'd come this far, accepted that his sexuality wasn't cut-and-dried. And deep down, there was part of him that wanted—no, *needed*—to know what it was like to feel another man's touch… another man's kiss.

A little exploration couldn't hurt, right?

Jesse's face was right there in the forefront of his mind, but Randy pushed it aside.

Can't think about him like that. Jesse's not an experiment. He's….

Fuck, he was so much more than that. But right then the thought of the party consumed him. Owen was offering him the chance to discover more about himself, and Randy was going to explore that chance to the fullest.

Chapter Thirteen

THIS IS a bad idea. What the hell was I thinking?

Randy stared at his reflection, seriously conflicted. As soon as he'd gotten into his own apartment the previous evening, the doubts began to creep in.

Why did I say yes?

A glance at the clock beside his bed only exacerbated his nerves. Owen would be knocking on his door any second, and Randy still wasn't sure if he was prepared to go ahead with this. He was ready to go, dressed in chinos and a pale blue shirt, because Owen had stressed casual, but his nerves just wouldn't quit.

Randy breathed deeply, attempting to force some semblance of calm into his body.

Look. What's the worst that can happen?

That definitely wasn't helping.

Okay, then what's the best thing? I have a great evening, meet some cool guys, and....

It was the *and* that bothered him.

A sharp rap on the door brought his internal conversation to an end. Randy picked up his dark blue casual jacket, left his bedroom, and opened the door. Owen looked his usual well-groomed self.

"Ready?"

You can still pull out. There's still time.

Except, when he pushed aside all his fears, doubts, and misgivings, Randy didn't *want* to pull out. He had to know.

Randy gave Owen a smile that was a damn sight more confident than he was feeling. "Ready."

"ADMIRING OUR view?"

Randy turned to one of the hosts, Martin, and smiled. "It's lovely. It must be nice to watch the changing colors in the fall." The apartment building stood on a corner on Central Park West, overlooking the park. Its location, along with the decor, told Randy his hosts weren't short of money.

Martin nodded. "We've been here twenty years now. Silas and I wouldn't live anywhere else." The men were in their fifties, Randy estimated, and both gave off an air of confidence.

"Your glass is empty." Silas appeared at Randy's side, holding out another drink. "More champagne?"

Randy exchanged his empty glass for the full one. "Thank you. Owen didn't mention anything, but are you throwing this party for a special reason?" He grinned. "Or do you just like throwing parties?" Randy felt at ease. There were maybe ten to fifteen men present, some more impeccably dressed than others, which made him glad he'd worn a jacket. Music played softly in the background, and a waiter dressed in black circulated throughout the large living room, holding trays of nibbles. The atmosphere was relaxed, and not at all what he'd expected.

Silas laughed. "Does it show? We love having parties, but yes, this is a special occasion." He held out his hand, and Martin took it. "This is our wedding anniversary. Well, kind of."

"It's complicated," Martin explained. "We got married five years ago, when it first became legal in New York, but we chose our wedding date specifically. Today was the day we met, twenty-five years ago."

Randy raised his glass. "Congratulations."

"Thank you. We're glad you were able to attend. Any friend of Owen's is welcome here. I believe you two are also neighbors?"

Randy nodded.

"Well, I hope you have a pleasant evening. We must mingle." Martin gave Randy a single nod, then walked off with Silas to talk to a couple sitting in a window seat.

"Having fun?" Owen said quietly from beside him, a glass in his hand.

"Yeah. I like your friends." They seemed like nice guys.

Owen stared across the room at Silas and Martin. "They're amazing men, Silas in particular."

"Why do you say that?"

Owen lowered his voice. "I met Martin when he accompanied Silas to an appointment at a clinic where I was working. I was being polite, just passing the time of day with him while he waited, until I realized

I'd seen him before. In a gay bar. I struck up a conversation, and he told me what had happened." He leaned in closer. "Silas was the victim of a violent attack."

Randy gaped at him. "Why would anyone want to beat him up? He seems like a sweet guy."

Owen raised his eyebrows. "And he is. He's also gay. That was enough reason to put him in the hospital for a couple of weeks, apparently. But once he'd recovered from his injuries, he was left with mental trauma. Martin persuaded him to seek help, and he came through it. We stayed in touch and became friends." Owen cocked his head to one side. "You must have come across such cases in your line of work."

"Yeah." Randy shook his head. "We still have way too many assholes out there." He didn't understand such hatred. What people got up to in their bedrooms had absolutely *nothing* to do with anyone else, and to beat the crap out of someone just because they were different made no sense in Randy's book.

"Anyhow, let's change the subject. You seem relaxed. That's good."

Randy chuckled. "That's because there's nothing going on here that would stress anyone out." Hell, they'd been there for nearly an hour, and so far all Randy had seen was guys talking, drinking, and snacking.

Yeah, definitely *not* what he'd expected from Owen's depiction of the party.

"Excellent." Then Owen's eyes gleamed as he stared past Randy's shoulder. "Except it seems the party is only just getting started."

Randy turned to look and was confronted by two men sitting on a couch in the corner, making out. Nothing heavy, just kissing, but things appeared to be getting quite heated between them.

That was one of the things Randy had liked about the Black Lounge—watching guys kiss. He couldn't account for why it turned him on in a way that watching a guy and girl kiss didn't. He glanced over to Martin and Silas, who'd also noticed the exhibition. Martin smiled, then carried on his conversation as if two men making out in his living room was an everyday occurrence.

Randy turned back in time to see the guys get up from their couch and walk out of the room. "Was I staring too much?" he murmured to Owen.

"Trust me, they weren't embarrassed. They've just gone into one of the bedrooms. And before you ask, yes, Martin and Silas know about that."

Randy chuckled. "Okay. Not so different from high school kids' parties, I guess, when their parents are away." What surprised him was that he could deal with it, knowing two guests had left to go fuck each other, with the hosts' blessing.

Then he noticed something. Now and again a guest would peer into one of several ceramic jars that were positioned around the living room, and smile. Randy had noticed them not long after he'd arrived. Intrigued, he peered into a jar that sat on a shelf near him.

Oh Lord. It contained condoms. And lube.

Okay, that *was* different. Not to mention convenient and incredibly thoughtful of the hosts. Wherever guests were in the room, protection was at hand.

I guess it really is *one of* those *kind of parties.*

The couple's exit seemed to provide some kind of catalyst. Around him, there was suddenly a lot of kissing going on, and more besides. Touching. Caressing. Then he noticed shirts were being unbuttoned, skin exposed.

It was as if someone had just turned up the heat.

Randy felt a little conspicuous, so he took a seat in a chair by one of the windows, unable to tear his gaze away from what was unfolding before him. Owen was talking in a low voice to a younger man, stroking his face and neck, occasionally leaning in to kiss him on the cheek.

It was fascinating. And definitely arousing.

A new soundtrack emerged above the music, that of soft sighs and low moans, and it took Randy back to the Black Lounge. How many times had he stood in that hallway, listening to similar noises coming from the rooms? How many times had he wanted to know what those guys felt when someone touched them so intimately? To know how much of what he heard was simply an act for the clients or sounds they couldn't keep inside because it all felt so fucking *good*?

What was happening before his eyes wasn't nearly as in-your-face as the kind of acts Randy had witnessed, but it was just as erotic, just as arousing. And Randy couldn't get enough of it.

Not all the guests were getting down with it. Some were watching, nodding, and discreetly adjusting themselves. *I guess some guys just like to watch.* Randy ached to do more than be a spectator, but he didn't dare. He wasn't that brave.

"Hey." A handsome man walked over to him, smiling. "What are you doing, all on your own over here? A guy as gorgeous as you shouldn't be alone." And before Randy could say a word in response, the guy leaned over and kissed his neck, a lingering kiss that was almost a nuzzle.

Holy fuck. Randy's dick sat up at that. Randy's heart, on the other hand, started pounding, and he sprang up out of his chair. "Excuse me," he croaked before making a dash for the safety of the bathroom. Once inside, he locked the door and leaned on the sink, his hands gripping the cool porcelain. He ran cold water into the bowl, then splashed his face, his breathing erratic. After a moment, he grabbed a towel and dried off.

What the fuck? Randy stared at his pale face in the mirror, trying to analyze his extreme reaction to that one sensual kiss. His stiffening cock made it impossible to deny the truth, however. He dropped onto the closed toilet seat and put his head in his hands. *Lord, but that was hot.* Randy felt light-headed, hyperaware of the cool temperature in the bathroom, the scent of lavender, the hardness of the seat he sat on....

He closed his eyes and breathed slowly... in... out... in... out....

A gentle tapping on the door made him almost jump out of his skin. "You okay in there?"

Thank God. It was Owen.

Randy lurched across the room and unbolted the door. He flung it open, grabbed Owen by the arm, yanked him into the bathroom, and locked the door after him. Randy sat back on the toilet, leaning forward, his elbows on his knees.

Owen placed his hand on Randy's shoulder. "I saw what happened. You bolted out of there like you'd been shot." He rubbed gently. "Breathe, Randy, breathe."

Randy gazed up at him. "And you bolted in here after me. Thanks."

Owen smiled. "I had to come see how you are." He glanced around the bathroom, smirking. "Ordinarily, if I'm in a bathroom with a guy at a party, it's certainly not to chat with him or check up on him." He gave Randy a sympathetic glance. "Nerves get the better of you?" Then he grinned. "By the way, I think you made quite an impression on Zac." When Randy gave him a puzzled glance, Owen grinned. "The guy who kissed you. I think you're in there."

Randy glared at him. "You're not helping." He drew in a long breath. "Fuck."

Owen's manner changed instantly. He crouched beside Randy, his hand on Randy's knee. "You're not all right, are you? Take as long as you like."

Randy gave him a grateful smile. "I'm fine. I just got a bit overwhelmed, that's all. No offense to Zac, but he's not my type. But that kiss… wow." He shivered as he touched his neck where Zac's lips had been.

Owen nodded. "I can understand that reaction. That's one of my hot spots. A guy kisses me there and I just… melt." He chuckled. "So, no point asking if you liked it. That much is obvious."

What bothered Randy was not the fact that he'd reacted to a stranger's kiss, but that what had been foremost in his mind at that moment… was Jesse.

"So… do you want to leave, or are you ready to rejoin the party?"

Randy drew in a deep breath. He wasn't ready to leave just yet. "I think if I left now, I'd regret it."

Owen beamed at him. "Good man. Let's get out there and have some fun."

Randy got to his feet, and after a glance in the mirror, he followed Owen out of the bathroom.

Owen paused at the threshold to the living room. "Remember. If you get uncomfortable, you can leave."

Randy barely heard his words. Something was going on in there. A group of men were standing around, plainly watching something intently. "What's happening?" he whispered.

"Your guess is as good as mine."

Randy walked across to join them, craning his neck to see what was captivating their attention. Owen came with him. When someone in front of him moved, Randy got a better look—and froze.

On the couch sat one of the guests, bare from the waist down, his pants around his ankles. In front of him was a kneeling figure who was obviously blowing him, his blond head bobbing furiously. Not that Randy could see much of him—his view was obscured by the guy standing behind him, totally naked, fucking him.

Oh…. Fuck.

Randy was spellbound. Watching Rear Guy's asscheeks jiggle and hollow as he slammed into the Kneeling Guy was… mesmerizing. The way his hands gripped Kneeling Guy's hips, pulling him roughly back onto his dick. The way Kneeling Guy's body jolted with each thrust into him. The moans that poured from Blown Guy's lips. The way he pushed down hard on Kneeling Guy's head, forcing him to take him deeper. The loud groans of pleasure that rolled out of Kneeling Guy.

And around them stood the guests, some focused on the developing scene, palming their own dicks through their clothing. One couple watched with one guy's hand down the back of another's pants, moving slowly, the sound of rapid, uneven breathing filling the room. Most of the guests were still dressed, though some had discarded their shirts and tops.

Randy's attention was pulled back to the three guys, who were plainly having a fantastic time. His skin was hot and cold at the same time. He was torn between wanting to know what it would be like to have a mouth on his cock, and wanting to be the one plunging his shaft into a tight hole. The situation was so… illicit, and yet he couldn't tear his gaze away. There was something about the guy on his knees that….

"Do you want to take a turn?" a voice murmured in his ear.

Randy jerked his head to stare at Martin, standing beside him. "What?"

Martin nodded toward the men. "That's what he's here for."

Randy was no clearer. "What are you talking about?" he whispered.

"The guy on the floor. That's what we're paying him for, so anyone can have a go."

"Paying him?" Ice crawled around Randy's heart. Owen was staring at him, shaking his head, and when Randy met his gaze, he mouthed, *I had no idea.* Judging by Owen's panicked expression, the same thought had to be racing through his mind too.

Holy fucking hell, this is really bad. They had to get out of there.

Randy stepped away from the onlookers, Owen and Martin joining him. "You mean to say," Randy began, speaking slowly and quietly, "that you and Silas are paying this guy to have sex with any or all of your guests?"

Before Martin could reply, Owen grabbed hold of Randy's arm. "Look, we gotta go, right fucking *now*! My license and your badge are on the line as of this moment!" His usual composure had fled.

Martin paled. "Oh shit. Owen, I wasn't thinking. God, I am so sorry." Then he gaped at Randy and stilled. "Badge? Are you a cop?"

Randy nodded. "Yeah, so you can see why I might have a problem with this." He glanced around as several more shirts were removed. This was beginning to have all the characteristics of an epic clusterfuck.

Martin took a deep breath. "What are you going to do?"

There was the million-dollar question.

Randy struggled to keep calm. "What you really want to know is, am I gonna arrest you?" It was what he *should* do.

All around the room were men enjoying themselves, supplied with condoms and lube in case the mood took them. And hadn't he been enjoying it just as much? Almost as much as the three guys who were fucking.

Randy breathed in through his nose and out through his mouth, trying to get his heart to stop hammering. "I'm going to leave now. I'm gonna pretend I didn't see any of this." At least that way, he didn't have to act on any of it. Randy caught Owen's gaze. "And you're leaving too."

Owen nodded vigorously.

Martin swallowed. "Thank you. Seriously. It was only meant to be a little entertainment, but—"

"Just don't say another word, all right?" Randy scanned the room for the chair where he'd left his jacket. He grabbed it and headed toward the door, his pulse racing. Owen followed him, leaving Martin with the guests.

"Look, I'm so sorry about this," Owen said as he unlocked the front door.

"Wait." Randy's heartbeat sped up. "Something's wrong here." *That blond guy....*

He went back to the living room doorway and stared at the crowd, which was shifting, murmuring, as if something was about to happen. Then he caught sight of a familiar face, and his blood turned to ice.

"Aw fuck."

Jesse was looking right at Randy, his eyes impossibly large, his mouth open, and white as a sheet.

Chapter Fourteen

RANDY COULDN'T stay in that room a moment longer. He pushed past Owen, opened the door, and got the hell out of that apartment.

"Wait!" Owen caught up with him. "Christ, you didn't have to run."

Randy came to a halt at the elevator. "Why? Did you want to stick around?" He was still shaking. *Of all people, why did it have to be Jesse?*

Owen scowled. "Of course not. God, what a mess." He peered at Randy, his gaze narrowing. "What's wrong?" he asked urgently.

Randy was trying his best to breathe, but the tightness around his chest made things difficult. "You're kidding, right?" He glanced back to the apartment, as if he half expected Jesse to come running after them. *Except, why would he?* Jesse was getting paid to do a job, right?

"I'm not talking about the fact that both of us could lose our jobs over this and probably never find work again." Owen took a deep breath. "And that's not understating the case, as I'm sure you know. I'm talking about what happened when you glanced into that room. And don't shit me, because you looked like you'd seen a ghost." The elevator arrived, and they stepped inside. Owen pressed the button, then leaned against the steel wall. "Well?"

Randy shuddered out a long breath. "That guy in there? The *entertainment*? That was Jesse."

Owen's jaw dropped. "You are fucking *kidding* me. Your Jesse? The one you—"

The elevator came to a halt, and as soon as the doors opened, Randy was out of there, striding through the lobby and spilling out of the building onto Central Park West. He stared into the oncoming traffic, scanning for a taxi, his stomach churning.

Owen caught up with him. "Can we talk about this?"

Randy gaped at him. "What the fuck is there to talk about?" He spied a taxi and hailed it. When it pulled up beside them, Randy got in, then stared at Owen. "Are you getting in or what?"

Owen got in beside him and rattled off the address.

Randy sank back against the seat, his head still spinning. *This is such a fucking mess.*

Owen twisted in his seat to look at him, and Randy shook his head. "We're not gonna talk about this. Not here. You got that?"

Owen said nothing, but nodded, then turned to stare through the window.

That left Randy with his thoughts, all racing through his head at breakneck speed.

Oh Christ. That was fucking close. The only saving grace about this whole sorry mess was that the guy they hired turned out to be Jesse. Because supposing it hadn't been? Supposing some time later, Randy ended up arresting the guy in a sting? *Hooker takes one look at me and it's game over.* At the least, he'd be outed at work. At worst? The hooker could've blackmailed him for fucking *years*, and all because of one lousy, goddamn party.

Never mind what Owen said about pushing boundaries and stepping out of comfort zones. Randy could admit to being curious, but he plainly wasn't ready to address that yet. What did it matter if he had feelings for Jesse if he was too fucking afraid to confront them? But what overrode those emotions was anger.

And Randy was fucking *livid*.

How the fuck could Jesse lie to me? Okay, so not *once* had Randy actually come right out and *asked* Jesse if he was soliciting, but that was just a technicality. All those times Jesse had talked about job interviews, waiting tables, pizza parlors… nothing but lies. And like a sap, Randy had believed him. All that time, he was selling his ass, all the while knowing what Randy did for a living, knowing Randy was a Vice cop. *Was he laughing at me? Was that it? Was it fun to pull the wool over my eyes?*

Randy clenched his fists. He didn't know for sure that the job interviews had been lies. And if he was going to lay the blame at anyone's door, he'd better start with himself, for going to that party in the first place. *I should have followed my instincts. I should have told Owen no, flat-out.*

And there was yet another focus for his anger. This was all down to Owen. Randy glared at the side view of Owen, who was still looking at the passing scenery, unaware of Randy's scrutiny. *He put me in that position.*

Except Randy knew he was to blame most of all, because what angered him more than anything was that he'd been turned on by the whole episode.

From the boner when that guy kissed him, to standing there, watching them fucking and wishing it was *him* in there, *him* with his mouth around that guy's dick, *him* with that guy's cock spearing into him.

Christ, he'd wanted that *so fucking much*, but not half as much as he'd wanted Jesse.

Right up to the point when he'd looked across that room and seen Jesse's face staring back at him.

He pulled out his phone, then stared at it. *What am I gonna do—send Jesse a text to ask him what the fuck he was thinking?* Like he could do that. Because that would mean further contact, and right then Randy was between a rock and hard place. How could he face Jesse after this? When Randy spent his days trying to *deter* guys from paying people like Jesse? *When what I really should be doing is arresting him?*

Randy forced himself to breathe. *This is such a mess.*

And he didn't know how to get out of it.

He was going to go home, shut out the world, and try to forget any of it had ever happened.

Yeah, right.

"Randy. Randy!"

With a start, he realized Owen was talking to him. Then he saw they were home. Owen paid the driver, and they got out of the taxi. Randy didn't wait around. He got inside and almost ran up the flights of stairs, with Owen close on his heels. When they got to the fourth floor, Randy turned to face him.

"Before you say another word, no, I do *not* want to discuss this. I wanna forget this whole sorry episode, and if you know what's good for you, you won't bring it up again."

"Randy, please." Owen appeared stricken. "Running away isn't going to solve anything."

Randy snorted. "Well, it works for me." And with that, he unlocked his front door, went inside, and slammed it shut behind him. Inside, he leaned against it, his shivers multiplying until he was quivering all over, his stomach tight.

Oh, Jesse, why? Why couldn't you tell me the truth?

JESSE STARED after Randy, his heart sinking, his breathing erratic. *Oh God. Of all the people....*

"Hey, you all right?" The guy on whose dick he was about to sit placed a warm hand on his waist.

All right? Jesse was in absolute fucking *turmoil*.

Is he going to arrest me? Why was he here? Was he on duty? Was he here on his own? How come I didn't see him when I came in? He wanted to grab his clothes and get the hell out of there, run after Randy, but he had a job to do, one for which Martin and Silas were paying him handsomely.

"I'm fine," Jesse murmured. He waited until the guy had gloved up, then slowly lowered himself onto his fat cock, ensuring he made all the right noises, moaning about how it filled him. Then the other guy was on him, aiming his dick at Jesse's already stuffed hole. Jesse tried to relax, waiting for the pinch he knew was coming, and finally he was there, as full as could be. He let the bottom guy take his weight, let the two men cradle him between them while they worked out who was moving and when, and shut himself down, retreating inwardly to fathom out this whole mess.

If Randy was here as a cop, then why did he leave? That part didn't make sense. But he knew one thing. He was never going to forget that look on Randy's face. The shock….

Jesse went through the motions, gasping when the guy on top picked up speed, grateful that they'd worked out the guy on the bottom had to keep still. *Thank fuck.* Guys who knew their way around a DP. Not that it mattered. Jesse was on autopilot, his mind still replaying what had happened over and over again. The more he thought about it, however, the angrier he became.

Why was *Randy here, if not as a cop?*

When the two guys fucking him finally withdrew, pulled off their condoms, and came, both with loud, messy cumshots that went everywhere, Jesse held his breath, knowing he was there to interact with anyone who wanted him. When only one guy asked, Jesse smiled and sat astride him on another couch, bouncing on his dick, moaning like it was the biggest goddamn cock he'd ever had, except he could barely feel it inside him. The guy seemed happy enough, especially when Jesse shot a load all over his chest.

Thank God some guys were *so* easy to please.

When Martin gave him the nod that he was done for the night, Jesse went into the bathroom, did a quick cleanup, got dressed, and prepared to hightail it out of there. Martin was waiting for him at the door with an envelope in his hand and a concerned expression.

"Was everything all right? I got the impression you were upset by something."

Dammit. Martin was a sweet man, and he and Silas had hired Jesse once for another party. They were a hooker's dream clients—they paid well, looked after him, and didn't invite any crazies.

Jesse gave him a hopefully reassuring smile. "I'm fine. Thanks again for the work. I know you didn't have to do that." He wasn't about to tell him about Randy.

Martin frowned. "I don't know what you mean."

Jesse kissed his cheek. "*Paying* someone for what I did? There are guys I know who aren't in my business who would line up to be on the receiving end of a night like this." He tilted his head to one side. "You were being kind, weren't you?"

Martin gave him a warm smile. "Let's just say I know what it's like to be in your shoes. And you earned every cent tonight. There's even a bit extra." When Jesse opened his mouth to protest, Martin shook his head. "I don't recall telling you double penetration would be on the cards, but you rolled with it. And you made our guests very happy." He kissed Jesse's cheek. "And if you ever need us, for anything, you call, okay?"

Jesse blinked back tears. Things like this did *not* happen in real life. "Thank you," he whispered. He stretched out his hand to take the envelope… and then withdrew it.

"Jesse? Is there something wrong?"

Jesse swallowed. "Keep it."

Martin frowned. "I don't understand."

In Jesse's head it made perfect sense. "I can't take it," he whispered. Whatever he had going with Randy, it was too good to let it get fucked-up. And if it came down to taking the money or holding on to Randy?

No contest.

Besides, some logical voice in his head kept telling him that if he didn't take the cash, then it wasn't really soliciting, and Randy couldn't have a problem with that, right?

Yeah. That voice was fucking delusional. And never mind Randy's problems—Jesse had a few goddamn questions to ask him, like what he'd been doing at that party in the first place.

Martin stilled. "Oh my God. This is about that cop, isn't it? How did you know—?"

Jesse stared at him. "What did he say to you?" His heart pounded.

"He isn't going to do anything… official about it. That's all I know." Martin gazed into the room where his guests chatted. "But it put the fear of God into me. That's for sure. I won't be doing this again."

What the hell? Jesse had to get out of there. He had to find Randy. "Take care," he said quietly, before kissing Martin's cheek once more.

Martin grabbed his arm. "I don't know what's going on in your head, but I am *not* letting you refuse me. You worked hard for this, Jesse. And if this is something to do with that cop…."

"It's… complicated." Lord, wasn't *that* the truth?

"I don't doubt it. But I also know you're in no position to refuse payment. Now, as for what you do with it, that's up to you. Keep it, donate it, whatever."

Jesse stared at the envelope. *Like it's gonna matter to Randy whether I take the money or not. In his eyes the damage is already done. Shit.* This was such a fucking *mess.*

He took the envelope and stuffed it into his bag. "Thanks," he said quietly.

"Are you all right?" The compassion in Martin's eyes almost undid him.

Jesse pasted on a smile that felt as fake as Donald Trump's tan. "I'll be fine." He left the apartment and made his way over to the elevator. While he waited, he got out his phone and composed a very short text to Randy.

WTF???

Like he'd really expected a reply.

Chapter Fifteen

WHEN HIS phone pinged for what had to be the tenth time, Randy ignored it. He didn't need to see the screen to know it was another text from Jesse. He'd already ignored four or five calls, and there was no way he was going to listen to his voicemail.

I don't want to hear his voice right now. Randy had gotten his anger under control, but he knew it wouldn't take much to have it resurface—along with a whole slew of other emotions that he didn't want to acknowledge right then.

Someone hammered on his door, and his heart lurched. Another loud rap.

It can't be Jesse. He can't get in without buzzing. Randy stood rooted to the spot.

Another dull thud against the door. "Randy?"

Shit. Apparently he could.

Randy walked slowly over to the door, unlocked it, and came face-to-face with Jesse, his eyes wide, face flushed. Jesse didn't wait for him to say a word but pushed past him into the apartment. Randy closed the door and followed him into the living room.

"How did you get in?"

Jesse arched his eyebrows. "That's really where you wanna start?" He dropped his bag onto the arm of the couch. "Okay, fine. I was at the main door when a guy opened it. He seemed to know me. Anyhow, he let me in, no questions asked. It was only when I was halfway up the stairs that I realized he'd been with you this evening." He cocked his head. "Friend of yours?"

"Neighbor."

Jesse nodded. "And now that we've got *that* out of the way… wanna tell me what the *fuck* a straight cop was doing at a gay sex party? And don't tell me you were there undercover, because I won't buy it." He speared Randy with a look. "Were you there for kicks? Didn't you get enough after all that time in the Black Lounge?"

Randy snorted. "Don't you *dare* get all indignant on me, not after tonight."

"Uh-uh." Jesse's eyes were the blue of a stormy sky. "We'll talk about me later. Right now we're talking about *you*, and that means *I* want to know what was going on in your head while you were undercover. Did it turn you on? Is that why you went to that party? You needed a fix?" His eyes widened. "Was that the first time, or is this something you do on a regular basis?"

"No!" Randy shouted. When Jesse flinched, he groaned internally. "Okay, tonight was a first, all right? You don't have to believe me, but it's the truth. And as for the Black Lounge…." Fuck, how the hell could he explain it? Randy took a deep breath. "Yeah, I saw a lot of stuff going on, I'll admit that, but… that was different."

"How? How was it different from watching me getting fucked tonight?" Jesse's face was still flushed.

"I was *working*, okay?" Randy flung back at him. "I could look at it all clinically. I just… filed it all into a box inside my head."

"Then what was tonight? You weren't working, I know that much. If you had been, Martin would have his ass in jail right now."

"So I have more than one box in my brain!" Randy exclaimed.

Jesse merely raised his eyebrows. "Oh yeah? And which box does the party fit into?"

That was the easy part. "Curiosity," Randy said simply. "And you're right. I wasn't there as a cop."

His reply appeared to unsettle Jesse, who blinked. "Okay. You were curious. Then why did you leave like you did?"

"Because I got *angry*, all right?" What remained of Randy's calm shattered. "At myself, for letting my neighbor persuade me to go to that damn party. At Owen, for bringing it up in the first place. At finding myself in that position. God, there were any number of things that got me mad. But most of all?" He was too far gone to keep the truth inside him a moment longer. "Because you were there."

"Because I was hooking?" Jesse's face was a picture of misery.

"Partly." Faced with Jesse's reaction, Randy deflated. *Tell him, for God's sake. Don't let him suffer when you know there's more to it than that.* His heart quaked at the thought.

"I see." Jesse looked like he'd been slapped.

That was more than Randy could bear. He summoned up every ounce of courage. "But mostly because up until the point where I glimpsed your face, I… wanted to be the one fucking you."

Jesse's mouth fell open, and he gave Randy a dazed stare. Randy didn't dare speak, his gaze focused on Jesse's rigid posture.

Finally, Jesse swallowed. "Did you know it was me? When I was…?"

Randy shook his head. But there had been *something*, hadn't there, about that blond head? Something that had stirred in his mind?

"So…." Jesse drew in a breath. "When I was just some faceless guy, you wanted to fuck me because you were curious." He didn't break eye contact. "When you saw it was me… did you still want to fuck me?"

Oh God. "When I saw your face, I was… shocked. Angry. I felt… betrayed."

Jesse took a step closer. "Answer the question. Did you still want to fuck me?" His voice was low, robbed of the rage that had laced it before.

Randy gazed into those stormy blue eyes, that earnest face, and had to tell the truth. "Yes. That's why I left. I… couldn't. Not there. Not like that."

Jesse's eyes were so fucking huge. "And what about now?" he asked softly.

Holy fuck. He can't mean… because that sounds like… oh fuck….

Randy pushed aside logic and reason, grabbed Jesse's head, and pulled him close, their mouths colliding, lips fusing in a frantic kiss with both of them groaning into it. Jesse's arms were around his neck, locked there, while he gave as good as he got, the noises pouring from him, leaving Randy in no doubt that he wanted this as much as Randy did. Randy slid his tongue between Jesse's lips, surprised by the fervor with which Jesse met his kiss.

Jesse broke free long enough to gasp out one word. "Bed."

Randy snickered. "Uh-uh. You're not calling the shots." Then he grabbed Jesse's ass and hoisted him up into his arms. "But seeing as I was already gonna take you there…."

Jesse moaned and wrapped his legs around Randy's waist, holding on to him as Randy moved swiftly toward the bedroom.

Randy came to a dead stop, however, before they reached the door. "Your bag!" He went back to the couch, lowering Jesse enough that he could reach it without letting him stand.

Jesse grinned. "You could've put me down, you know."

Randy shook his head. "Not letting go of you until I've got you where I want you." He nodded toward the bag now slung over Jesse's shoulder. "And we're gonna need supplies, which I'm assuming you have in there."

Jesse stilled. "You assume correctly."

That was it. They both knew where this was heading, and Randy didn't want to wait another second to get there.

JESSE CLAIMED Randy's mouth in a hungry kiss, not worried in the slightest that Randy was about to drop him. Randy's arms felt so strong around him, supporting him as he carried him through the apartment into his bedroom. Jesse was dizzy with anticipation, his head still spinning from the change in direction.

He wants me. He fucking wants *me.* Jesse's whole body tingled, and his heartbeat sped up. He wanted to tear the clothes from Randy's back, to kiss him all over that glorious body....

No. Not this time.

Jesse stilled in Randy's arms, breaking the kiss, and Randy gazed at him, his brow furrowed. "Something wrong?" He lowered Jesse onto the foot of the bed.

Jesse gave him a smile. "Far from it. You were right. *You're* calling the shots." His pulse quickened at the thought of giving up control, but he knew it was right. He had to let go. His heart pounded at the sight of Randy's face, his eyes so dark, his lips slightly swollen already. Then he snickered. "Well, when you get around to it...."

Randy laughed and proceeded to unbutton his shirt. "Clothes, off, now."

Jesse chuckled. "Now *there's* the bossy cop I know and love." Except he knew that last part was more than a line. He pulled his T-shirt up and over his head, loving how Randy's breathing hitched when he revealed his bare torso, thankful he'd cleaned up at Martin's place. His skin smelled of Ivory soap. Then Randy muttered under his breath when he couldn't undo the buttons on his cuffs, and Jesse laughed at the sight of him trying to free his arms from the shirtsleeves.

"Let me help." Jesse tossed aside his top and knelt up on the bed to wrestle with the buttons on one wrist, while Randy tried to open the others with his teeth. Jesse laughed, pulling at Randy's hand. "How about a little patience?" He gasped when Randy grabbed hold of his wrist and dragged his hand to Randy's crotch.

"Does *that* feel like I *want* to be patient?" Randy's eyes gleamed.

Fuck, he's hard. Any reply Jesse could have made died in his throat as Randy unbuttoned his fly, pushed down his pants and briefs to his knees, and a thick, meaty dick sprang up. Randy put one hand to the back of Jesse's head, pushing him down.

Like he could keep Jesse away from that gorgeous cock. Jesse dropped onto his belly, opened wide, and took Randy deep.

Randy shuddered, both his hands on Jesse's head, holding him in place while he slid in and out of Jesse's lips. Jesse relaxed his throat and went with it, his head bobbing as he let Randy fuck his mouth.

"Oh my God, how your mouth feels on my dick," Randy moaned. "So good."

Jesse poured his heart and soul into that blowjob, and was rewarded when Randy's low cries multiplied. He hummed around the thick length, exulting at the shivers that coursed through Randy's body, the gentle touch of Randy's hands on Jesse's back, stroking him, moving lower.

Then Randy pulled free, his dick glistening. He hoisted Jesse into a kneeling position, then pushed him onto his back, Jesse landing with a bounce. Before he could utter a word, Randy went for Jesse's jeans, unfastening them, yanking the zipper down, then tugging at them as he tried to free Jesse from them.

"Fucking hell, why would anyone wanna wear skinny jeans?" he muttered, pulling them over Jesse's hips.

Jesse burst out laughing. "Because they make my legs and ass look good?"

Randy had Jesse's feet in the air, tugging at the offending jeans, until finally his legs were free of them, his cock slapping against his belly, hard as a rock.

Before Jesse had time to draw breath, Randy spread him like he was a rag doll and dove between his thighs to take Jesse's dick into his mouth. Jesse arched up off the bed at the feel of that hot mouth, but Randy pushed him back down, pinning him there while he sucked hard on the head of Jesse's cock.

"Fuck, you're good at that," Jesse gasped out. Letting Randy take control was heady and exhilarating as fuck, like doing a trapeze act without wearing a safety harness. He marveled at Randy's self-assurance, the confidence he exuded as he pleasured Jesse, like he'd been sucking dick his whole life.

As if he'd read Jesse's thoughts, Randy pulled free and smiled at him. "Not bad for a first-timer, then? And I *should* be good at it, the number of times I watched guys do this. Amazing how it all gets stored away in here." He tapped his temple.

"Oh yeah?" Jesse grinned. "And what else did you learn?" Then he caught his breath as Randy slowly pushed his jeans all the way off, his stiff shaft curving up as he stepped out of them, finally, *gloriously* naked.

"That if I want something, I should just go for it."

Jesse's breath left him in a whoosh as Randy flipped him onto his stomach before covering him with his body, pinning him to the bed with his weight. Randy's lips were on his neck, making Jesse quiver. He could feel that hot, hard dick against his lower back as Randy kissed his shoulders and down his spine. When Randy shifted, his cock sliding between Jesse's asscheeks, Jesse shivered, surprised by his body's reaction to being held down by Randy's weight.

Why does this feel... different? Because there was no denying it. When Randy grabbed his ass and spread him, a moan escaped Jesse that he couldn't hold back. This wasn't new. Christ, how many johns had done this? Yet here he was, trembling at Randy's touch.

Jesse hadn't expected to feel this way, but *fuck*, he liked it.

"Want to be inside you," Randy whispered, rocking his dick over Jesse's hole, sending icicles of pleasure dripping down his spine and spreading out over his skin. His lips grazed Jesse's neck again, and Jesse shivered.

"Not stopping you," Jesse flung back. "My bag is on the floor. Condoms. Lube."

"Don't. Move." Then Randy's weight was gone, and Jesse missed it instantly.

When he heard the telltale crinkle, the snap of the lid on the lube, his heartbeat thundered in his ears and his hole tightened. As much as he ached to feel Randy's mouth there, Jesse wasn't about to ask him. No matter how much Randy had seen, Jesse was pretty sure that a rim job would be a step too far out of Randy's comfort zone, considering it was his first time. Besides, he didn't want to wait, not when he so badly needed to feel that slow press of Randy's cock inside him.

Randy seemed to be on the same page. He grabbed Jesse's hips, lifting him up off the bed. "Spread for me." Jesse barely had time to comply before he felt the slick heat of a wide head pushing insistently against his hole. Then Randy was in him up to the hilt, and *my God*, Jesse felt every blessed inch.

"Fuck." The word shuddered out of Randy, carried on a long breath, even as he slowly withdrew his dick. "Oh God, how that feels…." Strong hands gripped Jesse's shoulders, and the air was punched from his lungs as Randy slid into him with one long, deep stroke of his cock.

Three, four, five thrusts later, Randy pulled out completely and flipped Jesse onto his back. He scrambled off the bed, grabbed Jesse by the hips, and tugged him until his ass hung over the edge. Jesse got one look at that beautiful dick before Randy plunged it back inside him, holding on to Jesse's legs, spreading him wide, gripping him around his ankles. The sudden change of position shocked Jesse into a whoop of laughter that he couldn't hold inside him a second longer.

"Fuck, yeah, that's it," he yelled out in encouragement. Randy grabbed one leg and held it aloft, Jesse's ankle resting against Randy's shoulder while he fucked him, always going deep, lighting up every nerve ending and making Jesse cry out with the *sheer fucking pleasure* of it all. He reached for his cock, but Randy pushed his hand away.

"You're not gonna come yet." Randy's voice was raw. Then Jesse closed his eyes as Randy slowed to a crawl, the long, delicious slides into his body sending wave after wave of sensual bliss pulsing through him, until he was crying out for more.

Randy let go of his leg and climbed onto the bed beside him, lifting Jesse's leg once more so he was almost on his side before sliding into him again. Jesse slipped his arm around Randy's neck and pulled him down into a brutal kiss, while Randy began to thrust into him at a leisurely pace that lasted for all of three or four slow glides. Then he was fucking into him with long strokes, Jesse feeding him soft cries of sheer joy as Randy brought him to the edge.

Fuck, when had it *ever* been this good?

RANDY KNEW he was close, could feel it *right there*, and he didn't want it to end. He gazed at Jesse, taking in the glisten of sweat on his brow and chest, the scent that poured out of him, stirring Randy's senses. Randy let go of Jesse's leg and cupped his cheek, staring into those gorgeous blue eyes.

"I want to come like this, where I can see your eyes," he said breathlessly. *I want to see that look in your eyes, the same look you had at that concert, where you were lost in the moment, carried away by the beauty of it all.* He pulled out of Jesse, almost to the point where he was completely free of him, then slowly, exquisitely, he sheathed his dick all the way inside that tight body.

A shudder rippled through Jesse, and he grabbed his cock seconds before it erupted over his belly. "Fuck," he moaned softly, his skin laced with the creamy spatter.

Randy kept moving inside him, slow and steady, until Jesse's shivers had ebbed away. Then he picked up speed, his own need driving him as he thrust deep into Jesse and stilled, his balls tight as he filled the latex, his own shivers jolting him as his dick pulsed out its last drops, Jesse's body wrapped tightly around it. Jesse reached for him, and their lips met in an unhurried kiss while they lay there, touching, caressing, stroking, until Randy's heartbeat was once more back to normal.

He removed the condom, tied it up, and dropped it into the basket beside the bed.

"Wow."

Randy turned to stare at him, his pulse quickening, his chest tightening. "Wow?"

Jesse broke into a smile that lit up his eyes. "Sorry. All I'm capable of right now. I'll give you better feedback when I get more blood to my brain." He chuckled. "But if it helps? It's a really good wow."

Randy could live with that.

Jesse opened his arms wide. "Now come here."

He laughed. "Uh-uh. You're all sticky."

"And whose fault is that?" Jesse rolled his eyes. "A dainty cop. Who'd have thought it?"

To hell with that. Randy rolled on top of him, and cradling Jesse's head between his forearms, he kissed him, taking his time, loving how Jesse brought up those long legs and wrapped them around him, squishing their bodies together.

"Besides," Jesse murmured between kisses, "think of all the fun we can have in the shower."

Chapter Sixteen

THIS HAS to be a dream, right?

Jesse was in Randy's bed, curled up in Randy's arms like he fucking *belonged* there. It had only taken one word from Randy to have him decide where he was sleeping that night.

"Stay."

Like Jesse was gonna ignore that.

He was pretty sure there had been more kissing going on in Randy's shower than washing, but Jesse wasn't about to complain. Not that he indulged in a whole lotta kissing in his daily life. That was… intimate, especially the bare-your-soul kind of kisses he'd shared with Randy. Water cascading down on them, Randy's hands on his back, his belly, his ass, his lips locked on Jesse's, like he couldn't get enough of him….

One night was never going to be enough in Jesse's book.

Randy stirred behind him, his breath warm on Jesse's shoulder. "This feels good," he murmured.

Hearing his own thoughts echoed settled Jesse's few remaining doubts. He'd longed to ask if it had been everything Randy had expected, but hadn't dared. That left only one question.

"No regrets?"

"Just one."

Jesse turned in Randy's arms, seeking his face in the darkened room. "What?"

Randy huffed. "It was over way too fast. By the time I realized how amazing it felt, I was already on the point of shooting my load."

Jesse snickered. "Yeah, well, join the club. That was one hell of a frantic fuck." He sighed when Randy's hand caressed his cheek. *God, the simplest touch from him and my heart starts beating faster…*.

"And what if that wasn't what I wanted?"

Before Jesse could reply, Randy's mouth met his in a kiss that was worlds away from the fervent collision of lips, teeth, and tongues of a few hours previous. This was tender, gentle… sensual.

Then Jesse was pushed firmly onto his back and Randy moved to straddle his hips, the kissing not ceasing for a second. Randy rocked gently against him while he explored Jesse's mouth with exquisite attention, tugging on his lower lip before sucking on his tongue. He kept up that leisurely rolling of his hips as they kissed, his hand on Jesse's neck, until Jesse could feel the heat and steel of him once more against his own thickening dick.

Jesse held Randy's face between his hands, their breath mingling. "Don't stop kissing me," he begged.

Randy gave a soft chuckle. "Wasn't planning on it." Then it was right back to kissing, only now Jesse stroked his chest and neck, learning the feel of him, breathing him in with every inhalation. Randy, too, was lost in his own explorations, caressing Jesse's face and neck, pausing now and again to smile, as though it was slowly dawning on him that this felt *good*.

"I'm gonna have stubble burn after this, aren't I?" Randy chuckled again. "That might prove a little… interesting to explain."

Jesse grinned. "Now you know why I prefer being clean-shaven."

Randy kissed down his neck, sending shivers trickling through him as his cheek grazed the skin. He shifted position until he was staring into Jesse's eyes. "You like it when I kiss you there?"

"God, yes." Jesse bit his lip. "Turns me on."

Randy's eyes widened. "Where else can I touch you, if I want to turn you on?"

Jesse's breathing quickened. "My… my nipples. Love it when—" That was as far as he got before Randy's mouth encased his nipple, sucking at it, teasing it with his tongue. Jesse closed his eyes and moaned softly, catching his breath when Randy caught his other nipple between finger and thumb and tweaked it, sending waves of sensual pleasure surging all the way to his cock.

When Randy moved lower, shifting down Jesse's body, kissing his abs, his belly, down to the dip where his pubes lay atop his dick, he opened his eyes and moaned in anticipation.

"Fuck, I wanna see you." Jesse stretched out his hand, reaching for the lamp switch he knew was there somewhere. Suddenly the room was bathed in a soft apricot light, revealing Randy's face just above Jesse's dick.

Randy's gaze met Jesse's as he traced the stony length of Jesse's cock from the head to his sac with his tongue. "You like this too?"

Jesse snorted. "What man alive doesn't like having his cock sucked?" He couldn't resist. "Because I doubt my mouth was the first to encounter your dick."

Randy snickered. "Nope. That dubious honor went to Felicia Stevens, when I was eighteen and I lost my cherry."

"Was she any good?"

Randy laughed quietly. "Compared to you? Nope."

"Bye, Felicia." Jesse snorted again. "Sorry, I couldn't resist." Then all humor departed at the feel of Randy's tongue on the underside of his cock. He shuddered at the touch of Randy's fingers gently pulling on his balls.

"And if I really wanted to blow your mind?" Randy stilled, his gaze locked on Jesse, whose heartbeat went into overdrive.

Jesse spread his legs wide, his pulse rapid. "That depends...."

"On what?"

He swallowed. "On how willing you are to... push your boundaries."

Randy crawled up his body, until his face was inches from Jesse's. "Are we talking about a particular boundary?" His voice was low and hoarse.

Jesse couldn't break eye contact. "I fucking love it when a guy... eats my ass."

Lord, the heat in Randy's eyes.... Then he worried his bottom lip with his teeth. "Okay if we take it slow?"

Jesse reached up and cupped his cheek. "You don't have to, you know. This is just one of my hot buttons. I mean, you could probably make me come from just kissing me."

Randy's eyes gleamed. "Now *that* I'd like to see." He stroked Jesse's face. "Have to be honest here. I remember one time, you were kneeling on one of the red leather couches, between two guys, and...."

Oh fuck. "I was sucking one off, while the other tongue-fucked me."

Randy nodded. "Hottest goddamn thing I ever saw."

Heat crawled through Jesse. "Wanna see for yourself?"

"Fuck, yes." Randy kissed him on the lips. "Hands and knees, sweetheart." He rose to his knees.

Jesse's heart gave a stutter. The power in one small word.... He flipped over and got on all fours, spreading his legs wide and tilting his ass. Then he grabbed a pillow and held on to it, his heart pounding when Randy gently stroked his asscheek.

"God, look at you," Randy whispered.

Jesse shivered as Randy ran his finger through Jesse's crack, barely touching his hole. Then his finger was back, only slicker this time, rubbing over his pucker. When he felt the tip of Randy's tongue, so tentative against his entrance, Jesse let out a low moan, unable to repress the shudder that skated down his back.

Randy's chuckle reverberated against his skin, tickling him. "Wow. It's a bit… funky." Before Jesse would tell him it was okay and they could stop right there, Randy gave another lick across his hole, and the muscles in Jesse's stomach quivered.

God, please, don't let him stop!

OKAY, THE taste was *sort* of how Randy had thought it would be. What he hadn't counted on was his body's reaction to the moan of pleasure that tumbled from Jesse's lips. Because that was so fucking *hot*. Randy gave a few more licks, his hands full of firm flesh as he spread Jesse's hole wide. When Jesse pushed back with a groan, Randy grew bolder, pressing his face between Jesse's asscheeks, his lips finally coming into contact with hot skin.

"Oh, fuck." Jesse sank onto the bed, reaching out to grasp the edge of the mattress, gripping it tightly, his knees moving farther apart.

Fuck. This was…. Randy pushed his tongue against the ring of muscle and was rewarded by a string of soft *oh*s as Jesse tilted his ass higher still. Randy smiled to himself, licking over Jesse's hole with longer swipes of his tongue while he wrapped one hand around Jesse's dick as it pointed toward the bed.

Jesse's moans grew louder, and Randy kept up the double assault until finally he was kneeling between Jesse's spread legs, his face buried in Jesse's crack, licking and kissing his hole, and loving every minute of it. Jesse writhed beneath him, the noises a constant accompaniment to Randy's sensual onslaught. When Jesse lay there trembling, Randy kissed a trail up from his hole to his neck, taking his time. By the time he reached Jesse's head, Jesse was already turning to meet him, his eyes wide and lips parted.

"Taste yourself," Randy whispered, before taking Jesse's mouth in a kiss as he held Jesse's head in a firm grip. Jesse responded eagerly, their tongues meeting as Randy claimed his mouth again and again.

Jesse rolled onto his back. "Want you inside me," he gasped out.

Randy nodded, scanning the room for Jesse's bag. It didn't take long to get ready, and there he was again, slowly sinking his cock into Jesse's warm body. When he was fully seated, Jesse brought his legs up to wrap around Randy's waist, his arms around Randy's neck.

Fuck, this was so much better than the last time. They were locked together, a tight circle of flesh, their mouths meeting in kiss after kiss as Randy slid unhurriedly in and out of Jesse's hole, a gentle rock and roll as they moved together.

"Oh. Oh, yeah," Jesse murmured between kisses, stroking Randy's shoulders and back. "Fuck, that's…."

Randy kissed him, Jesse's heels resting on Randy's ass, his cock sandwiched between their bodies. Then he brought his legs up to lie against Randy's shoulders, lifting his ass up off the bed, almost bending himself in two.

"Now, baby," he murmured. "Want you deep." He cupped Randy's face in his hands. "Let me feel you."

Randy nodded, sliding nearly all the way out of him, then plunging back in until he was balls-deep.

"God, yeah, like that," Jesse groaned, his eyes widening. "Deeper." His hands were on Randy's nape, pulling him into a kiss. Randy rocked his hips, the friction just the right side of pleasurable. Jesse nodded, his lips parted, but no sound coming forth.

Randy braced his arms on either side of Jesse's head, buried his face in Jesse's neck, and slipped into a rhythm as he fucked Jesse, going deep with every single thrust. Jesse's moans and low cries rang out every time Randy drove his dick into him, until Randy knew he was about to come, and he was bringing Jesse with him.

With a groan, Randy shot hard, his body shaking with the force of it. Jesse clung to him, panting, fighting for breath, trembling as though he felt every throb of Randy's cock inside him. Randy shivered as the last drops pulsed out of him, a delicious ache crawling through him. Jesse lowered his legs, and Randy moved gently to lie fully on top of him, their mouths locked in a kiss, Jesse's dick so hard against his belly as they rocked together. Randy slid a hand between their bodies, his fingertips brushing against the head of Jesse's cock. Jesse moaned into the kiss as warmth spread between them, and Randy groaned to feel it. He didn't want to move, didn't want to pull free of Jesse's body, not when they were like this, as close as it was possible to be.

The words were right there, on his tongue. All he had to do was open his mouth and it would be out there, his soul, bared for Jesse. Because in the midst of the heat, the passion, the sensuality of it all, Randy knew the truth at last.

He loved Jesse Bryant.

What scared him to death was Jesse.

Yes, he'd seemed eager for them to fuck, but.... *This is what he does, remember? This is just... sex.* It didn't mean Jesse loved him. Randy wasn't that naive. It didn't matter that it had shaken Randy to his core. It was more than a confirmation of what he'd already known. So he was bi. So what? That didn't matter. What mattered was the confirmation of what lay in his heart.

How do I tell him? When doing that might make him run a mile?

Chapter Seventeen

SUNLIGHT WAS already edging its way through the blinds when Jesse opened his eyes and stretched, blissfully aware of the warm, sated feeling that pervaded every part of his body. Usually he never got the chance to enjoy such a luxury, and as for waking up in another guy's bed?

Yeah, this was bliss.

Beside him, Randy was sound asleep. Jesse smiled to himself, debating whether or not to wake him with a blowjob. It *was* the weekend, after all, and in Jesse's mind, that meant only one thing: two more days of making love. He'd switch off his phone and tell the world to go fuck itself for that. He'd do *anything* if it meant he got to experience more of what they'd shared in the early hours. If he closed his eyes and concentrated, he could still feel Randy moving inside him, so gentle, with such exquisite care that it brought tears to Jesse's eyes.

I truly gave myself to him last night. When was the last time I did that? All he knew was that he wanted to hold on to this wonderful feeling for as long as he could, at least until the bubble burst and Monday morning crawled around, when the demands of work would come knocking on their door.

Work….

Suddenly the light spilling into Randy's bedroom wasn't warm, but cold.

Yeah, think about that. Have a real good, long, hard think about that.

It was one thing to escape for a night in Randy's arms, to lose himself in heat and passion, to let his body soar. It was quite another to see how the world really was in the cold light of day.

This isn't gonna work, is it?

Jesse lay on his back and closed his eyes, trying to ignore the ache inside him. God, it was like some really cliched movie. A hooker with a heart, falling for a guy. Except this wasn't some Hollywood production.

In his case, it was never going to happen. A Vice cop in a relationship with a rent boy? What the hell was he thinking?

Jesse already knew the answer to that one. He'd let his feelings override his common sense. Because how could it ever work? Randy coming home from a hard day arresting johns, giving Jesse a peck on the cheek, and inquiring how many guys he'd screwed that day? Randy walking into a cafe where Jesse was meeting a guy, and giving him a cheery wave? Jesse coming home late from a trick, to find Randy in bed, reading, and asking him how it had gone before exclaiming how nice it was of the john to loosen Jesse up so Randy could fuck him?

Okay, so maybe that was exaggerating a little, but it didn't change the facts. Having Jesse in his life would ultimately hurt Randy's career. Whichever way Jesse looked at the situation, *both* of them were gonna end up hurt.

But what's the alternative? Taking money from Randy so Jesse didn't work on his back? Randy paying for him to finish college? Finding a job and giving up on the idea of ever finishing his MBA?

Jesse could be practical when the situation called for it. And right then what was needed was a practical decision.

He eased out from under the covers and crept around the bed, picking up his clothes from where he'd discarded them, trying to make as little noise as possible. He needed time and space to think, and being in Randy's bed wasn't conducive to either of those. When he was dressed, he gave the apartment one last glance to make sure he had everything, including his bag, and let himself out as quietly as possible.

Jesse shivered a little in the cool morning air, regretting leaving his jacket at home. He walked slowly down Broadway, his bag slung over his shoulder, turning the same thoughts over and over in his head. It didn't help that his heart was saying one thing, his head another.

Why couldn't it work? I love him. Surely that's all that matters?

Loving him isn't enough, not if it means Randy ends up losing his job. And he could.

Then I find a job. A regular job. One he could tell his coworkers about.

His coworkers. So Randy's gonna come out for ya? Announce he's gonna shack up with a guy? Besides, isn't that assuming a lot? Like, maybe, that he feels for you the way you feel for him? Listen, he just got his itch scratched. You just proved to him that he likes fucking guys too. That's all it was.

God, how Jesse longed for that cynical voice to be wrong on that last one. Because the previous night had been *so* much more than getting an itch scratched, and Jesse knew it. The shower, the tenderness Randy had shown him when they'd made love... all of that was so far removed from what Jesse experienced with his tricks that they might as well have taken place on different planets.

But if he cares for me, why doesn't he come out and say it? Then he sighed. *Yeah, like the way I came out and told him how I feel?*

Christ, this was fucked up.

When he reached West 181st Street, he spied a McDonald's. That meant coffee. Jesse crossed the street and went inside. It wasn't all that busy, but then again, it was a Saturday morning and still early. He bought a cup of coffee and chose a seat in the corner where it was quieter.

Jesse took out his phone and scrolled through his contacts. *Too early to call him?* Because what Jesse needed right then was some advice, and he knew one person who'd give it to him straight. He composed a text and sent it to Nikko.

You awake?

Seconds later, his phone rang. "Hey, you know me. Early riser."

Jesse heard something in the background that sounded like... gulls? "Where are you?"

"Taking a walk on the beach before I go back and make Mitch his breakfast. He's still sleeping." There was a pause. "Now suppose you tell me what's wrong?"

Jesse sighed. "Nothing gets past you, right? Even when I'm over three hundred miles away."

"Call it a gift. Now talk."

Jesse took a sip of the hot coffee and winced. "I think I just fucked up, and I don't know what to do about it."

"Wait a sec." Another pause. "Okay, I'm sitting down. What happened?"

Jesse related seeing Randy at the party and took it from there, not bothering to hide a thing. Nikko wasn't going to judge him.

Silence. "Wow."

That made him chuckle, despite his churning stomach. "That was my reaction."

"Still not seeing a problem here. I mean…." Nikko's voice softened. "You're in love with him, aren't you?"

If only that solved anything.

"Yeah," Jesse said with a sigh. "And that *is* the problem. My world and his? They don't mix."

"Then let's talk about your world," Nikko said practically. "Are you happy with what you're doing? Really? Is it getting you where you want to be?"

Jesse stared into the murky depths of his coffee. "No."

"Then why are you there? Why keep doing it if it's not working for you?"

"Because right now I have no alternatives!" Jesse glanced around as the patrons gazed mildly in his direction before going back to their breakfasts and coffee. He took a deep breath. "Look, I didn't mean to raise my voice. I'm just a little… overwrought right now." Which had to be the understatement of Jesse's year so far.

"Yeah, I get that." Footsteps sounded on gravel. "I'm just walking back to the house. It strikes me that you need to think things over."

Jesse had reached that conclusion shortly after waking up in Randy's bed.

"I have an idea," Nikko said suddenly.

"Uh-oh," Jesse quipped halfheartedly.

"I'm being serious. I just need to check something first. Can I call you back?"

"Sure."

"Okay, give me a couple of minutes." Nikko disconnected the call.

Jesse put down his phone, shaking his head. *What is he up to?* The intrigue was enough to banish his inner turmoil, just for a moment. Then he faced reality. *Nikko does* not *possess a magic wand. He can't fix this, no matter how badly he may want to.* Jesse's thoughts went to Randy, and his heart ached. *What's he gonna think when he wakes up and I'm gone?*

Swiftly he pushed the thought aside. *He's better off without me. I'll only bring him pain. He'll see that eventually.* Except Jesse wasn't going to be better off, not when what he truly wanted was Randy in his life.

It doesn't matter what I want. I can't just fuck up his life. And if I really love him, that means walking away and letting him have a successful career.

Being selfless sucked.

His phone rang. Before Jesse could get a word in, Nikko plunged ahead. "You're coming to Maine, to us."

Jesse blinked. "Excuse me?"

"You heard. You need space to think, with no distractions, and you're sure as hell not going to find that in New York. Right now you're stuck in a cycle that you won't break free from unless you do something drastic. I get that you like what you do, but it's plainly not working out. And nothing will change unless you do something." He paused. "You know what the definition of insanity is, right? Doing the same thing over and over again, and expecting different results."

Jesse couldn't lie to Nikko. "I did enjoy hooking—once. It's kinda… changed."

"Let me guess. It's different when your life depends on it?"

"Yeah." Fuck, Jesse had so many regrets. The halt to his studies. Letting Randy get under his skin—and into his heart. Not that he'd ever regret their night together.

Jesse was going to cling to that for as long as he lived.

"Look, about coming to Maine—"

His phone pinged, but Nikko spoke before he could investigate further. "You have mail."

"And what have you sent me?"

"The link to a bus ticket."

"What?"

"There's a bus at 1:45 p.m. out of New York. East Forty-Second Street, to be exact. It gets into Portland at 7:45 p.m. tonight. I'll meet you there. It's only fifteen minutes from the bus station to our place."

Aw fuck. "I can't let you do that."

Nikko laughed. "Too late. I've already done it. Now, you could ignore the ticket, but then I'll have wasted my money, and I don't think you'd like that."

"I have money," Jesse protested.

"Fine. You can pay me back when you get here."

"Here?" Mitch's voice rumbled in the background. "Who precisely is coming here?"

Nikko chuckled. "We got company coming."

Mitch laughed. "Now why am I not surprised?"

"Wait—you bought a ticket without telling Mitch first? Wasn't that what you needed to check?" Things were moving with a speed that took Jesse by surprise.

Nikko laughed. "I was checking the bus times. And as for Mitch.... Hey, sweetheart, Jesse is coming. That okay with you?"

"Like you have to ask."

"There." Nikko sounded awfully smug. "Happy now? All you have to do is get here."

Jesse couldn't believe this was happening. "You're serious."

"Of course. Think I'd go buying a ticket if I wasn't? Now, that gives you plenty of time to pack your bags. Make sure you pack something for the beach. Maine might not get temperatures as high as New York in July, but it's really pleasant right now, and you need some beach time."

"I am *not* coming to Maine to lie on a beach!"

Nikko's voice was gentle. "No, you're not. You're coming to Maine to give yourself time to make some decisions. And you can stay as long as you like. Right, Mitch?"

"Damn straight. Get your ass here, Jesse."

Tears pricked his eyes. "You two are unbelievable."

"No, we're not. We just love you. Now go pack. Let me know when you're on the bus." Nikko hung up.

Jesse wiped his eyes. *Maybe he's right.* Putting some distance between himself and NYC might be exactly what he needed. When his phone announced another text, he smiled. *Now what?* Except it wasn't from Nikko.

Hey. In NYC for the weekend. Any chance U can fit me in? Missed that ass. Before midday works if UR available.

It was a number Jesse recognized, a regular. For one brief moment, he contemplated messaging him back to arrange a time, before he stopped himself. *What the fuck am I doing?*

Nikko was right. Doing the same fucking thing over and over, expecting shit to change, was crazy. His thumbs danced over the keypad.

Sorry. Not available.

Right then he needed to get back to the apartment and pack.

And *not* think about Randy. He'd think about what the hell he was going to say to Randy when he was on the way to Maine.

He doesn't need this mess. He doesn't need me to screw up his life.

Jesse figured if he told himself that enough times, eventually he'd believe it.

Chapter Eighteen

RANDY OPENED his eyes and was struck immediately by the silence. He rolled over to find an empty space beside him, the sheets cool. "Jesse?"

No answer.

Randy sat up and scanned the room. No bag, no clothing. No sign that Jesse had even been there, except…. A couple of torn condom wrappers lay on the nightstand.

He threw back the covers and launched himself from the bed, hurrying into the living room. No sign there either.

What the hell?

Randy grabbed his phone from the coffee table and checked it. No messages. He brought up Jesse's number and clicked Call. When it rang and rang with no answer, he disconnected and threw the phone down onto the couch.

What are you playing at, Jesse?

This didn't make sense. Not after the previous night. *How could he just leave after…?*

And there it was, the heart of what really stung him. *How could Jesse leave, after we made love?*

His phone pinged, and Randy grabbed it.

Hey. Sorry I wasn't there when you woke up. I had to leave earlier than I'd intended. Will be in touch. xx

His heartbeat climbed down a little, but those last words hurt. *That's it? That's all I get?* If anything, they confirmed his fears, and his first thought was thankfulness that he hadn't told Jesse how he felt. Because that would have been painful.

Talk about unrequited love.

Randy sank onto the couch, his phone still in his hand. *Then it was just sex.* At least, it had been for Jesse, judging by the fact that he hadn't stuck around long. But for Randy, he felt… broken inside. There was a tightness in his throat that was almost painful, and just *breathing* hurt.

He tossed the phone onto the couch, put his head in his hands, and closed his eyes, as if that would take away the pain.

What pushed it aside was anger.

He ran out on me. He snuck out on me like I was one of his fucking tricks.

And as for that text…. There was nothing in those few lines that came even *close* to emotion, and that made a mockery of everything they'd shared the previous night. Because that had been more than just sex, and Randy knew it, with every nerve, cell, and fiber in his body.

When another ping sounded, he ignored it, until it hit him that it might be from Jesse. Randy seized the phone and peered at the screen. This time it was an email—from Jesse.

Hey.

Yeah, I know that text was a bit on the short side, but I needed time to think before I wrote this, and I didn't want you to worry when you woke up and found me gone.

Okay, not sure how to even start this, but….

Randy's heart sank. *Oh fuck.* Every instinct he possessed was screaming that this was *not* going to be good.

You're a sweet guy. You really are. A sweet, awesome guy.

Randy knew there was a *but* coming.

But we both know you being seen with me is not gonna be good for you. A Vice cop who goes to coffee shops / concerts / Coney Island, etc., with a hooker? There are only so many times you could explain that away, right? And because you're this sweet guy, you'd never let me know if you were catching shit for that. Neither of us is an idiot. We both know you could lose your job over this. And I like you too much to let that happen.

He likes *me? That's it?* Randy stared at the screen, his stomach churning. *What the fuck?* This amounted to "it's not you, it's me." It might as well have begun with "Dear John."

God, the irony.

About last night….

Randy caught his breath. *No. No. Don't tell me it meant nothing.* He couldn't bear that, not on top of the *I like you too much* business.

You were amazing. You took my breath away. And when you find someone who is worthy of you, who can stand by your side, someone you can be proud to be with… don't care if they're a guy or a girl, they're gonna be the luckiest SOB on this planet.

Be you, Randy. Be happy. And… don't come looking for me. Because you deserve better than me.

Thanks for everything.

Jesse.

Randy closed his eyes and broke, tears welling up beneath his eyelids. That one line hit him hardest of all.

You deserve better than me.

Randy took a moment to catch his breath. *That's what it all boils down to, isn't it? He's doing this because he believes a hooker isn't good enough for a Vice cop.* Then it hit him. *I took his breath away. Last night meant as much to him as it did to me.* And that meant….

Jesse was hurting too.

When Randy got himself under control, he wiped his eyes savagely and stared at the screen. "You think I'm just going to leave it there? Think again."

He was going to find Jesse. This was a conversation that needed to happen face-to-face, where he could look into those beautiful blue eyes—and know the truth.

And as for how easy it would be to find him? Randy had to smile.

Baby, I'm a cop. Just watch me.

RANDY TRUDGED up the stairs with his bags of groceries, reaching the fourth floor in time to see Owen locking his front door.

Owen swallowed. "Hey. I was just coming to see you." In one hand he held a bottle of wine. "Peace offering?"

Randy sighed. "Maybe later." He nodded toward his apartment. "Wanna come in?"

"You *are* still talking to me, then."

Randy put down one bag and unlocked the door. "Get your ass inside."

Owen heaved a sigh of relief. "I'll take that as a yes." He scuttled past Randy, through the open door, and into the living room. Randy followed him with the groceries, closing the front door with his butt.

He took one look at Owen, perched awkwardly on the edge of the seat cushion, and rolled out an exaggerated sigh. "You know where the glasses are. Is it a screw cap or have you bought the good stuff?"

Owen cleared his throat. "Peace offerings are required to be the good stuff. It's the law. Fancy you not knowing that. And for your information, the good stuff comes with screw caps, too, these days."

"I'll consider myself informed. The corkscrew is in the drawer, then." He waited until Owen had found it before placing his bags on the countertop and emptying their contents. "Drinking at midday. This has to be a record for us." He carried on unpacking, putting his groceries into cabinets and the refrigerator, while behind him, he heard the telltale glug of wine being poured. When everything was stored away, Randy joined Owen on the couch.

Owen held out a glass to him. "I'm hoping this is the part where we kiss and make up," he said with a hopeful look. "Well, maybe not actual kissing, but you get the idea."

Randy wasn't one to bear grudges. Besides, recent events had put a lot of things into perspective. "It's okay. I get it that you had no idea that was gonna happen. And I've moved away from the 'I shouldn't have listened to you in the first place' part."

"I see." Owen took a mouthful of wine.

"Feeling a little guilty, were we?" When Owen swallowed again, Randy nodded. "Yeah, *I'd* feel guilty, too, if I were you." Owen's face tightened, and Randy regretted his words, knowing he was being unfair. "Look, I'm a big boy. I make my own decisions." Randy sipped his wine, trying to ignore his churning stomach. "I hear you met Jesse." It had taken him most of the morning to get himself under control, resisting the urge to head down to West Forty-Second Street and look for him.

Owen's eyes widened. "Oh. Yes. He told you?"

Randy nodded. "He… stayed here last night."

Owen coughed. "I know." When Randy gave him an inquiring glance, Owen flushed. "Thin walls in this place."

Randy's face heated up. "I'll have to remember that."

"The important question is, will he be back?"

He took refuge in his glass, hoping the chilled wine would cool his hot cheeks.

"Randy?" When he glanced up, Owen's eyes were kind. "What happened?" he asked softly.

Too much had passed between them for him to even consider lying. Randy pulled his phone from his pocket, opened his email, and handed it to Owen. "This kinda sums it up."

Owen read it in silence, his brow furrowed. When he'd finished, he handed the phone back. "So now what? Are you going to leave things there?"

Randy gazed at him with interest. "You don't think I should, do you?"

Owen shook his head. "There's a lot here that he's not saying. Besides, reading something is not the same thing as an honest-to-God talk with someone. We lose so much in translation."

Randy nodded vigorously. "Yes. And as to your first question, no, I'm not going to leave things here. I'm going to find him."

Owen snickered. "How does the saying go? 'A Canadian Mountie always gets his man'?" He raised his glass. "Well, here's to a New Yorker copping his hooker."

Randy glared. "That was bad, even for you."

Owen smirked. "I do my best with the material available. Now, why don't you start by drawing up a list of contacts? People who might know where he is?"

"Now?" Randy stared at him.

"No time like the present," Owen said with a shrug. "So who's at the top of the list?"

That was easy. "A guy in Maine."

Nikko would know where Jesse was, if anyone did. And if he didn't, Randy had a few more names to work through, even if he had to find every guy who'd worked in the Black Lounge. He stared at Jesse's email, reading it for what had to be the tenth time.

I'll find you. And when I do, I'm gonna sit you down and make sure you don't move until I tell you that I fucking love *you.*

Randy had a plan.

Chapter Nineteen

August

RANDY WALKED into Nowhere, his eyes adjusting to the dim lighting as he scanned the tables and chairs at the far end of the bar. He recognized a couple of guys, and judging by their panicked expressions, they recognized him. Swiftly, he held up his hands, palms facing them, hoping they got the message.

Randy was *not* there in an official capacity.

He spied Steve in the corner, playing pool, and headed over there. Steve straightened to chalk his cue, and their gazes met. Steve shook his head. "Twice in one month? Better be careful, officer. People will say we're in love." The guy he was playing with jerked his head at that, staring at Randy with wide eyes, but Steve laid a hand on his arm. "Chill. He ain't here to bust your ass. Ain't that right, Detective?"

Randy nodded. "Just here to talk. That's all." He gestured toward the bar with a flick of his head. "Can I get you a drink?"

Steve blinked. "This a new kinda operation? Get a guy drunk, then get him talking?" He grinned to his fellow player. "Hey, you can buy me as many drinks as you like. I still ain't gonna tell ya squat."

"Let's call this a drink from one ex-coworker to another," Randy said quietly.

"Coworker?"

He smiled. "Once upon a time, we both worked in the same place. Different kinda work, of course."

Steve stilled. "Yeah. I guess we did at that. Okay. I'll have a beer."

Randy gave a single nod, then went over to the bar. By the time he had two glasses of beer in his hands, Steve had finished his game and was sitting alone at a table. Randy joined him, then raised his glass. "Here's to you."

Steve raised his glass in a similar gesture, then took a drink. He put down his glass and leaned back in his chair. "You're here about Jesse."

Randy arched his eyebrows. "You taking up mind reading?"

Steve snorted. "Don't have to be a friggin' genius to work *that* out. You've been asking questions all over Manhattan, so I hear. Not to mention Brooklyn and Queens." He smiled. "I got a lotta friends, and when a Vice cop starts askin' questions, you can bet word gets around." He took another drink. "I got nothin' to tell ya, same as last time."

Randy's heart sank. "You were one of the first guys I came to. I figured if anyone knew where Jesse was, it would be you. Since then I've seen Baz, Jordan—virtually everyone who worked in the Black Lounge. And every time I got the same answer. No one has seen him."

"So why are you back?"

Randy took a long swig of beer. "Because since I spoke to you, I've been to every guy I could think of who might possibly know Jesse, and I'm running out of names. Which, in a city the size of New York, is saying something. And the only reason I came back to you was to see if there'd been any news." He hadn't thought it possible, but Jesse had somehow slipped under the radar. What had seemed like an easy task a month ago now had him tearing his hair out. And he was starting to panic.

Where the hell is he?

Randy had called, sent texts and emails—all with no result. Jesse was staying silent.

Steve drained half his beer. "You really are worried about him, aren't ya?"

Randy huffed. "Gee, is it that obvious?" He wasn't about to divulge *why* he was looking for Jesse. That would be like committing professional suicide, not that he gave a rat's ass about his job right then. He was on a break from the sting operations, and that was just fine.

Steve stared at his glass, running his finger around the rim. "He was staying with me."

"What? When?" Randy gaped at him.

Steve shrugged. "Right up until I came home one Saturday a month ago, and he'd upped and left. He wrote me a nice note, left me some money to cover his rent, and that was it." His eyes met Randy's. "And before you ask, no, he *didn't* leave a forwarding address. I kinda got the impression he was… escaping something. Or someone."

Yeah. That would be me. Randy's gut was in turmoil. "Then I'm no better off."

Steve cocked his head to one side. "Did you call Nikko? Those two were pretty tight."

Randy sighed. "He was the first person I called. He hadn't heard from Jesse in a few weeks."

Steve stilled. "He said that?"

The hairs stood up on the back of Randy's neck. "Yeah," he said slowly.

"Then if I was you? I'd call him again. Because those two talked. A lot. The idea that either of them would let two weeks go by without a phone call? That's bullshit."

A light was finally beginning to dawn. "He lied to me." *Sweet little Nikko had lied his ass off.*

Steve rolled his eyes. "Duh." He emptied the rest of his glass. "We done here?"

"Yeah, I think so." Randy smiled. "Thank you."

"Don't mention it." Steve speared him with a look. "Seriously. Do *not* mention it. I don't want guys thinking I'm helping the cops." Then his expression softened. "Let's just call it a favor for an ex-coworker."

"Gotcha." Randy held out his hand.

Steve regarded it with a half smile, then shook it. "And now I'll get back to playing pool. Gotta win my money back, haven't I?" He grinned.

Randy left him to it and walked out of the bar. He pulled his phone from his pocket and glanced at the time—7:15. He'd gone to the bar straight from work, on the off chance that Steve might be there. Right then he was thankful he had. He scrolled through his contacts until he found Nikko, then paused.

Is it too late to call? They could be having dinner or something. Then he reconsidered. *Fuck that. He lied to me.* Randy hit Call. After three rings, Nikko answered.

"He's not here." The words rushed out of him.

God bless Steve. Randy cleared his throat. "What—I don't even rate a 'Hi, Randy, good to hear from you' now?"

"Oh. Oh, sure. Hi. How are you?"

Randy chuckled. "Sorry, Nikko, but the damage is done. You know where Jesse is, don't you?"

"Shit." There was a pause before Nikko spoke again, quietly. "He doesn't want to talk to you, Randy."

Thank God. "Then you do know where he is." When Nikko fell silent, Randy knew for certain he'd hit pay dirt. "Nikko, I've spent the last month trying to find him. I'm not gonna give up."

Silence.

"At least tell me he's all right."

Nikko's soft sigh filled his ears. "He's… okay. Actually, he's better than okay." Another pause. "And he still doesn't want to see you."

Randy wasn't about to be put off by that. "Where is he?"

"God, you're stubborn."

He chuckled. "You have no idea. And you can tell me he doesn't want to see me until you're blue in the face. I'm not giving up." Randy softened his voice. "I need to see him, Nikko. It's… really important."

"Why? Tell me that, and if I agree with you, then *maybe* I'll tell you where he is. Maybe."

He'd gotten this far. "Jesse walked out on me before I got the chance to tell him something. I should've spoken up sooner, told him how I felt, but… I was scared, I guess." He wasn't going to bare more of his soul. Only Jesse got to see that. Randy prayed Nikko could read between the lines. He knew what it was to be in love, after all.

If he could put two and two together….

"Oh." Nikko's soft exhalation filled Randy's ears. "Oh, wow."

Randy wanted to weep with relief. "Then tell me, please."

"He's here. In our house."

"Seriously?"

"He's been here since the day he left New York. But Randy… things have changed."

Randy barely took in Nikko's last words. "I'm coming there."

"What? When?"

There was no way Randy could keep away. "I need to go speak to my captain, take some vacation time, but yeah, I'll be there as fast as it takes to sort everything." Heaven knew he was owed enough time off. He hadn't taken a real vacation since before his stint in the Black Lounge.

"You're serious."

"Of course I'm serious. But I'll need some information, like the name of a motel or someplace local where I can stay."

"How… how long are you planning on staying?" Nikko sounded shocked.

As long as it takes to get Jesse to believe me. "A couple of weeks?" Right then he was playing this by ear.

"I see." Nikko paused. "You can stay here, as long as you don't mind sleeping on the couch. We've only got two bedrooms, and Jesse's in the guest room." He cleared his throat. "I'll let Mitch know."

"Don't tell Jesse," Randy blurted out. He didn't want to run the risk of him turning up and finding Jesse had decided to move on. "Please, Nikko, you can't tell him."

Nikko gave a long, drawn-out sigh. "Okay. Fine. Just… let me know when you'll be arriving, and I'll make sure we're ready for you. Without letting Jesse know, I promise. On one condition, though. If Jesse says he doesn't want you there, you are gone. No questions asked. Agreed?"

"Agreed." Randy owed Nikko the biggest hug. "Thank you," he said sincerely. "I know you're only looking out for him."

"You bet I am, so don't hurt him," Nikko blurted out. "When he first got here, he was a mess. But like I said, things have changed. You hurt him, and you'll answer to me. *And* Mitch."

It was hard not to laugh. Small, slim Nikko wasn't exactly bodyguard material, but Randy certainly wouldn't cross him. And as for Mitch? He could probably snap Randy in two.

"I promise you, hurting Jesse is the last thing on my mind."

"Okay." There was still that edge of doubt in his voice, but there was nothing Randy could do about that. "How will you get here?"

Randy laughed. "Not a clue. All I know right now is that you live in Old Orchard Beach. Where that is, I have no idea."

"I'll send you the link with the bus times. And we'll meet you in Portland."

"Nikko, you're a godsend."

He huffed. "I'm only doing this because… Jesse needs you. If he knew we were talking like this…."

"One day he might thank you for it." That was Randy's hope, at any rate.

"Okay, they're back. Keep in touch." And with that the call ended.

Randy put his phone away, his mind racing. Getting vacation time, even at this short notice, didn't concern him. His captain had been making noises about Randy taking some time off for the past two weeks. Randy had a good idea why.

No, what lay heaviest on his heart was Jesse.

What do I say to him? After weeks of having conversations in his head—which varied between trying not to sound resentful at Jesse's abrupt exit, to taking Jesse in his arms and kissing him till he was breathless—Randy was suddenly unsure of himself.

Maybe this is one conversation I can't plan for. Maybe I have to play this one by ear.

One thing Randy knew for certain.

He was going to do his best *not* to fuck up.

Chapter Twenty

RANDY YAWNED and rubbed his eyes as he awoke from his light doze. He'd grabbed an hour or so of sleep soon after pulling out of the bus station in New York—hardly surprising, seeing as they'd left at a quarter to four in the morning. Nikko had sent him a laughing emoji when Randy had messaged him the details. Like Randy cared about getting up at too-goddamn-early o'clock.

He just wanted to get to Maine as fast as he could.

He'd grabbed breakfast in Boston, where there was an hour's stop before changing buses. They were due to arrive at the Portland bus station within five minutes, and he gazed out of the window. Portland seemed a pretty busy place, not how he'd pictured Maine at all. Almost midday on Saturday, and the streets were crowded with people getting on with their daily lives, shopping, strolling, whatever.

"Here we are, folks," the driver called out over the PA system. "Greyhound bus station, Portland, Maine." The bus pulled into a large parking bay, at the end of which was a covered area where people congregated, some with suitcases and bags.

Randy got off the bus and collected his suitcase from the luggage compartment, then walked toward the exit. It didn't take long to spot Nikko, who waved at him from the edge of the parking lot. He looked like a poster boy for summer, wearing a thin white shirt open at the neck, cutoff shorts, flip-flops, and sunglasses. As soon as Randy reached him, he dropped the case and Nikko pulled him into a hug.

"It's good to see you," he whispered as he held Randy tightly.

Randy gave as good as he got. When they parted, he peered intently at Nikko. "He still has no clue I'm coming?"

Nikko shook his head. "And he won't be there when we get home."

From behind him, someone cleared their throat. Mitch had gotten out of the car and was walking toward him. He extended a hand to Randy, who shook it. "You're here to fix things, right?"

Randy had to smile. He really liked Mitch's blunt manner. "That's the general idea."

Mitch gave a single nod. "Okay then." He picked up the suitcase. "I'll put this in the trunk. You're in the back."

Randy got into the car and fastened the seat belt. It wasn't long before they were pulling out of the parking lot and heading south.

"Is that your nearest big town?" he asked as Portland's busy streets were left behind them.

Mitch nodded. "Portland's only fifteen minutes or so from our place. This is Scarborough," he said, indicating the view with a flick of his head. "Not much here. Next town is Saco, which is pretty. We're not far from there."

"So where has Jesse gone?" Randy was a little disappointed to know Jesse wouldn't be there.

"He's working."

Randy stilled, staring at the back of Nikko's head. "Working?"

"At the Old Orchard Beach pier. There's a restaurant and a bar. He's been there about three weeks now." Nikko turned and smiled. "He likes it."

"He'll be finished around six," Mitch added.

Randy wasn't sure he could wait that long.

"But he usually has a break after the lunch rush has died down, just in case you don't want to wait." Nikko's eyes sparkled.

"Are you two sure it's okay for me to stay with you?" Randy appreciated the offer, but they already had one guest.

Mitch chuckled. "I'll admit, I was a little... surprised to come home Wednesday evening and find out we were expecting another guest, but that's my Nikko. Heart as big as the ocean. However, I heard about his one stipulation, and I'm behind that 100 percent. If Jesse doesn't want you there, then I'm sorry, Randy, you'll have to leave. This is just a vacation for you. For him, it's more a case of getting some semblance of order back in his life."

Just a vacation. If only....

"Your captain was okay about you taking the time away from your job?"

Randy snorted. "Let's put it this way. I wouldn't have been surprised if he'd offered to pack my bags." His captain had been very frank. Randy's performance during the last couple of weeks had concerned him, enough that he'd reached the point of suggesting Randy take some leave. Randy knew he'd been distracted but hadn't realized to what extent.

His mind had been occupied with Jesse. And right then, he was praying Jesse would let him stay. Because they needed to sort things out.

"This is us." Mitch pulled the car into a parking space in front of a white-painted garage door. Randy got out of the car and gazed at the two-story house, covered in white boards. On the second floor, windows lined the front, their pale brown blinds lowered. A wooden staircase led up to the door. He glanced to his left. One street crossed the avenue, and beyond that, he could see the ocean.

"Wow. You weren't kidding when you said you were practically on the beach."

Nikko let out a happy sigh. "I love to go walking there."

Mitch came around the car and kissed Nikko on the head. "Yeah, you do." His eyes were warm. Then he popped the trunk and hauled Randy's case out of it. He pointed to the top of the house. "That's the attic room, for guests. You get the couch." He walked toward the staircase, still carrying the suitcase, and Randy followed him, Nikko close behind. "By the way," Mitch continued, "tomorrow we're going to my parents' house for Sunday lunch. We do this once a month. You're welcome to join us."

"Jesse will be coming," Nikko added. "And it's not like you haven't met Mitch's parents. You'll get to meet the rest of the family too." He grinned. "It's a lot of fun."

Mitch opened the screen door, and Randy stepped onto a cool covered porch. Two rocking chairs sat against the wall with a table between them. Wooden blinds covered every window.

"This is nice," he exclaimed.

Mitch huffed. "It's not huge, but it's perfect for the two of us." He opened the front door, and Randy entered the living room. Facing him was a small desk, loaded with books and papers, clearly where Mitch worked, and to the right was a cozy, square room with a couch along one wall opposite a brick fireplace, with comfortable-looking armchairs placed at intervals.

Mitch put the suitcase under the window. "I'll leave this here for the moment. Right now I'm assuming you'd like some coffee?"

Randy groaned. "Mitch, I love ya." Boston seemed a long time ago.

Mitch laughed. "Yeah, I figured. I'll get some going, while Nikko shows you the rest of the house, which will take less than a minute."

Randy had to admit, their home was delightful. Nikko, it seemed, had only one regret—that it wasn't big enough to house a grand piano. "That's a dream, which will have to wait," he said with a sigh. "Mitch did talk about making some changes to the attic room so we could fit a piano in there, but that would mean losing a bedroom. And I'm not sure I want to do that. I want to have somewhere to put Ichy—whenever he comes to visit."

Randy's heart ached for him. Nikko and Ichy had been so close before he'd gone into police custody, and he knew it had to be killing Nikko not to be able to see him now that he was in the witness protection program.

"You wait," he reassured Nikko. "Once things have quietened down and he's settled into his new life, you'll see each other again."

Randy would make sure of that, even if he had to bring Ichy to Maine personally.

THE ENTRANCE to the pier was colorful and quaint, with arcades and even a Ferris wheel. Randy strolled through the covered walkway, heading for the restaurant. Nikko had been right: the lunchtime crowd had dwindled to only a few diners. Through the door, he spied Jesse, cleaning tables and serving, and that was enough to get Randy's heart hammering. He entered the restaurant and was shown to a table looking out over the ocean.

It wasn't long before Jesse headed over. He came to a dead stop a few feet from Randy's table, his mouth open. "What… what are you doing here?" He narrowed his gaze. "Nikko told you, didn't he?" Jesse pressed his lips together.

"Don't blame him, please," Randy remonstrated. "He thought he was doing the right thing."

Jesse sighed. "Yeah, that sounds like him. Look, I can't talk to you."

Randy's heart took a dive. "I see."

"No, I mean, not right now. I'm working. But… I'll be on my break in about half an hour. If you want to stick around… we can talk then."

He's not sending me away. Thank God.

"In that case… I'd like a coffee, please."

"Latte?" Jesse asked, a familiar twinkle briefly visible in his eyes.

Randy just smiled.

"I'll bring it over. And…." Jesse swallowed. "I know what I said, but it *is* good to see you." He walked away.

Randy took the opportunity to breathe deeply. *God, don't let me fuck this up.*

A few minutes later, Jesse returned with a glass of coffee, together with two packets of cookies. He placed them in front of Randy and smiled. "There's sugar on the table if you need it, but I seem to recall you saying you're sweet enough. The cookies are because I know you have a sweet tooth." Then he walked off, only this time there was a definite sashay about those slim hips.

Randy had to stifle his chuckle.

Half an hour later, Jesse appeared at his table, his apron gone, revealing black jeans and a black T-shirt. "I've got thirty minutes. Let's go down onto the beach."

When they reached the beach, Jesse kicked off his shoes, tied the laces together, and slung them around his neck. Randy removed his sneakers and did the same. The sand was warm and soft beneath his feet.

"I can't remember the last time I did this," he said quietly.

Jesse smiled. "This is how I start my day. I get up early, make myself a coffee, and drink it while I walk on the beach at the end of the street where Nikko and Mitch live. Sometimes I watch the sun come up. It's so… peaceful." He stopped and gazed at Randy. "Okay, I'm listening. Why are you here? Especially after I told you not to come looking for me."

"I had to see you. I've been looking for you since the day you left."

Jesse blinked. "Seriously? I mean, I know you called Nikko, but I figured when you couldn't find me, you'd… forget about me."

Randy snorted. "Forget about you? That would be like… forgetting to breathe."

Jesse's breathing hitched, and Randy reined in his emotions. That outburst had come way too close to admitting how he felt, and this wasn't the time or the place.

"I still don't understand how you could have left the way you did, without a word."

"Call it self-preservation. Look, I said it all in that email. Yes, that night was… amazing, I can't deny that, but… it wouldn't work out between us."

"Why not?"

Jesse gave him an incredulous stare. "How many times do I have to state the obvious? You're a Vice cop."

"So?"

Jesse rolled his eyes. "C'mon, Randy, you're not stupid. How would it work? I mean, really?"

"You were hooking so you could save enough money to carry on your studies, weren't you?"

Jesse nodded.

Randy set his jaw. "I'd help you."

Jesse widened his eyes. "Hell no. You are *not* a cash cow." He sighed. "And if I carried on hooking, I… I couldn't be with you."

"If?" Randy stared at him. That one word was enough to make him believe Nikko was right.

Something *had* changed.

He tried a different tack. "Nikko says you've been working here a while."

Jesse nodded. "He and Mitch are both stubborn. They won't take any money from me. Nikko argues that I get most of my meals here, so it's not like I'm eating them out of house and home."

Randy took a good look at him. "You seem like you've put on a little weight since I last saw you." When Jesse stared at him, Randy smiled. "It looks good on you."

His cheeks had filled out a little, making him appear younger, and his hair was even more blond, clearly a result of the sun. He'd lost that lean look, but Randy didn't mind that in the slightest.

Jesse huffed. "I keep thinking I've let myself go. I haven't done any sit-ups since I got here, and I was always so careful about what I ate." He shook his head. "You should see some of the crap I eat nowadays. Pizza, subs, poutine, fried dough…." He grinned. "By the way, the bar at the end of the pier does a mean lobster roll."

Randy finally got what was different about Jesse. "You look... at peace."

Jesse's smile reached his eyes and lit up his face. "Yeah. Hard to believe, I know. Me, the original 'I heart NYC' boy, but here? I really like it. The air, the change of pace.... I'm saving every cent I make, and okay, so it's not nearly what I could make in New York, but it feels... good." He tilted his head to one side. "Where are you staying, and how long for?"

"I'm at the Hotel Mitch-and-Nikko too. I'll be sleeping on their couch." Randy paused. "For two weeks."

Jesse's mouth fell open. "Really?"

Randy reached for his hand and squeezed it. "I know you'll be working, but you don't work all the time, right? You could spend some time with me."

Jesse's face tightened, and he pulled free of Randy's grasp. "Why? Why prolong the inevitable? When your two weeks are over, you'll go back to New York. And right now, the way I'm feeling? I'm not sure I will."

Randy grabbed hold of his courage. "Do you want me to go?"

Jesse froze, his eyes wide, and for a moment, he said nothing. Finally, a breath shuddered out of him. "No. I don't want that at all. I want to make the most of what time we have."

Randy breathed a little easier. "Then I'll stay." He knew he was pushing things, but he reached out to stroke Jesse's cheek. "I missed you so much."

Jesse swallowed. "Missed you too." And before Randy could utter another word, Jesse leaned in and kissed him—a chaste kiss, but one that lingered.

Randy took Jesse in his arms and returned the kiss, holding him tightly, as though he feared letting him go would somehow burst this precious bubble they existed in right then.

Jesse smiled against his lips. "We're gonna get arrested, y'know. Causing a public disturbance."

Randy chuckled. "It's okay. You're kissing a cop, remember?" He released Jesse but took his hand. "How much longer have we got before you have to go back to work?"

Jesse's smile hadn't faded. "Enough to walk some more on this beach."

"And when you finish work, I'll be waiting for you."

God, the look in his eyes…. "That sounds perfect."

A lightness infused Randy, making him almost giddy.

It's going to be okay.

Chapter Twenty-One

JESSE STILL couldn't believe Randy was really there. He kept glancing across the table at him during dinner, just to make sure he wasn't dreaming. As soon as he walked through the door after work, Nikko had dragged him to one side and apologized profusely. Jesse had simply hugged him and reassured him it was all right.

Jesse should have realized by that point. Randy was one stubborn man.

"Jesse!"

With a start he realized Mitch was talking to him. "Hmm?"

"I asked if you wanted what's left of the wine." Mitch's eyes gleamed. "Or maybe you've had enough stimulation for one night."

Jesse gave him a warning glare. Like that was going to have any effect. Besides, Mitch—and Nikko—had given him plenty of hugs during the last month when Jesse had needed them. They knew exactly how Jesse felt about Randy. What intrigued him was the reason behind Randy's visit.

Please, don't let him be here just because he wants closure.

Except something niggled him. That remark of Randy's earlier, about forgetting to breathe? It had passed so quickly that Jesse had almost missed it, but now that he thought about it….

He didn't dare to hope it meant what he *thought* it meant. Finding out he was wrong would crush him.

Mitch's loud cough told Jesse he'd zoned out again. Only this time, Randy was watching him with amusement too.

Jesse seized the bottle and poured out the remains of the wine, glaring at both of them.

After dinner, he and Randy sat in the living room, listening to Nikko complaining about washing the dishes, both of them trying not to laugh when Mitch told him that no, they were *not* getting a dishwasher, which resulted in Nikko telling him he'd have Randy arrest him on the grounds of cruelty.

"They've invited me to come with you all to lunch tomorrow," Randy said quietly.

Jesse smiled. "I went for the first time last month. Talk about a houseful. They're great people. What I like most is how much they clearly love Nikko."

"What's not to love about him? He's one of the sweetest guys I've ever met." When Jesse gave him a pointed stare, Randy rolled his eyes. "I didn't say he was *the* sweetest guy. Besides, I hate to break it to you, but sweetness is *not* the first thing that comes to mind when I think of you."

Now he *was* intrigued. "Then what does?"

Randy blinked. "You really wanna know?"

Jesse laughed. "Hey, you started this."

Randy drew in a deep breath and leaned back against the seat cushion. "Okay… your… effervescence. Nothing brings you down—at least, not for long. Then there's your attitude. You're always ready to laugh and smile, even when life is kicking your ass. Your strength, because believe me, you *are* strong. Your resilience."

Jesse's throat tightened. He'd expected remarks about his looks, except that would have been… superficial? Then he realized Randy didn't care about the surface—he cared about what lay beneath.

Randy was staring at him, those beautiful blue eyes locked on him, and Jesse's heart beat faster.

"Then there's your sensuality."

Oh fuck. The hairs on Jesse's arms stood to attention, and something deep in his belly did a little flip-flop. His breathing quickened, and his chest rose and fell rapidly as he attempted to calm himself.

"The way you fill my senses when we're together. How you can arouse me with just a look, a touch… a kiss."

I arouse him. Heat crawled over Jesse's skin, seeping into his flesh and spreading through his body, a heat that seemed to center itself in his groin.

You need to stop, now. *Before I do something I'm gonna regret….*

God must have decided Jesse had taken as much as he could stand, because at that moment, Mitch and Nikko came into the room, carrying a tray laden with coffee mugs. Jesse jerked as though he'd stuck his finger into a socket, and Randy reacted similarly.

"Are you two all right?" Nikko asked with a frown.

Randy's gaze met Jesse's, and something flashed across his eyes. Then it was gone.

"We're fine," he said firmly.

Jesse was saying nothing. He didn't trust himself to speak just then. He grabbed a cushion instead and hugged it to his lower body, giving Nikko a smile.

He didn't miss Randy's snicker, however.

When Nikko turned his back to Jesse, and Mitch went to pull the blinds, Jesse gave Randy an evil glare. Randy just... smiled.

The evening passed without further incident, but when Mitch yawned and proclaimed it was their bedtime, Jesse deliberately avoided Randy's gaze. He said good night and went up to the attic room. Once inside, he closed the door with a sigh.

Two weeks. Randy was staying for *two weeks*.

Jesse wasn't gonna survive that long.

A gentle knock at the door made his heartbeat speed up. He opened it slowly to find Nikko standing there.

Jesse wasn't sure if he was relieved or disappointed.

"Sorry. I should have done this earlier. The spare sheets, blankets, and pillows are in the closet in here."

Jesse stood aside and let him enter. Nikko found what he was looking for and headed toward the door, then paused when he reached the threshold. "Is there anything you need?"

Jesse frowned. "Like what?" Nikko hadn't asked that since his arrival.

Nikko gave him an innocent look. "Oh, I don't know... toiletries, perhaps? You've not run out of anything?"

Jesse snickered. "Not since this morning, no."

"Yeah, but... you never know. Some things you forget about, because... you don't use them all that often, and then you come to look for them and realize you've not got any left, or what you have is... out of date, or... something." Nikko bit his lip. "I'll be going now." He hurried out of the room, closing the door after him.

It took a moment for Nikko's words to sink in.

Oh my God. Nikko did not just check that I had condoms and lube. Then an even more horrible thought occurred to him. *God, tell me I do. Tell me they haven't expired.* It wasn't until he found his bag, which had sat in the closet since he'd arrived, that he breathed more easily.

Wow. That's one way to get my heart rate up.

Then he pushed such thoughts aside. Randy was downstairs on the couch. He was up there. There was no way Jesse was about to go traipsing around the house in the middle of the night, armed with condoms and lube. That felt awfully… presumptuous. And in spite of Randy's earlier remarks, Jesse wasn't about to assume *anything*.

That didn't stop him from creeping down the small set of stairs to the attic door and opening it, however. *You know… just in case….* Nothing said *Go away* like a closed door.

It wasn't until he was under the covers, the lamp switched off, that Jesse realized how much he wanted to feel Randy's touch again. It had been four weeks since they'd made love, and a night hadn't passed without him reliving that blissful night.

Then it struck him. Since when did a night of sex stay with him *this long*?

RANDY LAY awake on the couch, his head propped by cushions and a pillow. It was comfortable, yet so far, sleep had evaded him. He was pretty certain the reason for his insomnia was the beautiful man in the attic bedroom, probably sleeping soundly, unaware of the turmoil he'd created in Randy's mind.

We need to talk. The conversation at the beach had at least gotten the ball rolling, but Randy hadn't said even *half* of the things he'd been rehearsing in his head during the bus trip. For one thing, he hadn't gotten close to letting Jesse know just how important he'd become to him.

Then maybe it's time to let him know. Randy gave a wry smile. *Why the hell should he sleep anyway, when it's thoughts of him that are keeping me awake?*

Yeah. Made perfect sense.

He pulled on a T-shirt and a pair of shorts, and crept past Mitch and Nikko's bedroom toward the rear of the house, where the door to the attic was located.

It was open.

Randy smiled. Either Jesse didn't care if someone walked in on him, or… it was an invitation. He stepped through the doorway and climbed the wooden staircase carefully, thankful none of the treads creaked, until he found himself in the attic, a fairly large space where sloping wood-lined ceilings met at the apex of the roof. There were windows at the gable ends, but apart from an oak chest of drawers, a nightstand, and a bed, there was nothing else in the room. It was narrower than Randy had expected, but that was because part of it had been turned into a closet or possibly a bathroom—a door was set in the middle of the constructed wall.

Light flooded the room, coming from a lamp beside the bed, where Jesse sat. "Don't tell me. You got lost," he said quietly, smirking. He seemed wide-awake.

Randy walked carefully across the varnished wooden floorboards toward the bed. "I couldn't sleep." He sat on the edge of the mattress.

"So you figured you'd come and disturb me instead," Jesse quipped. He shrugged. "As you can see, I couldn't sleep either." He gave Randy a gentle smile. "I hoped you'd come."

Randy cocked his head to one side. "Are we talking me coming to your bedroom, or to Maine?"

"Definitely the former. The latter? Maybe a little."

Randy nodded slowly. "Sure. Tell me not to come looking, then hope I'd ignore you. That makes sense." He should have stopped right there, but something in him was still stinging. "Waking up that morning to find you gone? That hurt."

Jesse winced. "I guess I deserved that. And I *am* sorry it took me a while to send that email. I just needed a little time to figure out what I wanted to say."

"The email took away the sting of your text. Because receiving that, after...." Randy swallowed. "After we made love.... And it *was* that, for me. I know you said I was amazing, but... hell, you must say that to a lot of guys... after."

Jesse's mouth fell open, and his eyes widened. "You... think that was a line? Fuck, no."

"Well, what was I supposed to think? When you hightailed it out of there?" Randy's chest tightened. "And as far as I was concerned, yeah, that night was amazing. I'd finally gotten you where I wanted you."

"In your bed?"

Randy shook his head. "In my life."

Jesse leaned back against his pillows. "So what happened to Mr. Straight Cop?"

Randy smiled. "Uh-uh. That would be Mr. Bi Cop."

"Wow." Jesse blinked. "You just flicked a switch, huh?"

"Nope." Randy sighed. "I never once considered I might be bi before the Black Lounge. But that whole experience opened my eyes. It made me look at myself. Then when my neighbor Owen challenged me, I—"

"Challenged you?" Jesse seemed more alert.

Randy chuckled. "Long story, which ended up with me taking some online tests."

Jesse was grinning. "Let me guess. 'Am I gay?'"

"Kind of. And I kept doing them until I got the results I wanted. But I knew, all right. They only confirmed what I'd come to realize. Still, I had to know for sure." He stared unblinking at Jesse. "And I found out, that night with you."

"What did that teach you?" Jesse asked softly, throwing off his covers and crawling across the bed to where Randy sat. He knelt beside him, hands resting on his thighs.

Randy groaned. "Did you *have* to sleep naked?"

"Answer the question." Jesse reached out and cupped Randy's cheek.

Randy locked gazes with him, his face held steadily in Jesse's warm hand. "I learned that it felt good to hold a man in my arms. More importantly, it was *you* I wanted there. I learned that your kiss made me tremble. It made me want more. I learned that… being inside you felt so good… so right. That listening to you, hearing you laugh, holding you…. *This* is what's important."

Jesse nodded. "I learned some things too." His fingers were gentle on Randy's cheek. "That it was possible to give myself to someone, heart, body, and soul. To… lose myself in them—in *you*. And it scared me to death, because I couldn't have what I wanted."

"And what was that?"

Jesse swallowed hard. "You… in my life."

Randy's heart pounded. "Why not? We can make this work. We… we have to."

"Why?" Jesse demanded.

"Because I love you!" God, it felt so goddamn good to finally say the words.

Jesse's breathing hitched. "You… love me?"

Randy pulled Jesse into his lap, his hands on Jesse's back. "With all my heart. And no, I don't have a clue how to make this work. I only know I can't lose you." He took a deep breath. "The question is, do—"

"Like you have to fucking ask," Jesse gasped out as he fused his mouth with Randy's, lips locked in a kiss that set Randy's soul alight.

Randy slipped his hands under Jesse's ass, supporting him as he rose from the bed, Jesse clinging to him, arms looped around his neck. Randy turned and lowered him carefully to the bed before removing his T-shirt and shorts, his own dick already reacting to the sight of Jesse on his back, slowly pumping his cock, his gaze trained on Randy.

Jesse held out a hand. "Let's make love."

Randy had never heard sweeter words.

Chapter Twenty-Two

"GOD, I feel like a cop in a donut factory. I don't know where I wanna start first," Randy joked as he gazed at Jesse's prone body.

Jesse laughed quietly. "Decisions, decisions. Is it gonna be frosting, sprinkles, or the creme filling?" He waggled his dick in the air, and that got a laugh. Then he had an idea. "Can I do something for you?"

"I thought we'd be doing that already," Randy quipped.

Jesse smacked his leg. "Let me give you a really good massage." He let go of his cock and flexed his fingers. "I'm good at it, honest. You'll be so relaxed by the time I'm done." He grinned. "Which is precisely how I want you when I slide my dick into your ass."

Fuck, that hitch in Randy's breathing was hot. What made it amusing was the way he immediately lay facedown, legs spread.

Jesse let out a low chuckle. "I'm guessing you like that idea."

Randy turned his head to one side to stare at him. "You're still here? Go get the massage oil or whatever it is you're using."

Jesse was still chuckling when he found the oil in the closet. He climbed onto the bed and knelt beside Randy as he poured a little oil into his cupped palm.

"Don't I need a towel to cover my butt?" Randy mumbled into the pillow.

Jesse slid his hands leisurely over Randy's shoulders and back. "It's not that kinda massage," he murmured. "This one definitely comes with a happy ending."

He caught Randy's muffled chuckle. "You said *comes*."

"How old are you?" Jesse pressed his thumbs lightly on either side of Randy's spine and moved down his back.

"Old enough that I'm getting hard at the thought of what's coming my way."

Jesse leaned over and kissed the back of his neck. "Enjoy getting there." He sat astride Randy, his shaft resting on Randy's crack as he made circles with his thumbs into the flesh at the base of Randy's neck before rocking gently as he manipulated Randy's back, moving up and down.

"Feels like I'm not the only one who's hard," Randy muttered, his head slightly to one side.

Jesse smiled to himself as he continued working Randy's back, just above the swell of his ass. Then he changed position, shifting to one side while he worked his fingers into Randy's thighs and calves, moving toward his feet.

"Hey! You missed a bit." Randy sounded indignant.

"Oh, hush. You know I'm gonna get there. Now will you stop focusing on me fucking you, and concentrate on melting into this mattress? Switch off your mind and enjoy it, for God's sake." He couldn't help smiling as he listened to Randy grumble about it being difficult to switch off anything when a sexy fucker was sliding oily hands all over his body.

Jesse figured he had a point. But it was when he got to Randy's feet that things got interesting.

"Straighten your legs," Jesse instructed. "Let your feet hang over the edge of the bed." Randy complied, and he rubbed his knuckles into the arch of Randy's foot, kneading it, before moving to his toes, where he pressed his fingertips into the gaps between each toe, rubbing gently.

"Oh." Randy's soft moan had lost all of its former irritation. "Yeah."

Jesse didn't react but supported Randy's foot carefully while he used his thumbs to rub the heel, the arch, and the ball of his foot. Smiling, he got off the bed and stood at the end of it, lifting Randy's feet until they met Jesse's dick, where he pushed his hard shaft between them, the oil helping it to slide through.

"Oh fuck," Randy whispered.

Jesse held Randy's feet together while he gently thrust his dick between them, moving slickly, keeping the pace unhurried. When Randy began to dry hump the bed, Jesse guessed it was time for a gear change. He climbed onto the bed and gently parted Randy's thighs until he was able to kneel between them. Jesse trickled oil over Randy's asscheeks and into his crease, then put the bottle aside and began the slow, sensual process of working those firm globes. He dug his thumbs into the swell of his ass, gently pulling his cheeks apart, revealing more and more of that pink hole.

Randy lifted up slightly to adjust himself, then lay back down, only now, his balls and the head of his dick were visible between his legs. Jesse smiled at the hint before stroking the tops of Randy's thighs, making sure his fingertips grazed Randy's balls and cockhead.

"I like your technique," Randy murmured.

"I'm glad." Jesse used his thumbs to manipulate the firm flesh, each time stretching Randy's hole a little wider. He concentrated on one asscheek, sliding the side of his hand through Randy's crack, his fingers stroking his balls, before applying the same attention to the other cheek. With every pass of Jesse's hand over his hole, Randy let out a low sound of arousal and desire. Finally, Jesse spread his cheeks wide, bent over, and gently brushed the tip of his tongue across Randy's pucker.

Randy's soft exhale was music to Jesse's ears.

Jesse continued to focus his attention on Randy's hole, alternating between tongue and fingers, listening as Randy's moans became more frequent, accompanied by the gentle rolling of his hips as he chased the sensations.

"Stop!"

Jesse halted instantly and drew back as Randy flipped over, his cock rising, a hard exclamation point of flesh.

"Now, please," he begged.

Jesse shifted to lie beside him, stroking Randy's dick. Then he leaned over to kiss him, Randy's hands in constant motion on Jesse's nape and chest. There was so much hunger in that kiss that Jesse shivered in anticipation.

When he broke the kiss, Randy reached for Jesse's dick, stroked it, cupped his balls, and squeezed them before he tugged on Jesse's shaft. "I want this, now."

"Then suck it, babe, while I get you ready."

Randy wasted no time getting onto all fours and taking Jesse's cock into his mouth. Jesse reached into the nightstand drawer to grab the lube and a couple of condoms, momentarily distracted when Randy took him a little deeper. Jesse gave a shudder, forgetting his intentions as he placed his hand on Randy's head, Jesse's hips in motion as he thrust up into that glorious mouth.

"Yeah, that's it. You've got me so hard."

Randy pulled away for a moment and grinned. "Your fingers. My ass. Get busy." Then he went back to his task, seemingly hell-bent on making Jesse shoot his load into Randy's mouth.

Jesse chuckled and opened the tube. "This what you want?" He slowly pushed his index finger deep inside Randy's tight hole. Randy groaned around his dick, his head bobbing faster. Jesse kept the motion slow and steady, loving how Randy's body tightened around his finger, hot and silky….

God, how he ached to slide his cock into that heat.

By the time he'd added a second finger, Randy was pushing back hard, riding it, rocking between Jesse's slick fingers and his dripping dick—and Jesse didn't want to wait a second longer. He pulled free of Randy's body and grabbed his cock around the base.

"Ride me?"

RANDY WAS off his shaft in a heartbeat. He grabbed a condom packet from where Jesse had left them on the bed, tore it open, and tried to unfurl it down Jesse's solid length. His fingers trembled.

"Hey, go slow," Jesse said softly. "We're gonna take our time, okay?" His hand joined Randy's, unrolling the latex to its full length.

Randy fought to breathe evenly as Jesse squeezed more lube onto the head, slicking up the shaft. "That's it. Can't have too much lube." He held his arms wide. "Now come here and kiss me."

Randy straddled Jesse's body and bent down to kiss him, Jesse's hands on his head and neck as their tongues met. Jesse stroked his back, moving lower to his waist before finally caressing his ass. Randy shivered as Jesse's dick rubbed through his crack, hot against his hole, but Jesse simply stroked his ass and thighs, seemingly in no hurry to penetrate him.

His calm proved infectious. Randy's breathing slowed, and he lost himself in Jesse's tender, lingering kisses.

"Yeah, that's it," Jesse murmured against his lips. "Just enjoy this."

Randy smiled. "I could kiss you all night long."

Jesse chuckled. "And with your scruff, I'd end up with swollen lips and beard burn. This is how it should be. Slow, hot, toe-curling…. And when you're ready, guide me in."

Randy sat up, reached back, and brought the head of Jesse's cock to lightly kiss his hole.

Jesse didn't break eye contact. His hands were on Randy's waist, gentle and warm. "Now sit back on it, as slow as you like."

Randy pushed back a little, meeting resistance.

Jesse nodded. "Breathe. That'll help."

In spite of his nervous state, Randy chuckled. "Breathing always helps, I find." He pushed a little harder, until— "Oh, fuck, you're hard." He stilled, conscious of being stretched and filled. Jesse didn't move, his hands so gentle on Randy's chest and belly, his gaze never leaving Randy's. Eventually, Randy eased down a bit more, breathing deeply.

"It's gonna feel so good in a minute," Jesse assured him.

Randy sank down until his ass met Jesse's thighs, and Jesse was all the way inside him. "God, I feel that," he moaned. "Like I'm sitting with a tent pole up my ass."

Jesse chuckled. "I'm flattered, but I'm nowhere near that thick. Or long, if it comes to that. Now lift yourself up a little, then sit back on it." He grabbed Randy's ass and pulled his cheeks gently apart. "That might feel a bit easier."

Randy made a few experimental movements and let out a sigh. "Oh yeah." That felt a *whole* lot better. He rocked slowly, aware that the initial burn was fading with each press of Jesse's dick inside him. He grinned. "You were right. This… this feels good."

Jesse nodded. "Now hold still and let me do the driving for a while."

Randy did as instructed—and gasped as Jesse tilted his hips and slid deep inside him, his asscheeks still spread by Jesse's gentle hands. Randy braced himself, his hand flat to the wooden-clad wall, gazing down at Jesse's earnest, sweet face.

He smiled. "You can go faster."

Jesse grinned. "You might wanna reconsider that. I can go pretty damn fast." He thrust up into Randy, a little harder, and what felt like a hell of a lot deeper, and Randy moaned.

"More."

Then Jesse was sliding in and out of his ass, making him shudder, making him hotter, until his awareness had narrowed to the wonderful friction they were creating between them, the heat that increased with every thrust.

"Think I wanna ride some more," he gasped out. With one hand still braced against the wall and the other planted on the bed, he started to rock a bit faster, loving the feeling of impaling himself on Jesse's shaft in short, quick bursts.

"Can't stop touching you," Jesse blurted out, stroking his chest, his waist, his ass. "And fuck, your ass feels amazing." In the midst of all that passionate rocking, they kissed, over and over again, Jesse's fingers teasing his nipples and sending shock waves of pleasures darting through him.

"Gotta slow down," Randy choked out, pressing his hands to Jesse's chest and reducing his motion to a gentle rock-and-roll of his hips. *Fuck, that felt even better.*

"Oh wow." Jesse gazed up at him, his lips parted. "My favorite—nice and slow." They moved together, their bodies synchronized in a leisurely undulation. Then Randy leaned back, his hands braced on Jesse's thighs, and the change in angle brought him that much closer to the edge.

"Want to come when I'm inside you," he murmured.

Jesse stroked his belly, his eyes wide. "How do you want me?"

"On your back." Randy eased out of him, and Jesse grabbed the remaining condom packet and eagerly tore it open with his teeth. It felt like mere seconds had passed before Jesse had his knees to his chest, his legs hooked over Randy's arms, and Randy was sliding his gloved dick deep inside him. His lips met Jesse's in a long, sensual kiss before he whispered, "Nice and slow. I remember."

Then they were kissing without ceasing, Jesse's hands on Randy's thighs as Randy rolled his hips, slowly stroking his cock in and out of Jesse's body, Jesse breaking the kiss to gasp that Randy was *so fucking deep*, before seeking Randy's lips yet again.

Fuck, the heat…. Sweat dripped from Randy's body, mingling with Jesse's, both of them slick, which only added to the sensuality of it all as skin slid against skin. Now and again Randy sat back, his hands firm on Jesse's thighs, keeping up that gentle rocking motion while Jesse tugged at his dick, both unable to keep silent. Then it was back to kissing, only now Randy picked up a little speed, thrusting into Jesse with short, quick strokes, until Jesse was shaking, his hand a blur on his shaft, and Randy knew they'd reached the end of their erotic dance.

Jesse came with a harsh cry, his fingers tight around his dick as he shot hard, and Randy kissed him until the tremors subsided. "My turn," Randy whispered, moving gently inside him, knowing he was close to his own climax. He ran his fingers over Jesse's torso, scooping up his come. Randy locked gazes with Jesse as he brought his hand to his lips and tasted him, loving the low moan that rolled out of Jesse.

Too many sensations. Randy shuddered as he came, his back arched, his cock pulsing as he filled the latex. Jesse held him, his hands on Randy's shoulders, and as the last of the mini jolts ebbed away, they kissed, slow and sweet and oh *so* tender.

"You taste of me," Jesse murmured against his lips. "Not fair. I don't get to taste you."

"Next time," Randy promised. "I'll feed you every drop."

For a long time, they lay together, arms around each other, neither saying a word. The only sound was their breathing. Randy knew they couldn't stay like that, but he didn't want to break the spell, to shatter the peace that surrounded them, to lose the warm contentment that spread through him.

Let me hold on to this for as long as it lasts.

Chapter Twenty-Three

JESSE DECIDED he liked these kinds of dreams. He was warm, strong arms enfolded him, and soft lips pressed kisses to his shoulder and neck, while lower down, there was definitely *something* going on. Then he opened his eyes and realized it was no dream.

Thank God.

He shivered as Randy's lips brushed over the back of his neck. "It's on days like these that I'm glad I got my hair cut," he murmured.

Randy chuckled against his nape. "So I get easier access?"

"God, yes." Then Jesse shuddered as Randy moved his hand higher, and he was caught between two hot spots, both of them competing to drive him out of his frigging mind. "You… you keep doing that, and I am gonna be shooting my load all over this bed."

In a flash Randy flipped him until Jesse was on top of him, then reached for the lube. "Get ready," he barked out, thrusting the tube into Jesse's hands. Jesse didn't waste any time. He straddled Randy's waist and reached back with slick fingers while Randy gloved up. Less than a minute elapsed before he sank onto Randy's dick, groaning at how *fucking hard* it was inside him.

They were both too close to make it last, and it wasn't long before Randy thrust up into him and shuddered as he shot into the latex, his hands tight on Jesse's hips as he held him there. Jesse gave his cock a good tug and creamed Randy's chest, his breathing rapid and harsh.

Jesse bent over and kissed him softly on the lips. "Do I get this every morning during your stay?" As soon as he'd uttered the words, however, he instantly regretted them. Randy only had a finite amount of time in Maine. Sooner or later, he'd have to go back.

Can't think about that. Not now.

Randy's face tightened for a moment, then relaxed. "Well, that depends on two things," he said with a smile. "One, if I get to share this bed with you every night, and—"

"You'd better, if you like your balls where they are," Jesse growled.

Randy winced. "Ouch. And I was *about* to say—two, only if we take it in turns." He craned his neck and kissed Jesse on the lips. "Tomorrow morning, *I* get to ride again." He bit his lip. "Although, what Mitch and Nikko will have to say about the sleeping arrangements remains to be seen."

Jesse chuckled. "One thing you can count on with Mitch—you always know what he's thinking, because he damn well tells you."

Randy laughed. "Yeah, I had noticed." He sighed. "One of us has to make a move, babe. And seeing as you're the one sitting on my dick...."

Jesse's sigh echoed his. "Damn. Okay." He lifted himself higher, and Randy's softened cock slipped from his body. Jesse leaned over again and kissed him. "Tonight. Here."

Randy cupped his cheek. "It's a date."

Jesse would be counting the hours.

"I TAKE it you didn't like the couch." Mitch's gaze met Randy's in the rearview mirror. Beside him, Nikko smacked Mitch's thigh, and Mitch jerked his head to stare at him. "What? You said the same thing this morning."

"Yes, but that was to you. And it wasn't for sharing."

Jesse snickered. "I'm amazed you kept quiet about it as long as you did. We're almost at your parents'."

"Yeah, I'm becoming more… restrained in my old age."

Nikko made a choking sound.

Randy didn't know where to look. Jesse covered Randy's hand with his own and squeezed it gently. Randy cleared his throat. "So, how many people will be there for lunch?" Anything to change the subject.

"All the family, from what Mom said. Apparently, some of them can't make it for the Labor Day weekend, so this will be a substitute. We're talking my brother, Gareth—you met him at the trial—my sister Deirdre, her husband, Eric, and their kids, Ben and Debbie, and my sister Monica, her husband, Shaun, and their kids, Lisa and Cal. The kids are all in their twenties except Cal—he's nineteen." He chuckled.

Nikko smacked him again. "You promised. Your best behavior, all right?"

Randy was intrigued. "What's going on?"

Nikko twisted in his seat to look at Randy. "Cal's bringing someone with him, and it's a big deal." He smiled. "His first boyfriend."

Randy had to smile back. "Aw, that's great."

"And speaking of boyfriends…." Mitch caught Randy's eye in the mirror again. "You two. Is it official?" Nikko smacked him yet again, and Mitch glared at him. "What? We need to know these things before we get there. I mean, we know they're fu—"

"Mitch!" There was a warning note in Nikko's voice.

Randy glanced across at Jesse, who was staring at him. What struck Randy most was his questioning gaze, the way his hand rested over his heart, his eyes, wide and shining….

Randy smiled and took a step out over the precipice. "I guess it's official, seeing as we love each other." Then his heart melted when Jesse lifted his hand to his lips and kissed it.

Nikko twisted around again, his jaw dropping. "Love…. Oh wow. That's wonderful."

"See?" Mitch said triumphantly. "That makes me feel better. *Now* I know what to say when Mom asks me why Randy and Jesse keep sneaking off to be alone today. I'll tell her, they have an excuse. They're in love." He grinned at Randy in the mirror. "Best excuse ever."

Randy couldn't argue with that.

It wasn't long before Mitch pulled into a long driveway with a pale blue-painted house at the end. He parked behind a line of cars. "Looks like we're the last to arrive."

"Ready for mayhem?" Jesse asked him with a grin.

Randy kissed his fingers. "I'm ready for anything." It wasn't a line. Right then he felt fucking *invincible*.

LUNCH WAS over, and Randy was sitting by the piano, listening to Nikko play, lost in the beautiful harmonies. "I had no idea."

"That I played piano?" Nikko smiled. "I've played since I was a child." His fingers danced over the gleaming keys, and Randy was mesmerized. Nikko nodded toward the living room through the french doors. "I'm in awe of Valerie right now. How she managed to seat *and* feed sixteen people is just amazing. I don't think I've ever seen so many of us here at one time."

Randy followed his gaze. Not everyone had congregated in the living room—some were in the kitchen, talking with Valerie, or sitting at the dining room table. Both couches were fully occupied, along with the armchairs, and the younger members of the family were sitting on chairs and floor cushions, taking animatedly. Mitch's nephews and nieces were about the same age as Jesse, and he'd obviously warmed to them right away. The chatter from their end of the table during lunch had been lively. Cal and his boyfriend, Dale, had sat together, Dale joining in the conversations now and then, but mostly his attention had been focused on Cal. Randy liked the way Dale put his arm around Cal's shoulders, letting Cal lean against him.

"Dale seems nice," Randy murmured. They both looked so young. Randy liked the idea that they felt confident and relaxed enough to be themselves. It said a lot about Mitch's family.

Nikko nodded. "I like him a lot. But then again, I've known him for a while. He's at college with Cal, which is where I met him."

"Are you nearly finished with your master's?"

Nikko sighed. "Yes, and then the hard work really begins. Sometimes I think Mitch is right. I must be crazy for wanting to teach."

"Any kid who gets you as his teacher will be lucky," Randy said sincerely. Nikko's eyes shone.

"Nikko? You got a minute?" Mitch hollered from the living room. "You, too, Randy."

Nikko rolled his eyes. "Now what? If Valerie wants to organize family games again, I may decide to take a walk in the yard." He squeezed Randy's arm. "A word to the wise. Don't get on Mitch's team. He's really competitive."

Randy laughed. They got up from their seats and went into the living room, where everyone had gathered. Mitch was beside the fireplace, his gaze focused on Nikko as he beckoned him over. Jesse stood in the doorway to the dining room, smiling at the assembled family. Randy went over to stand beside him, and Jesse automatically took his hand.

"Having a good day?" Jesse asked him.

Randy shook his head. "Nope. I'm having a great day." The atmosphere was laid-back, and Mitch's family was a delight. Everyone had been so easygoing and friendly, and by the time a couple of hours had passed, Randy felt like he'd known them a good deal longer.

He inclined his head toward Mitch and asked Jesse under his breath, "What's going on?"

"No idea."

Mitch held up his hand, and the room fell silent. He turned to face Nikko, his expression gentle. "This weekend is a kind of anniversary. A year ago, you first came here and met my family." He smiled. "Well, I guess they're your family now." Murmurs of agreement echoed around the room. "We've all come to love you, and sometimes it's difficult to remember a time when you weren't around. I knew, back then, that you were a very special man, and if anything, this past year has only reinforced that."

Nikko's face had a glow to it, his eyes alight. "Look who's talking," he said softly.

Mitch smiled. "You've changed my life, sweetheart, to the point where I couldn't imagine you not being in it. So that got me thinking."

He reached into the pocket of his jeans, and suddenly Randy knew *exactly* where this was heading. He gripped Jesse's hand tightly, unable to tear his gaze away as Mitch got down on one knee, accompanied by Nikko's soft gasp.

Mitch held out the small black box, opened to reveal a white-gold band. "Nikko Kurokawa, will you make me the happiest man alive? Will you marry me?"

Nikko clutched his chest. "You sneaky...." His face erupted into a wide, beaming smile. "Like you don't already know the answer." He bent over and slowly kissed Mitch, his hand on Mitch's cheek. Mitch rose to his feet, took Nikko's hand, and slipped the ring onto his finger. Nikko gazed at it, tears sparkling in his eyes, before throwing his arms around Mitch's broad chest and hugging him tightly.

The onlookers burst into rapturous applause, and Randy lost sight of the couple as they were surrounded by family members, all wanting to exchange hugs and kisses.

Once she'd gotten her share of hugs, Valerie wiped her eyes and gazed at Malcolm. "Now I know why he told me to make sure we had champagne in the house." She shook her head. "He told me we were celebrating Nikko finishing his master's."

"I'll go get the glasses out," Malcolm said, kissing her cheek. He gazed back at Mitch and Nikko, and smiled. "You finally get to plan your baby's wedding."

Mitch cleared his throat. "Er, Dad? Not exactly. I've already planned it."

Nikko blinked, then grinned. "*Someone* was awfully confident I'd say yes."

Mitch beamed. "Didn't doubt it for a second. And yeah, the wedding is already booked." His eyes twinkled. "Think garlands, lights, snow, sleigh bells…."

Nikko's eyes widened. "We're getting married at Christmas? This year?"

"Well, I'm not gonna wait around until next year." Mitch stared at Randy and Jesse. "And you two are gonna be there as well, so you'd better make a note in your diaries."

Randy laughed. "Can't wait." The joy in the room was infectious. He pulled Jesse into a hug, kissing him on the lips, loving how Jesse threw his arms around Randy's neck and returned the kiss wholeheartedly.

"Hey. Is there about to be another announcement?" That came from Gareth.

Randy grinned at him. "Only if *you're* about to make one."

Guffaws erupted from Deidre, Monica, and Mitch, while Valerie glared at them.

Deirdre snorted. "Sorry, Mom, but we all know that's not going to happen."

"Yeah," Monica agreed. "Besides, Gareth doesn't need a woman. He's got his dogs—"

"His house, with the forest right up against his backyard," Shaun added, his eyes bright.

"His pool," Eric interjected.

Mitch gave Randy an amused glance. "My brother is happy as he is. Just because his siblings are all married—or about to be—doesn't mean he has to follow the trend."

Randy gazed at Gareth, who appeared to take all the amusement in his stride. Except… when everyone had gone back to congratulating the happy couple, Randy couldn't help but notice a couple of things. How Gareth's mouth turned down slightly. His gaze narrowed. His eyes tightened underneath. *Gareth is* not *as happy as Mitch thinks.* For a moment, Randy's heart went out to him. Then Gareth caught him looking, and all trace of whatever emotion Randy thought he'd glimpsed vanished, lost beneath a warm smile.

"Champagne!" Malcolm announced. "Come into the kitchen, everybody, and grab a glass. Then we'll have a toast to Mitch and Nikko." He glanced at Randy and Jesse, his eyes warm. "And maybe a toast to wish our best for the other couples here today." He cleared his throat. "Yes, Cal, that means you too."

Laughter rang out, and Cal flushed. Dale kissed his cheek and smiled. "I think that's a great idea."

Randy held back as the family filed into the kitchen, his hand on Jesse's back. When they were alone, he took Jesse in his arms. "I know I don't have all the answers right now as to how this is gonna work. I'm just playing this by ear. But I meant what I said last night. I love you, and I'll find a way to *make* this work, because… we have to."

Jesse locked gazes with him. "I love you, too, and I'm holding on to that, because…." He sighed. "I just keep thinking these two weeks are gonna fly by, and then—"

Randy stopped his words with a gentle kiss. When they parted, he held Jesse's face in his hands. "Let's not think about that, all right? Let's just enjoy the time we have. We'll deal with reality in a little while." He smiled. "Now, how about a glass of champagne?"

Jesse chuckled. "Just so you know? Champagne always goes straight to my head, so if you're considering having your wicked way with me tonight…." He waggled his eyebrows. "You'll definitely be in luck."

Randy snorted. "Who are you kidding? I knew I was getting lucky way before there was any mention of champagne."

Jesse gave a mock gasp. "Are you suggesting I'm easy?"

Randy gave him an intense look. "Nope. I'm saying neither of us can keep our hands off each other, and I can't wait to get you alone tonight, because I'm gonna—"

It was Jesse's turn to stop his words with a kiss. "Don't spoil it," he whispered against Randy's lips. "Surprise me."

Randy grinned. "I aim to."

Chapter Twenty-Four

THE FIRST week of Randy's visit went by slowly, which was just fine as far as he was concerned. Every morning, he and Jesse got up early and went for a walk along the beach, drinking coffee and talking. *So* much talking. Jesse spoke of his high school days and his family, and Randy knew him well enough to catch the pain in his voice. He longed to do *something* to ease that pain, but it wasn't his battle. Randy spoke of his parents, living in Florida, where they'd both taken early retirement. In that respect, he envied Mitch the closeness of his family. Both Randy's parents were content with their lives, playing golf, sailing, his mom's charity work, his dad's hobbies…. They were proud of him, he knew that, but they were happy for him to live and work in New York. Come to think of it, they hadn't been all that close-knit a family when Randy was growing up. He'd spent more time with his Aunt Carol and her family than his own.

After their walks, it was back to the house, where they stayed out of the way. Nikko worked on his music and studies, and Mitch was up to his eyeballs in getting ready for the new school year—September sixth loomed ever closer on the horizon. Randy and Jesse would sneak up to the attic, where they'd make out like teenagers, more often than not ending up under the covers, making love.

There was a *lot* of that.

In the afternoons, Jesse went off to work, and Mitch and Nikko took Randy out in the car, showing him around Maine—or as much as they could in the time available. He got to see more of Portland and other small towns along the coast. Randy could understand why Nikko had been so keen to move there. It was certainly nothing like New York. Randy loved the peace and quiet of the inland towns, their… desolation, almost, but it was the coast that seemed to seep into his bones, filling him with a contentment he'd rarely known.

Evenings were spent watching TV, reading on the porch with a glass of wine, or going for yet another walk along the shoreline. That had become their favorite way to spend time—at least, with their clothes on. There was something about the breeze that came off the ocean, the sound of gulls overhead, the waves crashing.

Nights were spent in Jesse's bed. Long nights where they slept in each other's arms, awaking with the dawn, and other nights where neither of them got any sleep, and that was just fine too. For a man who'd gotten laid rarely, Randy seemed to be making up for lost time. Either that, or Jesse's sexual appetite was infectious.

During the second week, however, something changed.

Randy had a good idea what lay at the root of it. Neither of them wanted their precious time together to come to an end. Tempers were frayed, nerves were on edge, and more than once they snapped at each other, only to apologize instantly. Nights became times to hold each other, as if they were clinging to a fragile reality that was about to be ripped away. Neither of them mentioned the future. Randy couldn't bear to bring up the subject, because if he couldn't see a way to make this work, then why bring it up? It would only make matters worse.

Mitch and Nikko said nothing, but Randy knew they were concerned—he could see it in the glances they gave each other, in the awkward silences that fell sometimes when he or Jesse had snapped, and in the murmured conversations that ended abruptly whenever he or Jesse entered the room.

By the time it got to Friday, with only two days remaining until Randy was due to head back to New York, Mitch apparently had had about as much as he could take.

Jesse left for work as usual, looking pale and drawn. Neither of them had slept well and, unusually for them, for all the wrong reasons. Randy sat on the porch, a book that he couldn't work up enough enthusiasm to read open and facedown in his lap.

Mitch opened the front door, stepped out onto the porch, and speared him with a look. "You and I are going for a walk. Now."

Randy blinked, but one glance at Mitch's stony expression had him biting back a retort. He got to his feet and followed Mitch through the screen door, down the stairs, and onto the avenue, where they headed toward the beach. Mitch said nothing but walked with long, quick strides, Randy struggling to keep up with him.

"Are we late for something?" he joked.

Mitch came to a halt and sighed. "Sorry. I've got a lot on my mind. Most of it because of you and Jesse, but not all." He resumed walking, but at a more sedate pace.

"The part that's not related to me… wanna talk about it?"

Mitch stared at the sidewalk. "It's Ichy. I want to invite him to the wedding, but I have no idea how to go about it. And I don't want to say anything to Nikko, in case it doesn't happen."

Randy considered the problem. "Right now he's settling into his new life. I don't know where he is, but I can try to find out. Why don't you leave this with me? I can't promise anything, but at least I can look into it."

Mitch nodded. "Okay. It *is* your area, so to speak." They reached the path that led to the beach, and both of them kicked off their shoes. Once they were on the sand, Mitch turned left and headed along the shore, walking slowly. Randy said nothing, figuring he'd get to whatever troubled him eventually.

After a few minutes, Mitch cleared his throat. "What was I doing when we first met?"

Randy blinked again. "Teaching English." *What the hell?*

"Where was I teaching?"

"Er… New York?" Randy had no clue where this was going.

Mitch nodded. "And what am I doing now?"

"Teaching."

Another nod. "Except now I'm in Maine."

"Yeah?" Randy was starting to think Mitch had flipped.

Mitch came to a stop and faced him, folding his arms across his broad chest. "And what do *you* do?" The expression in Mitch's eyes told Randy this was no joke.

"I'm a New York cop."

Mitch stilled. "But… you could be a cop anywhere, right? Even in Maine?"

"I suppose," Randy said slowly. "Where are you going with this?"

Mitch arched his eyebrows. "I have to spell it out? Fine. I'm suggesting you could be a cop in Maine."

"Is there much call for cops in Maine?" Randy quipped. "Coast guards, maybe. Inland, I'm not so sure."

Mitch's jaw dropped, and he gaped. "Oh my God. I didn't know that."

"Know what?"

"That Maine is the crime-free state of the US. Wow. When *this* gets out, people will be moving here in droves." There was a twinkle in his eye.

Randy chuckled. "Okay, okay, *now* I get it. Yes, I'm sure Maine has its fair share of crime, just like everywhere. But it would be a different kind of job to the one I'm used to."

"And would that be a bad thing?" Mitch narrowed his gaze. "Because it strikes me you aren't happy in your work."

Randy opened his mouth to deny it, but the words died in his throat.

Mitch regarded him steadily, his head tilted to one side. "Why did you go into law enforcement?"

"Because… I wanted to make a difference. I wanted to make New York a safer place for people." It was all he'd ever wanted to do, both him and Donna.

Another slow nod. "And are you doing that?"

That stopped him in his tracks. Because there *had* been a time, right, when he'd felt like he really made a difference? Back when he first became a detective. Before he joined Vice.

Before the lines blurred.

Randy didn't know what to say.

Mitch reached into the back pocket of his jeans and pulled out a folded piece of white paper, which he handed to Randy. "This is for you. I printed it off this morning while you and Jesse were walking."

Randy opened it and smiled. "Wikipedia?" Then he took a closer look. *List of law enforcement agencies in Maine*. He jerked his head to stare at Mitch, who smiled.

"What you have there are your state agencies, your county sheriffs' offices, and a ton of police departments all across the state. There are even three campus police departments." He narrowed his gaze. "Now, are you gonna stand there and tell me not *one* of them would have a vacancy for a cop who wants a transfer?"

Randy's heartbeat sped up. *Could it be that simple?*

Mitch laid a hand on Randy's shoulder. "I've been where you are, remember? Right now, you're faced with a choice. Jesse, too, for that matter. You both have some talking to do, but I just wanted you to see that there *are* options. All you have to do is consider them." He squeezed

Randy's shoulder. "Nikko and I, we think the world of you two. And we want you to be happy. Now Jesse, he's happier here, there's no doubt about that. Or at least he *was*, until this past week." Mitch's face fell. "I know what you're going through. The thought of being apart cuts into you like a knife, doesn't it?"

Randy couldn't argue with that.

Mitch nodded. "Then you need to think seriously about making some changes. Life is too short to waste it in the wrong job, the wrong city… or with the wrong gender." His eyes sparkled. "Although I think you've pretty much made your mind up on that score, right?"

Randy bit his lip. "Gee, what gave it away?"

Mitch arched his eyebrows. "The noises I've been hearing above my bedroom ceiling every night for the past two weeks," he said gruffly. "And that's another thing. Much as we love Jesse, and love having him stay with us? We need you two to get a place of your own, if you catch my drift. Because I'm not sure I could put up with my sleep being disturbed whenever you come to visit."

Randy winced. "That bad?"

Mitch rolled his eyes. "Christ, I swear I was never that horny, even when I was a teenager. You two are just at it like bunnies." He coughed. "Sorry. Nikko made me promise not to say too much. I guess I let my mouth run away with me." He grinned. "Hey. What say we go grab a bite to eat at the Old Orchard Beach pier? There's this really cute server I think you'd like." Mitch winked.

Randy waved a hand. "Nah. I know the one you mean. I hear he's spoken for. And I also hear his boyfriend's a cop."

Mitch laughed.

"Still…." Randy rubbed his chin. "At least I'd get to see him in black. Because his ass in those tight jeans?"

Mitch glared at him. "On second thought, I don't wanna give you ideas. You already have way too many of your own." He patted Randy on the back. "Seriously, I'm thinking a beer and a lobster roll. How does that sound?"

Randy nodded. "Sounds delicious." And while he was waiting for the food to arrive, he'd be on Google Maps, checking out which police departments were on or near the coast. Because *that* was a given. He folded the sheet of paper and put it into his pocket. "I'll talk to Jesse tonight."

Because where Randy could transfer to another police department, Jesse's future was not so simple.

Chapter Twenty-Five

RANDY PUT away the last of the dishes and hung up the towel. "How about we go for a walk?" he suggested. "It's a beautiful evening."

Jesse shrugged. "I guess." Not that he was really in the mood for a walk. There were only two more nights left before Randy would have to leave, and as the time for his imminent departure drew closer, Jesse grew more despondent.

It didn't matter what angle he looked at their situation from, the view didn't improve. Long-distance relationships sucked and stood little chance of success.

Randy grabbed Jesse's jacket from the closet, along with his own, before addressing Mitch and Nikko. "We're gonna go for a walk. We won't be back late."

Mitch nodded, saying nothing.

Randy held the door open for Jesse, then followed him down the staircase onto the street below.

Jesse pulled on his jacket and waited for Randy to do the same. "Do you have a particular destination in mind, or is this just an aimless stroll?"

"I thought we'd walk down to the beach."

Jesse let out a happy sigh. "Like I'm gonna argue with that."

They walked at a leisurely pace, side by side, in silence. Above, the gulls circled, their harsh cries piercing the quietness of the evening. The sun had almost set, and the sky was aglow with orange and red.

"So what did you do with *your* day?" Jesse said lightly. "Apart from turning up at my restaurant to bug the crap out of me."

Randy snorted. "I didn't hear you complaining when we left you a tip."

"Duh." Jesse sighed again. "Seriously? It was good to see you." He liked his job, but right then, with Randy staying, it was robbing him of precious time they could be sharing.

"You really like working there, don't you?"

"Yeah." They reached the path that led to the sand, and Jesse immediately kicked off his flip-flops. Any excuse to get the sand between his toes.

"But it's not where you wanna be for the rest of your life, right?"

Jesse came to a halt. "That depends. If we're talking geography, then yeah, I'd live here in a heartbeat." He stared out at the ocean, at the way the sun's dying rays sparkled on its surface. "This place really gets to me. I don't necessarily mean Old Orchard Beach, but the ocean. Take last weekend as a for-instance. There are some beautiful places farther up the coast." He smiled. "Look at me. New York City boy through and through, and yet...." Jesse peered at Randy. "You know what? I don't miss it. When Nikko used to talk about living here and how much he loved it, I thought he was nuts. I mean, who'd live in *Maine*, for Christ's sake?"

Randy laughed. "Yeah, I know the feeling. It kinda gets under your skin, doesn't it?"

Jesse stared at him. "You too?"

Randy gave a slow nod. "Which is why...." He paused, taking a deep breath, and Jesse wondered what the hell was coming. Then Randy locked gazes with him, and Jesse's scalp prickled. "I'm seriously considering transferring to Maine."

Jesse froze. "Wait. You wanna do what?"

"You heard me."

"Well, yeah. I'm just not sure why you said it." Jesse's mind was reeling from Randy's U-turn. *Where did this come from?* He prayed it wasn't a knee-jerk reaction to what Jesse had just said.

"Let's sit down for a minute." Randy lowered himself to the sand and sat cross-legged. Jesse joined him, the sand still warm from the day's heat. Randy pulled something from the pocket of his jeans and handed it to Jesse. It was a piece of folded paper.

Jesse opened it and stared at its contents. "Oh my God. You're serious." The list of police departments was huge. *I had no idea Maine was this big.* He glanced at Randy. "Now tell me why." He handed the paper back.

Randy folded it carefully and put it into his jeans pocket. "Mitch got me thinking today."

Jesse chuckled. "Now why does that not surprise me?"

"He asked me two questions that made me reconsider why I was working in New York. And I had to be honest. My goals haven't changed, but everything else has. I didn't get into policing to improve some government statistics. I got into this job to make a difference in people's lives. To make them safer. And whereas I have no problem tracking down guys who were into human trafficking and sexual slavery, I do have a problem with depriving sex workers of their livelihoods. That was down entirely to my stint in the Black Lounge. I've come to see matters in a different light."

"That's why when I said it would never work because you were a Vice cop, you said, 'So?' You really didn't have a problem with me escorting?" Jesse gave him a hard stare. "Come on. Level with me, if we're being honest here."

Randy sighed heavily. "Yeah, I've thought about that part since then. I *maybe* could have gotten my head around you selling yourself to make a buck, because you were working toward a goal and you weren't gonna do it forever, but… I'd have lost my job for sure once someone found out."

Jesse nodded. "And I couldn't let you do that. You're a good cop."

"Then I can be a good cop here, in Maine. The change of pace would do me good."

"Wait a minute. Going from working in Vice in New York, to a cop in Maine? The change of pace might end up killing you."

"Huh?"

Jesse chuckled. "You'd die of boredom."

Randy shook his head. "Sorry to disappoint you, but Maine isn't all that quiet. Crime is on the up, has been for the last six years, even if it does have the second-lowest violent crime rate in the US." He shrugged. "I did some research this afternoon. And transferring isn't all that cut-and-dried. I'd have to become a Maine state trooper first, and that means eighteen weeks of training. I don't know if my years of service would count for much." Randy sighed. "So many questions that need answering. But I have to be honest. The prospect… excites me. I relish the challenge." Randy reached out and cupped Jesse's cheek. "Maybe we both need that. I'll get back to good old-fashioned policing—and *you* can get back to your studies. Here."

Jesse blinked. "Excuse me?"

"You said you weren't sure if you would go back to New York. You love it here. And the University of Southern Maine is right on the doorstep. They have an excellent MBA program too. Plus there's always the option of studying online. That might work out cheaper."

Jesse had to laugh. "Wow. You *have* had a busy day, haven't ya? Mitch's laptop got some use, it seems." What warmed him was that Randy had gone to the trouble of looking all this up.

Randy took Jesse's hands in his. "That MBA will open so many doors for you."

"Oh, I agree. It's just *paying* for it that's the issue." He'd been saving every cent he earned, but it was a slow business.

"Then you work for it. Take on another job."

"Really?"

Randy laughed. "Sure, why not? You can take on as many jobs as you want—or…." He leaned in and kissed Jesse on the mouth. "You consider the alternative."

"You kissed me to distract me, didn't you?" Jesse said softly.

"Did it work?" Randy's eyes gleamed.

"Kiss me again, and I'll tell you." Jesse closed his eyes as Randy's lips met his in a gentle, tender kiss, Randy's arms going around his waist. It was a serene moment, sitting in the middle of the beach, not a soul in sight, lost in a kiss.

Randy broke the kiss but didn't let go of him. "Let me help. I'll transfer here, we can find a place to live, and I'll pay the bills *and* your tuition until you finish your studies. When you're a hotshot consultant or whatever you end up doing, you can pay me back." He smiled. "You'll probably be earning more than me anyhow."

Jesse frowned. "I said I—"

"I know what you said, sweetheart, but this is different."

"How? *How* is it different?"

"We'd be here, not in New York. We'd be together. And if you *really* wanna work, then I'll help you find a company that might be interested in letting you work for them while you finish your MBA. You'd get a foot in the door that way." Randy smiled. "And it would pay better than working in a restaurant."

"You really *have* thought about this."

Randy nodded. "I don't wanna lose you. I said I'd find a way to make this work, and I'll do anything it takes to keep you in my life." His fingers were gentle on Jesse's cheek.

"I never thought I'd be hearing this." Jesse's throat tightened. It really was like a dream come true. "All those times I thought about you in the Black Lounge, hoping you'd smile at me, cursing the fact that you were straight and you'd never want me the way I wanted you…."

"Well, now you've got me."

Jesse's heart sank. "Yeah, but for how long? You have to leave on Sunday."

Randy kissed him again, his lips lingering on Jesse's, while he cupped Jesse's nape. "Now listen. I have to go back to New York so I can set things in motion to move here. I don't know how long it will take to organize a transfer—and right now I have no idea where I'd be transferring to, or if I can. If I can't, then it's eighteen weeks' training in Vassalboro. But I promise you, I'll be here every weekend. I'll be here Labor Day. And I'm gonna be praying it won't be long before we're together. For good." He kissed the tip of Jesse's nose. "And in the meantime, you have a big, important task to complete. You have to find us somewhere to live."

Jesse laughed. "What you *really* mean is, I have to find us a place so Mitch and Nikko can get their house back."

Randy coughed. "And while we're still under their roof, it might be a good idea if we were a little… quieter?"

Jesse stared at him, aghast. "Oh God. They said something, didn't they?"

"Possibly." Randy's eyes twinkled in the light. "But you have other stuff to occupy your mind. You need to put the wheels in motion to see about transferring here too. Transcripts, documentation, letters, whatever you need…. Can you lay your hands on all that?"

"Yeah, I think so."

"What about your parents? Do you think they might come around?"

Jesse huffed. "Who knows? I'll tell them what my plans are. If they wanna make a move, that's up to them. I'm not gonna get my hopes up." He took Randy's hand. "As long as I got you in my corner, I'm good." He tried not to think about them. It only got him upset.

"You have a lot of people in your corner, sweetheart. Mitch and Nikko. Mitch's family. And when they meet you, my folks are gonna love ya."

"Your…."

Randy grinned. "Have you ever been to Florida? Because you're gonna get to see it. I'll take you to meet them as soon as we can fix a time."

"Florida might have to wait a while." Jesse's mind was already working. "We're gonna be strapped for cash. I don't imagine a police officer makes all that much."

"Not at first, but I'm aiming for the Criminal Investigation and Forensics Division. From there, I'll have lots of options." He smiled. "And you'll *still* be earning more than me."

Randy's words were finally sinking in, and with that a whole new window opened up in Jesse's mind. It really was a fresh start, for both of them. Randy's excitement about his future was almost palpable.

Jesse took Randy's face between his hands and kissed him softly. "I love you," he whispered. "And I want this."

A long sigh shuddered out of Randy. "Thank God." He returned the kiss. "Love you too." The light had faded, and the sky had darkened. Randy glanced around them. "Wanna go back to the house and snuggle?"

Jesse laughed. "Nope. I wanna go back to the house and start looking at rental properties."

Randy was on his feet in an instant, brushing sand from his jeans. "Then what are we waiting for?" He held out a hand and hoisted Jesse up. "We also get to give Mitch and Nikko the good news." When Jesse snickered, Randy smacked his butt. "I was talking about our change in plans."

"Oh, sure," Jesse replied, his eyes wide. "But *they'll* be thinking about something else entirely. And while we're on the subject… I think *you* telling *me* we need to be a little quieter was a bit self-righteous. After all," he added with a grin, "*I'm* not the one who—"

Randy covered Jesse's mouth with his hand. "Not. Another. Word."

Jesse was still grinning when he removed it and they walked back to the house.

Epilogue

December 23, 2016

"Well? How do I look?"

Jesse cast a critical eye over Nikko. His dark blue suit fit his slim figure, and the blue silk tie against the white shirt complemented it. "You look wonderful." He cleared his throat. "For the fourth time."

Nikko stared at his reflection. "My hands are shaking."

Jesse got up out of the armchair beside the window and took hold of Nikko's hands. "I don't know why. You look amazing, and you're about to marry the man you love. Sounds perfect to me." He smiled. "I'd give you a hug, but I'm too scared of wrinkling your suit. Now come away from that mirror. You have a wedding to go to." His phone vibrated in his jacket pocket. Jesse removed it and glanced at the screen.

Good to go. Where are you?

He grinned. "Looks like they're ready for you."

Nikko drew in a deep breath, then nodded. "I'm ready, best man. Have you heard from Randy yet? It's a hell of a day to be running errands."

"Oh, I'm sure he'll get here on time." Jesse smiled to himself.

"As long as he's not this late for his own wedding." Nikko's eyes sparkled.

Jesse coughed. "Neither of us has even considered marriage yet—unless you know something I don't." Hell, they'd only been living together for two months. Randy had finally moved into the little house Jesse had found them, at the beginning of November. Jesse had been living there since early September. It wasn't huge, and it was a winter lease until early June, but it was comfortable and, more importantly, within their budget.

Nikko laughed. "Don't look so panic-struck. Anyone would think you didn't *want* to marry him."

Jesse chuckled. "Listen, Mr. I'm-Getting-Married-Any-Second-Now, we have other priorities. If you could see the list of things Randy has to do...."

Nikko laughed. "I know *exactly* what he's had to do, remember? I have this neighbor who keeps coming to my house and updating me on everything Randy is doing." He counted off on his fingers. "Like when he got his Maine driver's license, when he passed the background check, the written test, the medical exam, the psychological exam, and even the lie detector test. Surely there can't be all that much left to do."

Jesse arched his eyebrows. "Are you complaining about the fact that we live a few blocks from you? Because that can be changed, y'know. We can move."

Nikko chuckled.

"But he's still got his physical fitness test to do, plus his oral board exam, *and* the oral interview with the chief of the Maine State Police."

"He shouldn't have any difficulties with the last two, surely." Nikko bit his lip. "He's good at oral, isn't he?"

Jesse gasped. "Whatever happened to that sweet, quiet guy who sat reading in a brothel?"

Nikko grinned. "He met Mitch."

Jesse shook his head. "Does he know what a handful you are?"

"Maybe that's why he's marrying me."

There was a soft knock at the door. "Guys? Mitch wants to know where you are."

"We're coming, Gareth. Tell him to chill."

From the other side of the door came a muffled snort. "Yeah, right. Only if I want to wear my balls as earrings."

Nikko sighed. "And I thought *I* was nervous. We'd better get out there."

Jesse rolled his eyes. "What have I been saying for the last ten minutes?" He walked with Nikko to the door, then along the carpeted hallway to the elevator. As they descended, Jesse laced his fingers through Nikko's. "Breathe, babe."

Nikko laughed. "Good advice."

The doors slid open and they walked through the lobby of the Cliff House Hotel to the Cape Neddick Salon. Jesse paused at the doors, where Cal and Dale stood, looking very smart in their suits.

"Uncle Mitch said I was to let him know when you arrived," Cal said quietly. He opened the door slightly and looked around it. Seconds later Mitch was there, and Nikko let out a gasp.

"You sneaky man."

Jesse had to admit, Mitch looked awesome in a kilt. He wore a white shirt with a ruffled front under a black jacket with lapels that swooped down to his waist where it fastened. His kilt was green check with lines of black and white, on top of which sat a gilt sporran, adorned with tassels. His almost-knee-high thick socks had tassels, too, and his black boots shone.

"D'ya like it?"

Nikko snickered. "Please. Do *not* attempt a Sean Connery impersonation during our wedding." He stroked the sporran. "I didn't know you could wear tartan."

"There's Scottish blood on my grandfather's side," Mitch explained. "This is the family tartan."

"And are you wearing it like a true Scotsman?" Nikko's eyes twinkled.

Mitch leaned in and whispered, "You'll find that out tonight." He straightened and held out his hand. "Ready?"

"I will be, once Jesse goes in and stands with Gareth."

Jesse kissed his cheek. "See you in there." He stepped into the Salon and quickly made his way to the window, where the justice of the peace stood. To one side was a gleaming black piano, its pianist seated on a bench. In front of the justice stood Gareth.

Jesse stood to the left of the assembled guests, peering along the front row. Randy gave him the thumbs-up, grinning.

The air was suddenly filled with soft chords as the pianist began playing Debussy's *Clair de Lune*, and the doors opened to admit Mitch and Nikko. They walked solemnly toward the wall of windows, outside which lay a white landscape, the coastline obscured by a thick covering of snow. Inside the room, Christmas trees stood at regular intervals, covered with tiny white lights and deep red garlands. About fifty people sat on either side of the aisle, marked by red ribbons and small white flowers.

Mitch and Nikko reached the front and stood side by side before the justice of the peace. Mitch nudged Nikko, who turned to look at the front row where Randy sat, next to Valerie and Malcolm. Suddenly

Nikko's eyes filled with tears, and he left Mitch's side, heading for the man seated on Randy's other side, who lunged to his feet. The two men embraced, both crying, and Jesse had to fight hard to hold his own tears in check.

Mitch held up his hands. "Sorry, everyone, but this is the first time Nikko has seen his brother in a long while."

There were murmurs from the guests, and a few people wiped away tears.

Nikko and Ichy said nothing, just held each other, as if they were afraid to let go. After a minute, Mitch gently rubbed Nikko's back. "He'll still be here when we're done. And in case you missed them, there's a room full of people here who came to watch us get married."

Nikko laughed and wiped his eyes. Ichy squeezed his arm and sat down again next to Randy. Then Mitch took Nikko's hand, and they faced the justice together.

Jesse watched the proceedings, his heart full of joy for his friends. Now and again he glanced over and caught Randy staring at him. Jesse couldn't help staring back. Randy in a formal dark suit was a sight to behold. His smooth-shaven jawline had Jesse yearning to kiss and stroke it. Then a lovely thought crossed his mind.

There'll be dancing later. I get to dance with Randy for the first time.

Now *that* was something to look forward to.

RANDY TOOK two glasses of champagne from the waiter, then made his way across the floor of the Atlantic Ballroom to where Jesse stood talking with Nikko and Ichy. He smiled as he passed members of Mitch's family, who greeted him with a wave or a raised glass. As he drew nearer, Nikko's eyes lit up.

"And here's the man I have to thank. So this was your *errand*?" He gestured to Ichy.

Randy smiled. "When I was here in August, Mitch mentioned how badly he wanted Ichy to attend the wedding. All I did was talk to the right people." He nodded to the bar, where a tall man dressed in black was watching them, smiling. "And *that* is Ichy's personal detective. He's the one responsible for making sure Ichy stays safe, as a favor to me."

"I was telling Nikko, I'm doing all right. He doesn't have to worry about me. I have this whole new life, and it's working out." Ichy chuckled. "I thought having a cop bring me was a bit too much."

"Hey, the trial only finished in June," Randy said quickly. "We couldn't be sure you weren't being watched by friends of Richards. You know what they told you at the start—absolutely *no* contact with old friends or family."

Ichy nodded. "Doug—the cop who came with me—made it clear the authorities weren't happy about me coming here. I knew it was a risk, but hell, it's your *wedding*. And if I can't even come to my brother's wedding, see the only family I've got left, then I'm not really living, am I? So yeah, it's a risk, but like I said to Doug—fuck it." He grinned when Nikko gasped. "Oh, don't give me that. I'm sure you've heard worse."

Randy chuckled at Nikko's horrified expression as he handed a glass to Jesse. "I knew I had to try to get him here, if only because it was the best wedding present I could think of."

Nikko nodded. "The best." He turned to Ichy. "I think it's time we had some champagne." He led his brother toward the waiter, who was still carrying his tray of glasses.

"There was only one thing we didn't see coming," Jesse murmured, his gaze focused on Nikko.

"Their grandmother, you mean?"

Jesse nodded. "Nikko hoped she'd be well enough to be here."

It wasn't to be. His grandmother had passed away at the end of November.

"I'll see what I can do about bringing Ichy here again. Maybe I can persuade Doug that he can stay with us for the holidays. I mean, who better to keep him safe than me? And Christmas is only two days away." Randy hated the thought of the brothers being apart.

"Better with us than with Mitch and Nikko," Jesse said with a grin. "I mean, they may be family, but this *is* their honeymoon, right?"

Randy laughed. "And they'll be spending two days with Mitch's family. I'm sure Valerie could find room for Ichy."

"What's this about Valerie finding room?" Mitch appeared behind them, his hands on their shoulders. Randy repeated his idea, and Mitch nodded. "I'm sure she wouldn't mind, as long as you can square it with Doug. And, er, thanks for volunteering to put Ichy up for the holidays. Ordinarily I wouldn't hesitate to offer him our guest room, but...." He gave them a sheepish grin. "A little alone time right now would be appreciated."

"Can't think why," Jesse said with an innocent expression.

Randy skewered him with a look.

"Anyway, why aren't you two lovebirds dancing?"

Randy narrowed his gaze. "Because there's no music? We'd look a little strange, don't you think?"

Mitch sighed. "I suppose even a band has to take a break. Well, the break's over." He strode across the room in search of the musicians.

Jesse chuckled. "You know, earlier, I was asking Nikko if Mitch was aware of the handful he was about to marry. I take it all back. They're as bad as each other."

Soft music filtered through the air, and Randy smiled. "Don't you think it's time you danced with me?"

Jesse took Randy's glass and placed it, along with his own, on a nearby table. "I thought you'd never ask."

Randy put his hands on Jesse's waist and pressed his cheek to Jesse's. "Having a good time?"

Jesse sighed. "I like weddings. Such happy, romantic occasions."

"I'm glad to hear that, because there'll be another along shortly." When Jesse pulled back and gave him an inquiring glance, Randy smiled. "My cousin Donna is getting married next year. You get to meet all my family."

Jesse chuckled. "Can I at least meet your parents first?"

"I think that can be arranged." Randy held him close as they moved slowly together to the music. He shook his head, smiling.

"What's amusing you?"

"I was just thinking, that's all. Little did I imagine, this time last year, that by Christmas I'd be head over heels in love—with a guy—living with him, and training to be a state trooper."

"No regrets, then?"

Randy laughed softly. "What is there to regret? I'm happier than I've been in a long time. I get to wake up every morning next to you. Our friends live a few blocks away from us."

Jesse snickered. "Mitch still can't believe we found a house in Old Orchard Beach."

They'd spent a lot of time going through lists of properties, but their hands were tied by the available budget. The little house on Evergreen

Avenue was perfect for them. Jesse had a solid job in Portland, and his prospects were good once he finished the MBA.

"I knew there was something I'd forgotten to tell you. Owen called."

"Don't tell me. He's moving to Maine, too, to start up a new practice," Jesse said with a grin. "He's missing your Friday night drinks and gossip."

Randy laughed. "Possibly, but no, he's staying put. His job is working out well. But he *was* hinting heavily about paying us a visit in the new year."

Jesse shrugged. "I don't see why not." He glanced around the room and sighed. "I love the holidays. I *was* looking forward to my first Christmas alone with you, but you're right. Letting Ichy stay with us is the nice thing to do. And we'll have other Christmases."

"That's what I love about you," Randy said quietly. "Your generous nature." He brushed his lips against Jesse's ear. "And what about you? No regrets either?"

Jesse pulled back to look him in the eye. "I don't miss my old life. Let's face it, you nailed it. I got into escorting because I figured getting paid to do what I love had to be a dream job, right? Well, now I go to bed every night with a gorgeous man who loves sex as much as I do." He grinned. "Maybe more."

"What about your parents?"

Jesse's face darkened a little. "They know the score. It's up to them now." He lowered his gaze, but Randy lifted his chin with a couple of fingers.

"At least your mom called, right? That's gotta be a good sign."

"Yeah, you're right. Who knows? They might come around, now I'm working in a job they can actually tell people about." Jesse smiled, the light returning to his eyes. "All right, so the life of a product manager is a hell of a lot less glamorous than the life of a hooker, but you know what? I can live without the glamor, because it had its darker moments too. I feel safer than I did back then. There's food in our cabinets and refrigerator. I don't have to worry about money. It might only be our home until June, but who knows where we'll end up living? I can walk a few blocks and there's the Atlantic Ocean." He stroked Randy's cheek. "And okay, so your career involves a certain amount of risk. At least you're doing what you *want* to do." Jesse sighed. "Nothing's perfect in this life, but you know what? We've got each other. I'll help you carry your burdens because you're there to carry mine."

"For as long as you want," Randy said wholeheartedly.

Jesse leaned in closer, until their lips were almost touching. "How about forever?"

Randy could deal with that.

K.C. WELLS started writing in 2012, although the idea of writing a novel had been in her head since she was a child. But after reading that first gay romance in 2009, she was hooked.

She now writes full-time, and the line of men in her head clamoring to tell their story is getting longer and longer. If the frequent visits by plot bunnies are anything to go by, that's not about to change anytime soon.

K.C. loves to hear from readers.

Email: k.c.wells@btinternet.com
Facebook: www.facebook.com/KCWellsWorld
Blog: kcwellsworld.blogspot.co.uk
Twitter: @K_C_Wells
Website: www.kcwellsworld.com
Instagram: www.instagram.com/k.c.wells

A Love, Unexpected Tale

Two months after Mitch Jenkins had the rug pulled out from under him when his two-year relationship came to an abrupt end, he is still hurting. A colleague's attempt to cheer him up brings Mitch to a secret "club." Mitch isn't remotely interested in the twinks parading like peacocks, until he spies the young man at the back of the room, nose firmly in a book and oblivious to his surroundings. Now Mitch is interested.

Nikko Kurokawa wants to pay his debt and get the hell out of the Black Lounge. Earning his freedom isn't proving easy, especially when he starts attracting interest. Life becomes that little bit easier to bear when he meets Mitch, who is nothing like the other men who frequent the club. And when Mitch crawls under his skin and into his heart, Nikko figures he can put up with anything. Before long he'll be out of there, and he and Mitch can figure out if they have a future together.

Neither of them counted on those who don't want Nikko to leave….

www.dreamspinnerpress.com

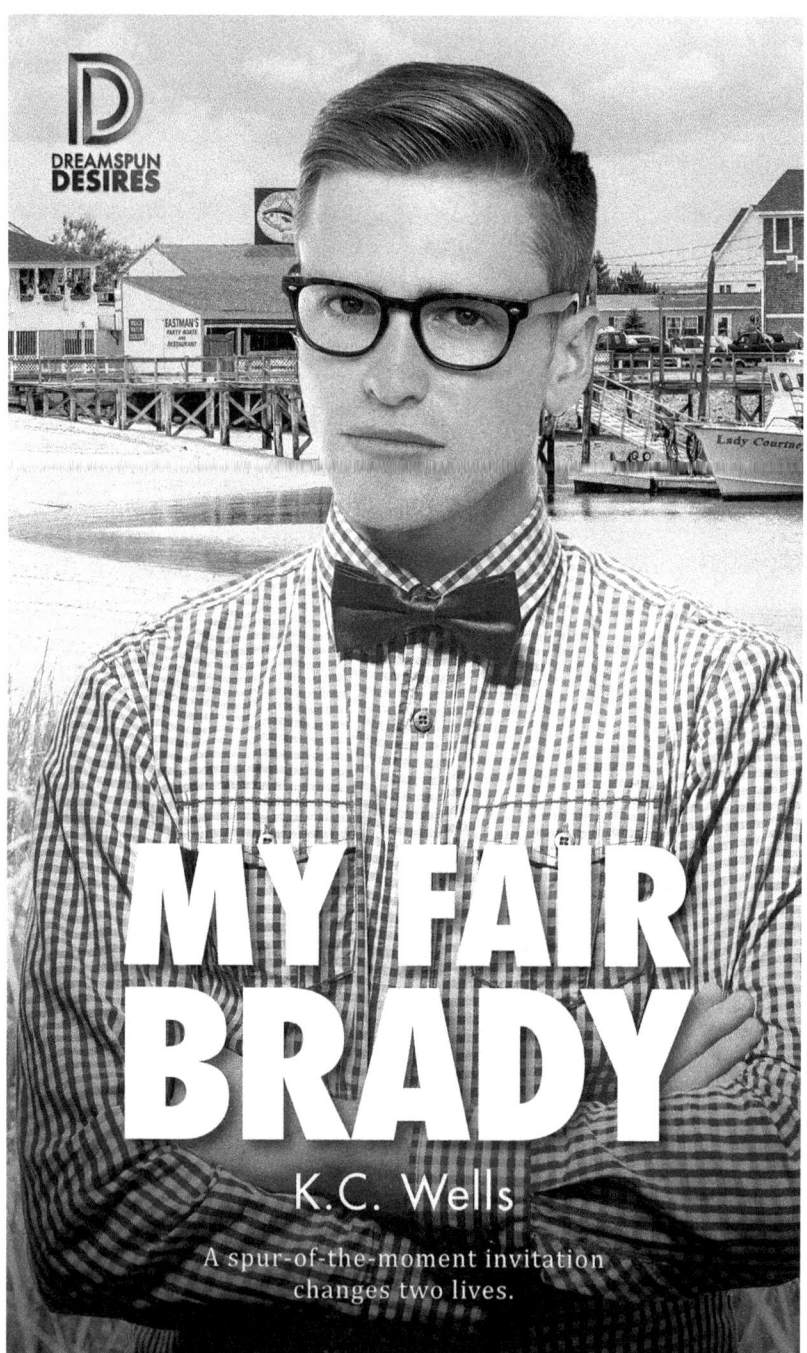

A spur of the moment invitation changes two lives.

Jordan Wolf's company runs like a well-oiled machine. At least until his PA, Brady Donovan, comes down with the flu and takes sick leave. Then Jordan discovers what a treasure Brady is and who really keeps his business—and Jordan in particular—moving like clockwork. So when Jordan needs a plus-one, Brady seems the obvious choice to accompany him. After a major shopping trip to get Brady looking the part, however…. Wow.

Brady has a whole new wardrobe, and now his boss is whisking him away for a weekend party. Something is going on, something Brady never expected: Jordan is looking at him like he's never seen him before, electrifying Brady's long-hidden desires.

But can the romantic magic last when the weekend is over and it's back to reality?

www.dreamspinnerpress.com

Truth Will Out

K.C. Wells

Jonathon de Mountford's visit to Merrychurch village to stay with his uncle Dominic gets off to a bad start when Dominic fails to appear at the railway station. But when Jonathon finds him dead in his study, apparently as the result of a fall, everything changes. For one thing, Jonathon is the next in line to inherit the manor house. For another, he's not so sure it was an accident, and with the help of Mike Tattersall, the owner of the village pub, Jonathon sets out to prove his theory—if he can concentrate long enough without getting distracted by the handsome Mike.

They discover an increasingly long list of people who had reason to want Dominic dead. And when events take an unexpected turn, the amateur sleuths are left bewildered. It doesn't help that the police inspector brought in to solve the case is the last person Mike wants to see, especially when they are told to keep their noses out of police business.

In Jonathon's case, that's like a red rag to a bull….

www.dreamspinnerpress.com

OUT OF THE SHADOWS
K.C. Wells

DREAMSPUN DESIRES

Can he step out of the shadows and into love's light?

Can he step out of the shadows and into love's light?

Eight years ago, Christian Hernandez moved to the Jamaica Plain area of Boston, took refuge in his apartment, and cut himself off from the outside world. And that's how he'd like it to stay.

Josh Wendell has heard his coworkers gossip about the occupant of apartment #1. No one sees the mystery man, and Josh loves a mystery. So when he is hired to refurbish the apartment's kitchen and bathrooms, Josh is eager to discover the truth behind the rumors.

When he comes face-to-face with Christian, Josh understands why Christian hides from prying eyes. As the two men bond, Josh sees past his exterior to the man within, and he likes what he sees. But can Christian find the courage to emerge from the darkness of his lonely existence for the man who has claimed his heart?

www.dreamspinnerpress.com

 FOR **MORE** OF THE **BEST GAY ROMANCE**

dreamspinnerpress.com

CPSIA information can be obtained
at www.ICGtesting.com
Printed in the USA
FFHW010623050419
51525841-56968FF

9 781644 052327